The Glass Guitar

The Glass Guitar

By

Marshall Riggan

www.Penmorepress.com

ISBN-13: 978-1-957851-54-9 (Paperback)
ISBN: 13: 978-1-957851-53-2(E-book)

BISAC Subject Headings:
FIC002000 FICTION / Action & Adventure
FIC064000 FICTION / Absurdist
FIC060000 FICTION / Humorous / Dark Humor

Stained Glass Guitar by Elana Pierkowski www.oddballartist.com.
From Pattern Designed by Tiffany Ard – wwwtiffanyard.com

Address all correspondence to:

Penmore Press LLC
920 N Javelina Pl
Tucson AZ 85748

Dedication

To Kelly, Todd, Laura and Jessica,
My children who dared

Author's Note to the Reader

Walter Woodrow Pillow's guitar plays a significant role in this novel. It is the instrument of his protest against just about everything. However, it is not glass, as the title would suggest. It is wood. So I suppose I have some explaining to do.

The title is derived from the fact that Wally's protests never really succeed; they are irrelevant, hollow, transparent and fragile. He also can only play minor chords and the only two songs he knows by heart are "Foggy Foggy Dew" and "When Johnny Comes Marching Home Again". So for all the heft and substance of effective protest, Wally's guitar might as well be glass. Besides, *The Wood Guitar* would be an awful title. And it wouldn't provide an opportunity to use artist Alana Piekowski's wonderful stained glass image on the cover.

The madman shouted in the marketplace
And no-one stopped to answer him.
Thus it was confirmed that his
Thesis was incontrovertible.
—Dag Hammarskjold

CHAPTER 1
THE SABOTEUR

As Walter Woodrow Pillow watched the worshippers coming through the great bomber factory, he wondered if it was he or the world that was going mad. They came on bicycles and electric scooters, jaws pressed forward, eyes alive with holy fire. They wore faded blue denims, steel-toed boots and shirts with the names of bowling teams emblazoned on the back. Some walked, carrying Bibles. They moved through the mile-long defense plant; they passed the white jigs and wing-mating stations where the supersonic *F111* fighter-bombers were being assembled. Now, the harsh howl of the midday whistle came, and there was the sound of things winding down. It was noon on a fine spring day at the Fort Worth General Dynamics Bomber Factory and time to praise the Living and Everlasting Lord.

The worshippers settled down among the machinery, the forklift trucks and the components of the unborn bomber. They asked of each other's families, and they looked upward, where the grey corrugated metal roof hid the watching angels, and then they began to sing. Pitiful at first, this human sound, so small and lost within the factory's immensity. High above, a yellow crane crawled, fishing with its great hook, and through the congregation, an Air Force pickup came, bound on some unknowable armorer's mission deep within the factory. The voices of the singers rose.

Wally listened to the worshippers. He was almost invisible among the many other engineers and professionals, who, like Wally, were wearing the standard uniform of the young professional of the 1960s: khaki slacks and a white dress shirt, sleeves rolled up above the wrist and no tie. Outwardly he might have appeared calm, but the voices of the worshippers touched something deep within him and that something stirred and roiled and made him feel ashamed and angry.

'Why are they here?' he wondered, and he wished he had the courage to tell them how obscene it was to praise God in a factory where they make machines that kill human beings. 'Isn't this a plane designed to drop an atomic bomb? Aren't they manufacturing death here?' But he knew, really, why they turned to prayer, and maybe, deep down, the worshippers knew as well. They were tormented by the same guilt he felt, so they turned to Jesus to wash clean their souls. Unfortunately, Wally and Jesus had not been on speaking terms in years.

The factory whistle howled noon away and the worshippers scattered like startled sparrows. Wally turned and began the long walk back to the department they called the "Mock-up Area." He passed the long line of squatting aircraft in various stages of assembly, each submitting to the noisy attention of riveters, grinders, welders, and other Vulcans. The planes, which he had once loved, seemed to him somehow malevolent as if each was an evil will observing its own creation. It was as if they waited calmly to become whole and then they would turn and devour their creators.

At Final Assembly Station Number Three, a group of Air Force Officers wearing flight suits were watching a wing-sweep demonstration. Wally paused to watch the silver wings glide to their aft position. 'It could be a beautiful plane,' he thought. He remembered the original design and the graceful soaring models he had created as part of the design team. But the Air Force wanted the pilot and co-pilot to sit side by side, causing the plane to lose its slim, almost sensual profile. And the Navy needed beefed-up landing gear for carrier landings, so the aircraft got even more bulky. And then they began hanging rockets and bombs from its lovely wings. "Shit!" he said aloud, and he moved on, whistling to drown out the tumult in his mind.

The Mock-up Area was separated from the main factory by a high plywood wall on which were pasted posters demanding that everyone be more accurate and conscientious in their work and that they try to avoid waste. There was a large cardboard barometer announcing that *F-111* production was on schedule.

There was a guard at the door to the Mock-up Area and he signaled Wally to stop before entering. "Name?" the guard asked, glancing at a clipboard.

Wally sighed. "How many times do you figure I go through this door every week? At least fifty. You know damn well what my name is."

"You know I got to ask, Wally."

"That's the first part."

"Don't give me trouble, Pillow."

Once again Wally cringed at the sound of his name, both first and last, not to mention his middle name. Walter

Woodrow Pillow. 'Disgusting,' he thought. How could a person achieve anything, be anything, worth a damn with a milquetoast name like Walter Woodrow Pillow? Why couldn't he have been named Casey Jones or Bart Starr or Jack Armstrong or Huckleberry Finn or something with some heft, some substance, some flair. He thought about that for a while and it did nothing for his mood, which, as usual these days, was abysmally rotten.

"Another secret night illumination test?" the guard asked, writing something down.

"Can't say. It's a secret," Wally said, and he waited for the guard to push the buzzer, signaling that the door was unlocked. He passed into the highly restricted area. Wally had once loved this huge room, essentially a museum of the history and romance of flight. Along its walls and on pedestals were scale models of the most beautiful and significant flying machines ever devised by man. Here was the delicate *Wright Flyer;* the *Bird of Prey* designed and flown by Santos Dumont, the tough little machine in which Louis Bleriot first flew across the English Channel; and the iconic *Spirit of St. Louis*. And, of course, here were displayed the elegant fighters of World War I: the *Newport*, the *Sopwith Camel*, the various *Fokkers* and the French *Spad*. The displays followed the evolution of aircraft design from Icarus's wings of wax to the menacing little *Sputnik*, a satellite no larger than a beach ball that would change the world forever. How many hours had he spent in the company of such marvelous planes, he wondered, building his *Spitfires* and *Mustangs* and *Lockheed Lightnings*, alone with his dreams in the basement of his childhood home. As he looked at the models, he could almost smell the balsa, hear the whispery sound of the tissue he used to cover the wings, and feel the dried airplane glue on the tips of his fingers, a crust that would take days to peel away. Major features of the room's exhibits were dozens of scale models showing the evolution of the *F-111* design, from concept to production model. Most of the models he recognized as his own work and, again, he felt a momentary breath of shame as he remembered how much he had enjoyed building them.

Dominating the area was a full-size wooden *F-111*. It was like the actual aircraft in nearly every respect except the material of which it was made. Bombs were slung snugly beneath its wings; all the control surfaces were there—it looked quite real and nearly was. Wally looked around to make sure he wasn't being observed and then he climbed up the wooden stairs to the cockpit, raised the canopy and climbed into the model.

"Hi, Wally," said the girl in the co-pilot seat. She grasped his tie and pulled him to her and kissed him. She tasted like peppermint Certs. "What's wrong?" she whispered when he pulled away. She opened her purse to show him—her bra and panties were in there.

Her name was Jasmine and she was the only person at General Dynamics that he liked and trusted. There were many secrets in the Fort Worth bomber plant, but the one he shared with Jasmine was that every Tuesday noon they met to talk and make love in the cockpit of the wooden facsimile of the super-secret *F-111* supersonic bomber. Now he pulled down the black canopy shades to simulate night flight and he switched on the instrument lights. The cockpit was kissed with a gentle glow of blue and green.

"You haven't been down there with those religious nuts again, have you?" Jasmine asked.

He admitted he had.

"Why do you keep going down there?"

"I've just got this thing bothering me."

"I know," she said softly, settling back into the contoured seat. "But I tell you, Wally. You're listening to voices that don't exist. And getting all uptight about those Jesus people won't help."

"It's just that those people down there feel the need to pray. You don't find prayer services in soup factories, oil refineries or places where they make cars, so why do they pray here? In a fucking bomber factory! It's because all that crazy stuff I talk about isn't crazy at all. By building this killing machine we are killing ourselves. I'm not the only one who feels guilty about what we're doing."

"Why don't you leave, then?" she asked and immediately appeared to regret it. "I'm sorry, Wally." She touched his hand.

"Because I'm just like all the other bastards here. All I know how to do is make model airplanes. Now where in the hell else can I make a living doing that? And all these other people who work here, ten thousand of them, all they know how to do is build bombers."

"It's for their country."

"Bull! How often do you say to yourself in the morning that you're going to work to serve your country? Nobody thinks that! Nobody stops to think that they are accomplices to mass murder. For instance, what did you think when you helped design this cockpit?"

"As a human factors engineer, my job is to bring about a harmony between man and machine. Those lights, for instance, were designed to minimize fatigue and maximize exterior night vision."

"You sound like some kind of handbook."

Jasmine sighed and for a moment remained silent. "Wally," she said, "I like you too much to fight. I put up with a lot to be with you because I like the way you think deeply about things. But you are going to drive yourself crazy. The world is as it is. You and I can't change it. God! When I think of all I do for you!"

"What?"

"Well, for one thing, why can't we make love in a bed like everyone else? Why does it have to be in a goddamned fighter-bomber, just because you've got some nutty, overblown sense of irony?"

"It's not that, Jasmine. I like you. I like doing what we do here every Tuesday. It's like, you and me against the world. Here in the dark, we can be human for just a little while. Out there, everything is about war and killing."

"But don't you feel this is a little bizarre, Wally? Even perverse?"

"I feel that it's a small way of striking back, of throwing a pie in their face. As long as we make love in their death-dealing bomber, I believe maybe we can cling to a little bit of our humanity."

"Oh, Wally, you are truly crazy."

"I just get so sick of how serious everyone is about their self-deception. Everybody talks about this plane as if it were some kind of god. One time I went up to a propulsion engineer and I said, 'Have you ever noticed how ugly this airplane is?' And he looked at me like I'd let out a fart, and he turned me in, to my supervisor. And anybody can see that it is really, very, very ugly."

"Wally," Jasmine whispered, "for my birthday can we make it in a bed?" She leaned far back in the co-pilot's seat and unbuttoned her blouse. The instrument lights painted her flesh rainbow-colored, like the titles of a James Bond movie.

Wally had to admit to himself that Jasmine was a fine-looking woman for a human factors engineer. And she was a very good friend and a fine person. And she was the only person he knew who hadn't been driven away by his abysmal lack of self-respect and his rants against the industrial-Christian-military complex. He also respected her important, yet futile, profession as a human factors engineer, bringing to the sharp corners and hard edges of technology something softer and familiar, to fit the contours of the pilots who would fly the plane against enemies both real and imagined. Perhaps her crowning achievement was located low on the left side of the instrument panel above the nuclear release handle. It was a tiny compartment labeled SANDWICHES. He envisioned a pilot nibbling on a peanut butter sandwich as he released mass destruction on a city. It was so horrible that he had decided Jasmine had sketched in this astounding juxtaposition as a joke, but some humorless fools had taken her design seriously and had built it into the cockpit. Maybe that's why he liked her so, in addition to what was so sensationally revealed in the glow of the instrument lights. She was just as insane as he was.

Now Jasmine helped Wally pull his pants down. "Just imagine how easy this would be in a hotel room." She laughed and raised her skirt. Just as she had managed to straddle his legs and he was kissing her breasts, the canopy flew open, and the factory's fluorescent lights exploded into the cockpit like runaway suns. Never had Wally seen so much revealing light. When he was over his shock he could see the Air Force Colonel there, his eyes showing white all the way around, his red mustache quivering, his mouth slack as a wet flag. With deep dread, Wally watched the Colonel's struggle for composure.

"What great holy mother of..." he began, as the impaled human factor engineer covered her breasts with her hands.

"It's not what you think, Colonel," she said. "Someone has to do it."

"Wha?"

"Look in your requirements. Human Factors Category 15c6b."

"Category what?"

"Erection Testing," the quick-thinking engineer said, slip-sliding off Wally's lap, climbing back into the co-pilot's seat, fully revealing the subject of their test. "I don't recall the exact words but it's something to the effect that combat pilots who control great destructive power have often been observed to have erections during the moments of unleashing said power. Obviously, this must be taken into consideration when designing the seat harness, to say nothing of the possible obstruction of other gear such as oxygen tubes, etcetera."

The Colonel rubbed his chin and Wally noticed his mustache had stopped quivering. The Colonel's victims were pinned in colorful rows upon his chest and Wally wondered if he was familiar with the difficulty outlined in Human Factors Category 15c6b. He probably was, because he said, "Hmmm." And then glancing to where Wally was cupping his privates, he asked, "And the testing, how is it proving out?"

"This isn't the kind of test one can discuss with just anyone who comes along," Jasmine said.

"I have top-secret clearance," he replied.

"But there's the matter of privacy."

"Of course," he said, his face drained and strange. Then he added, "I'm sorry."

"You'll have access to my report."

"Yes. Please carry on," the Colonel said, and then the canopy closed, the sun went out, and the work to keep America free continued.

When Wally returned to his office there was a covey of officials gathered around the new model he had just completed. A man whose name he couldn't recall, but had something to do with public relations, caught his eye and called his name. The intrusion annoyed him because he was still aglow from the test he and Jasmine had conducted.

"This is the man you'll want to talk with, Senator," the public relations man said. "Senator, meet Walter Woodrow Pillow, he's had as much to do with the success of the *F-111* Program as anybody."

Wally was doubly annoyed because he hated to hear his lily-livered name called out, especially all of it, especially in public this way. Feeling diminished, Wally shook hands with the senator and despite himself could find no immediate reason to dislike the man. In fact, he seemed rather pleasant, with an open, youthful face. The senator brushed his hand along the smooth surfaces of Wally's latest model and Wally was impressed with the tenderness of his touch. "So, tell me how this model is used in testing?" the senator asked.

Wally took a deep breath and launched into his memorized spiel. "It's designed so that any measurable dynamic phenomenon on the model can be scaled to full-size aircraft values by some known law. It's called a dynamically similar model. We put it in the wind tunnel and actually fly it." Usually, Wally resisted explaining his strange and complex specialty, but he sensed the senator was interested, maybe even fascinated. He also had the strange feeling that this was a man he could talk to, about the concerns about life that he was reluctant to reveal to anyone other than Jasmine.

"Since the model is like the real thing in such critical areas as stiffness, weight distribution, mass movements of inertia and unbalance, if the model experiences vibration at a critical speed in the wind tunnel, then we can predict a similar vibration in the real plane during actual flight."

Encouraged by the senator's apparent interest, he droned on, ceasing to hear what he was saying. Instead, his imagination began to play with a conversation he would rather have with the senator. He imagined that he and the senator were walking in a meadow. It was immensely peaceful and there were wildflowers, mostly yellow against the green. After a while they paused and folded onto a smooth flat boulder, and Wally played his favorite minor chords on his guitar.

When he had exhausted his repertoire of random minor chords, Wally said, "There's something that's bothering me, Senator. And I thought maybe out here, away from distractions, we could talk about it. I sense we can be honest with each other; express how we really feel."

"If you like."

"In a way it's sort of embarrassing, because it will probably sound crazy. I mean I don't want you to think that I'm a radical nut or something, because I don't think I am. I'm just trying to get down to the truth of things."

"We can talk about it here, Walter. And don't be afraid to say what you feel."

"Well," Wally continued, "I've been having this feeling that what we're doing here at General Dynamics is wrong."

"Wrong?" The senator shifted his position.

"I mean in a moral sense."

"Go on."

"Well, I just don't think we should be building the *F-111*. I think it's destroying us."

The senator looked away; his eye caught the soaring of a raven. The wind played in his fine white hair and his kind eyes reflected the blue of the sky. "Destroying us? How could it be destroying us, Walter?"

"Well, the purpose of the *F-111* is to kill, isn't it?"

"Yes," the senator said. "Yes. I understand how you feel. I had similar thoughts when I was young. It's disturbing to real-ize that we must sometimes do things that are against our na-ture , but you're still young. That's part of youth."

"You mean when I'm older I won't worry about it?"

"You'll mature."

In his imagined scenario Wally thought about that for a moment. The sun eased behind a cloud and came out again. "What you're saying is that when we grow older, we lose the ability to tell right from wrong?"

"No, Walter. That's not it at all."

"Then we must lose the ability to care. It has to be one or the other."

"I'm trying to follow you, Walter."

"Okay. Take General Dynamics. All of us here earn our living, actually devote our professional skills and our lives to the building of an instrument of death. Jesus said we shouldn't kill. Reason tells us we shouldn't kill. Simple compassion says the same thing. Yet we continue to create the instruments by which this commandment can be broken."

"Walter, my friend," the senator said, smiling sadly, "there are times when killing is necessary for survival. It's the law of nature. An animal will protect its own kind unto death."

"But we're supposed to be better than animals. And human beings are all one kind. But here we are building a weapon to kill people halfway around the world who have never done us one little bit of harm. And that's what really bugs me, Senator. General Westmoreland, McNamara, Nixon, they are probably far more intelligent than I am, yet I know, just as sure as I was born, that they are wrong and on the wrong side of history." Wally was finding it difficult to catch his breath and felt his heart rate climbing dangerously. The senator regarded him as one would regard a tarantula in the doorway.

"I think I've heard enough, Walter. Don't you see you are talking like an insane man?" In Wally's imagination, the senator rose and began to pace through the wildflowers. Wally wished he could identify the names of the flowers, or the grass in which they grew, or the distant, smoky trees. Perhaps it would make things clearer if he were on a first-name basis with his environment.

The senator stopped and his face was dark and very close. "You have really made me angry, Walter! It takes more to run a world than what you call simple compassion." And then, rising to his full height, he added, "You Commie piece of shit!"

"Fuck you!" Wally shouted in his imagination.

"Fuck you twice!" the senator added in the imaginary dialogue.

"Fuck you 'til the cows come home!" And it went on like that for a while. The words rattled down a long hollow corridor, the blue sky turned grey as an old man's beard, all the petals fell from the flowers, the distant soft trees burst into flame and dead birds rained from their branches. Rats crept from the senator's trousers, and he turned to rotting straw. The wind blew cold on the strings of Wally's guitar.

Then, suddenly, he was back in his model shop, strangely out of breath and light-headed, but explaining how the little models he made had led to the development of McNamara's weapon system. There was nothing in the senator's manner that would suggest he had a moment ago called Wally a Commie piece of shit. In fact, he had placed his arm around Wally's shoulder. "I want to congratulate you, Walter, on your service to our country. And I don't need to tell you what this contract means to the economy of this area. And I will certainly do all that I can to convince Congress we need more, many more, of these marvelous bombers to provide more and more jobs." The senator thanked everyone and shook hands all around.

The hours ground away at the afternoon. In his office, Wally listened to the monotone voice of the factory and searched his mind for signs of insanity. 'To be insane,' he thought, 'is to be unable to control your behavior.' He decided he was in strict control of his and could do or not do anything he might ask himself to do or not do. He might sometimes do what other people might consider weird things, like making love in a fighter-bomber, but he could stop doing them at will. It was not his behavior that he couldn't control, rather it was his thoughts. They came and went like uninvited guests, roaming around the corridors and rooms of his mind, opening drawers, knocking over chairs, stealing silverware and then leaving without a fare thee well. But madness was to express these vagrant thoughts in action. He had thought about all that anti-American stuff and about saying fuck you to the senator, but he didn't actually say any of it out loud. So, *ex post facto*, he was as sane as any human being could hope to be.

He knew an old man in the General Dynamics Motion Picture Department, a gifted animator, whom he liked very much. He, too, had often mentioned the possibility that he might be overcome by insanity one day. To guard against this he committed small daily ritual acts of insanity, a strategy he compared to the practice of forest rangers starting a line of small fires to combat the spread of the huge fire that threatened the whole forest. He called this practice the Psychology of the Silly. Occasionally, Wally would get a telephone call, and a voice on the line would gobble like a turkey or bray like a donkey, and Wally would know it was the old man still fighting hard against madness.

As Wally thought about what he didn't say to the senator, he was engulfed in a profound unhappiness that very nearly stopped his heart. It rushed in unexpectedly like a deep, dark tide, driving him down in his chair and beneath fathoms of sorrows. He was at the bottom of the sea, down where no light could reach. Around him moved the unseen presences of great, cold, blind beasts. And he cringed in fear that their awful antennas would brush against his face.

"God in heaven!" he quietly called, tears beginning to flow from his eyes. "What can I do?" He laid his head upon his arms and remembered the advice of Norman Vincent Peale about such sorrows. Each day, Peale advised, make a list of all the positive things in your life. And so, with eyes closed, Wally began. 'I'm an American, a Caucasian. I have a good job. I am very good at designing fighter-bombers.' But as he counted, he realized that all these things were somehow on the wrong side of the ledger. 'All of the things I am and have been are foursquare against what is right and good and noble. To be me is to be in the company of those who restrict freedom, deny justice, imperil what is best in human nature, and even imperil life itself. How do other people deal with this dilemma?' he wondered. They close their eyes and pray. But he couldn't pray. So, he reached into one of the rooms of his mind where he had nurtured a monumentally exciting and life-affirming thought for more than a year. And he knew now it was time to convert the thought into behavior. And if that was madness, then fuckadoo!

Late that afternoon, as the shifts were changing, Wally walked across the great concrete runways to the run stations where the twelve completed *F-111s* were housed. Dozens of people crossed the concrete expanse in shifting, orderly patterns, some moving to their cars, others to their jobs. They were like ants, the patterned paths always the same. The run stations were all in a row, facing the active runway, and in each of them, mechanics and engineers fussed and tinkered and readied the planes for tomorrow's flight. Carrying a large briefcase, Wally entered Run Station Number One.

"Hey, Wally!" the crew chief called. "What can we do for you?"

"Just want to check the air intake spoilers. Got a little problem with my dynamically similar model."

"Okay, Wally. It'll give you a chance to see what a real plane looks like."

Wally pushed an access ladder under the wing and climbed into the air intake. It was cool inside and his breathing echoed around him in the metal cavern. He opened his briefcase and removed an object covered in Reynolds Wrap and he wired it to the aft spoiler, near where the intake narrowed to meet the engine. He closed his briefcase, climbed down, then visited ten other run stations and wired packages to each of the *F-111*s. The Number 12 *F-111*, he did not visit that day.

Then he walked to the parking lot, got into his Morris Minor convertible, and drove home to his garage apartment overlooking the Fort Worth Zoo where at night he could hear the lions roaring their discontent. He stepped through the door and encountered all there was of his adult life, face to face. Here was the sanctuary where he had lived ever since he graduated from design school. Here were his model airplanes hanging from the ceiling—some of radical and ingenious design, far ahead of their time. Here were his books on every aspect of aviation, including biographies of significant aviators, his books on the religions of the world, shelves containing bronze Buddhas and statues of Hindu and Mayan and Zoroastrian deities, and his complete collection of *Playboy* magazines from that initial December 1953 issue featuring a nude Marilyn Monroe as its centerfold.

Here were his record albums: Pete Seeger, Peter Paul and Mary, Buffy Sainte Marie, Phil Ochs, Bob Dylan, and all the others who protested the war in Vietnam. On one wall hung his guitars and his collection of anti-war posters. For a moment, he stood in the door, looking at the eclectic clutter and supposed it adequately reflected the state of his mind. He moved to his desk where he had created a scrapbook of articles and information on the horrors of the Vietnam War. Just last month, an 82-year-old woman in Detroit had burned herself to death to symbolize the horror of the war. Just a few days ago, Lyndon Johnson was burned in effigy. It was here at his desk that he had written letters to Dow Chemical Company, demanding they stop manufacturing the napalm that was burning thousands of people to death in Vietnam and to Monsanto Chemical Company pleading they stop producing Agent Orange that was killing and maiming thousands more. But he had not written a letter to General Dynamics insisting they quit producing their supersonic fighter bomber.

He looked around at the evidence of his hypocrisy and his guilt. Until today, his life had been four-square against everything he believed. "Until today," he said aloud, and he wondered if his mad act would set him free. He knew he had to leave the country. Soon the CIA, the FBI and who knows whom else would be on his tail. But what would he do with all this stuff, the artifacts of his life? He knew he had to abandon it all, leave it for someone else to pitch in the dumpster. He had to travel light, seek a new life, maybe even redemption. What would he miss? Maybe he would miss the model airplanes, maybe the zoo, certainly Jasmine on Tuesday afternoons. And so he sighed, threw some jeans and t-shirts into an old suitcase, grabbed his favorite guitar from the wall and his Peter Paul & Mary and Bob Dylan song books and the May issue of *Playboy* from his shelves, took one last look around, then closed and locked his door for the last time. Then he drove south, through the city, out into the flats and away.

As the little black Morris Minor ripped like a zipper through the grasslands, Wally felt an almost giddy elation, as if he had just left a painful dental appointment. It seemed like something deep inside emptied, dark shadows fled from his soul, like all the Lords of Darkness and all their minions escaped onto the vast Texas prairie. He felt so good and free that he sang, one after another, all the songs he knew by Peter Paul and Mary, Phil Ochs, and Bob Dylan. He sang so loud and so long and so joyously that he lost his voice.

CHAPTER 2
THE ASSASSINATION OF POPEYE

Below Uvalde, the road cut south through fields flat and orderly and green, as far as the eye could see. There was a vegetable fragrance in the air and something else, perhaps chemical sprayed upon the crops. After a while, Wally was enveloped in a sweet, melancholy communion with the earth and the natural green all around; he slowed the car and crept along, the low sun casting the car's long shadow upon the crops by the side of the road. He wondered if that was broccoli growing there, or cauliflower, or what, and he deeply regretted his inability to call natural things by name. 'Can you love something you can't name?' he wondered, and he thought about that for a while.

He stopped the car and walked out into the fields. It was so very still. The earth had a spongy feel beneath his feet as he walked toward where the rows were green. He came upon an irrigation ditch between the road and the fields, and when he tried to step across, his foot slipped down into the mud. With difficulty, he pulled his foot out of the muck, sank to the ground, removed his muddy shoe, and began to poke at the gumbo with a stick he had found. The earth was still warm with the memory of noon, and there was an essence in the air so laden with life that he felt it had substance and that he might float in it, like in a stream, if he tried. He lay back, flat against the earth and it felt as alive and supple as flesh. Overhead a few fragile clouds waited to receive the first rose of sunset. Beyond, the green rows fled away to the horizon. Then he heard a voice.

"I see you there," a man said. His voice was soft and deep with the musical cadence of one whose native language was Spanish.

Wally saw the shadow of the man, and then the man himself, standing above him. "You must not stay here," the man said, and he helped Wally to his feet. "This field is marked for spraying. A plane will be here soon to spray the spinach. He comes now because the air is still and the spray will not drift away on the wind to where it does not belong." Then he asked, "What is your name, son?"

Wally told him his name and was surprised when the man extended his hand with easy formality. He said his name was Augustus Salizar. He was very dark and very thin and there was, on his upper lip, a dark stubble where a full sweeping mustache should have been. He was not very imposing but was somehow completely at ease. His eyes were set deep and they regarded Wally with both humor and curiosity. He could have been, Wally decided, a wise and kindly head of state, living incognito in a country not his own. Augustus Salizar took Wally's arm and led him from the field. As they reached the road, an angry little airplane ripped down to within inches of the earth and farted fog on the spinach.

When they got to the car, Augustus looked long at the tortured old Morris convertible, the guitar, and the torn plaid suitcase in the back. "I watched you when you were lying in the field," he said. "I can tell that you are a man who loves the earth."

"Well, yes, I suppose," Wally said, embarrassed.

"I can always tell a man who loves the earth, even if he does not know her ways." Augustus reached for the guitar and plucked the lowest string. "You are a singer," Augustus said, as if it were a known fact.

Wally was silent.

"Do you have a home?"

"No."

"Do you hate injustice?"

Wally nodded. "Of course."

"Do you believe a man should act as his conscience tells him he should act?"

"Yes. I believe that."

"Do you believe a man should have the right to earn a living wage so that his children will have enough to eat?" He punctuated this question with a hard-struck cacophonous chord and then there was a long silence, in which Wally tried to decide if the man was making fun of the gringo he found lying in the spinach field. "Of course you do," Augustus answered. "You have a guitar." Then after another pause, Augustus said, "I am going to gamble on you, my new friend. I am going to gamble that you will not betray me when I tell you who I am."

"You're not Augustus Salizar?"

"It is not who I am but what I am. I am a revolutionary. You are looking at the guiding force of SLAY, the Stooped Labor Action Association." And then he asked, "Are you going anywhere important?" When Wally said he wasn't, Augustus climbed into the car. "Come," Augustus said, "I will show you how a revolution is made. Perhaps you can write a song for SLAY. Every revolution must have its song." Wally thought of "One Horse Open," but said nothing, and they rattled away down the darkening road.

For several miles, there were only the vegetable fields and the garish billboards along the road leading to the city. Giant, handsome people with paper-white teeth the size of barrels smiled at each other and held sweating bottles of Coca Cola in flat hands. Pall Mall offered an anthology of old slogans that some cowardly advertising agency had refused to discard. And behind the signs were the ocean fields, not so deep and infinite now, because they were about to reach the city, Crystal City, widely known as the Spinach Capital of the World. Augustus pointed out the ludicrous concrete statue of Popeye that had been erected, like some giant fertility symbol, in the center of the town square. Then he indicated a turn to the left, down a narrow, rutted street, deeply shadowed by encroaching adobe walls. There was dust in the air and shapes moved in the half-light and a jukebox somewhere hurled bad brass out into the street.

Augustus directed Wally to a large stucco building—an old theater, it seemed—with walls of earth held up by generations of tattered posters announcing a thousand forgotten events. They stopped, left the car, and as Wally followed the Chief of SLAY through the door and into the lobby, he could hear the low, doomful synthesis of many male voices. And then he saw them, perhaps a hundred men, standing in denim clusters, breathing great billows of white smoke toward the naked bulbs high above. He was immediately aware of an electric urgency in the hall.

Their entrance drew a warm and animated acknowledgment from the crowd. Augustus shook hands with those who gathered around him, and Wally could sense a deep mutual affection in the brief exchanges. Augustus took Wally's arm, and they entered a small anteroom and closed the door. Augustus slumped into a red plastic chair with Coca Cola printed on the back, and his fingers played in the stubble of his mustache. "All they await is a word from me," he said. "One word from me and the revolution begins."

Wally noticed a change in mood, as if Augustus had just remembered the death of a close friend. "What's going to happen?" Wally asked, and he looked around the room that seemed very small and very empty. There was only the plastic chair, a table, a small high window where a pale light leaked down from above.

Augustus sighed. "I don't know. Jesus Christ... I don't know." This he said softly, almost as if speaking to himself. "There is no plan. There is no word I can give them. They will forever be slaves to the landowners and there is nothing I can do."

"But the revolution?"

"The revolution is a thing I invented to give them hope. I am, you see, a very cruel man. I give them hope and there is none to give." He rose and began to pace as a condemned man might measure his cell.

"There's always hope," Wally said, automatically.

Augustus turned abruptly. "Ah, that is where you are wrong. There is not always hope. It is only those who have it that say there is. But let me tell you this, for you to write in your songs about the earth. Most of the people on this earth have no hope. They are hungry and they starve and they are more sick and miserable than you can imagine. Only those who have hope, have hope."

"Augustus, I can't believe what you're telling me." Wally said, and something deep within him was strangely offended. "Those men out there are depending on you. I can tell how much they respect you. They—"

Augustus interrupted. "There is this about those men. A year ago they worked for eighty-five cents per hour in the vegetable fields. And they were glad to get it, because their fathers told them about working for half that. They had little, perhaps enough to eat, but nothing more. They were merely existing. Then I came along and convinced them that they were men, native-born citizens of the world, due more than mere existence. I told them to throw off their chains, to rise up against the rich Texas landowners who grew richer and richer while the laborer grew poorer and poorer." As Augustus told his story, Wally thrilled to the essential rightness of the cause. "I convinced them there was a better life. I promised them there was a better world."

"There must be some way. A demonstration or something."

"They want a revolution, not a demonstration. Non-violence is not in the nature of things here. A man who loves a cockfight does not turn the other cheek. They want a revolution, a radical shift in who holds the power here on the land."

There was a sound at the door, someone knocking, and then the door flew open, and a man backed in, pushing a cart filled with what appeared to be a great quantity of motion picture equipment. He turned, recognized Augustus and greeted him warmly.

"This is Mario Rossetti," Augustus offered, and Wally shook hands with a dapper, wild-eyed young man whose elegant Italian shoes were caked with mud from the spinach fields. Even standing still, he seemed constantly in motion, as if energized by some inner dynamo. His dark eyes were alive with excitement and his smile added at least a thousand lumens to that provided by the high window.

"Ah, I understand you are a ballad singer," Mario said in a thick Italian accent. "It will be good for the film," he added, busying himself with his equipment.

Augustus explained that Mario was making a documentary film on the migrant workers' fight for better wages.

"We have enough fiction in the world," Mario said, as he spread the legs of a large wooden tripod. "Realism! I am dedicated to what is real, what is actually happening here and now. In the end, the documentary film will live. The theatrical will be doomed to the garbage dump. Hollywood will become little more than a theme park." As he worked with his equipment, he explained how his documentaries were in the tradition of Robert Flaherty and Sergei Eisenstein and all the early filmmakers who revealed the human condition in some of the most unexplored regions on earth. "By telling the stories of these people I preserve their lives, human lives that otherwise would perish and be forgotten."

"But how are you going to film something that apparently is not going to happen?" Wally asked, again feeling somehow betrayed.

"With utter realism and candor," Mario said as he placed an impressive-looking camera on the tripod and screwed it down. "Now," he asked Wally, "What about the score?"

"What score?"

"The sound track. We are going to use natural sounds. A lot of sounds, voices, coughing, cries of anger and pain, the shouts of many men. But we'll also use your ballads. You'll be the American ballad singer who has come to help the migrant workers in their fight for justice. You will be the conscience of the movement."

"But I'm not really a ballad singer," Wally countered. "I can barely remember lyrics. I've got to use a song book. I only know minor chords."

Mario seemed undeterred. "All the better. It can't seem too slick. What do you know? What ballads?"

Wally was acutely embarrassed. He decided he had let the ballad singer thing go too far. "With music or without?"

"Without."

"I know "When Johnny Comes Marching Home Again" and "Foggy, Foggy Dew"."

"How about with music?"

"Anything in my Peter Paul and Mary Songbook. But I need a music stand. I don't suppose it would be right to march in the revolution with a music stand."

Mario unpacked an extremely complex-looking tape recorder. He then suggested Wally get his guitar and they would lay down a few tracks.

As Wally moved back through the crowd of off-duty migrant workers to get his guitar, he was acutely aware that he would soon make a fool of himself. But it was irresistible. He *had* to play the guitar for the revolutionary meeting and for the revolution itself. He remembered a time, many years before, when he was riding on a bus with a group of strangers through Switzerland. It was winter and it was night and the snow closed in until there was only the womb of the bus with its light alone, the light of the world. All that existed was there in the bus with its snowbound passengers. A bottle of cognac was passed, and they soon were enveloped in a community of what Wally could only call love. He had never felt so much connection with other human beings. To belong in this small, isolated, family was extraordinary. He had been so overcome by emotion that he struggled to the front of the bus, grabbed the tour guide's microphone and began singing a negro spiritual, because there was more heartfelt emotion in this sound than any other he knew. After a while, a few voices joined in, probably out of embarrassment, and then the bus grew silent. There was only the whisper of the wheels on snow, and he was left more alone than ever as he drank the rest of the cognac and closed his eyes. Now he was not snowbound with strangers, but isolated from the world by the spinach fields, yet the feeling he had was much the same as when that cognac bottle had first been passed. He simply *had* to play the guitar for the revolution.

When he got back to the small room, Augustus's eyes were again blazing with revolutionary zeal and Mario was dancing around his camera, shouting Sicilian proverbs. "We have a plan!" Augustus shouted when Wally entered the room. "A symbol that will make our cause known in every corner of the world!" He was pounding his fist in his hand now. So intense was his mood that both Wally and Mario moved forward to calm him, Mario shooting close-ups of the emotional Chief of SLAY.

Augustus kicked over the Coca Cola chair and shouted: "Death to Popeye!"

Wally remembered the great statue of Popeye in the center of the town square of Crystal City, the Spinach Capital of the World. He felt his heart lifting and fluttering with excitement. "I don't care if there isn't any hope," Augustus said. "We may lose the war, but we will win one magnificent battle! The world will know how we are being enslaved." And then more quietly, almost with reverence, he said, "we will assassinate Popeye."

Mario was ecstatic. "This is the guts! This is the guts!" he shouted repeatedly and then asked when the attack would be made.

"Tonight," Augustus answered.

"Can't be," said Mario.

"Why not?" Augustus asked, somewhat taken aback.

"I can't light the whole outdoors, baby. If you want your revolution documented on film, you have to make a daylight revolution. Broad daylight. Preferably between nine and ten in the morning. We'd have great cross lighting. Vivid colors."

"Then it is settled," Augustus said with finality.

By the time Augustus and Wally reached the stage in front of the crowded old theater, the substance of the revolutionary plan had been leaked and the word "Popeye" could be heard over and over above the crescendo of sound. Mario had lighted the podium area and Wally could occasionally hear the whine of his camera. Wally viewed what happened next through a prism of emotion so overpowering that he lost his grasp on reality. He knew there was a great deal of shouting and there were strong men embracing. And there were the great, welling "Hoorah, Hoorah!"s shouted by the membership of SLAY at the end of each chorus of "When Johnny Comes Marching Home Again" and after "We'll give him a hearty welcome then." Someone kicked over his music stand, and Mario scurried around madly, shooting close-ups and shouting "Marvelous face!"

And then, almost as if they were suddenly submerged, deep within the earth, there came a stillness, a silver secret silence, where a few moments before, there had been bedlam. Augustus had ordered the men back to their homes to spend this last night with their families. Few by few, they moved off into the night, and Augustus, Mario and Wally were left alone with echoes.

"Marvelous," Mario whispered. "It will be an epic film, a documentary that will live forever, like *Nanook of the North* or *Battleship Potemkin*."

"It will go well," Augustus agreed. "I am a cruel man, but it will go well."

They left the theater through a back door and passed through a courtyard crowded with orange trees. The moon cast lace upon the ground and lit the fruit, like ornaments. Wally glanced at Augustus's face, the shadow of his wide hat hiding the expression there, and he wondered if he was a cruel man. Is it a cruel or evil thing to give people hope when here is none? The church promises a kind of hope, which most churchmen know, deep down, does not exist. The promise of personal salvation is history's great white lie. But just because it's a lie, is it evil? The church dresses the lie in pageantry, just as Augustus's

SLAY movement will decorate their hopeless cause with fragments of a concrete Popeye. Yet, Augustus's cause is just and
beneficial and human. The church's cause is irrelevant, negative
and has little to do with the human condition. Augustus is dealing with morality. The church is dealing with immortality. But
then, he considered, the church has never been much of a moral
influence anyway.

Behind the courtyard there was a row of small adobe buildings. They entered one and the cool darkness within was
fringed with the soft reds, blues and greens of a Lone Star Beer
display. They moved to a table, groped for chairs, and sat down.
Augustus explained that he would soon leave them and go
home to be with his family, but there would be a place for them
to sleep in a small room behind the bar. Wally began to play
minor chords on his guitar. As his eyes became accustomed to
the darkness, he noticed there were three other people in the
place. An extremely large, earth-motherly woman leaned with
eyes closed against a wall behind the bar. When Augustus called
her name, which he translated as Little Dove, the woman
heaved herself to semi-wakefulness, reached into an ancient
refrigerator—the kind with the round coil on top—and brought
them three Lone Star Longneck beers. Then she returned to her
somnambulistic station against the wall. There was another
strange heap of motionless matter in a far dark corner, a shape
of vaguely human proportion. Wally wondered if it might be
someone who came in and died there on the floor, unnoticed in
the dark. There was definitely a cloying trace of putrefaction
radiating from that corner of the room.

And there was the girl. She moved through the rainbow cast
by the Lone Star beer sign like a goddess and Wally was certain

she was Maria and he was the dynamiter or she was Ava Gardner or Loren Bacall and he was Gregory Peck or Humphrey Bogart and they soon would be madly, dangerously in love. Then, quite suddenly she was gone, swallowed by the shadows, and Wally wondered if he had seen the girl at all. From the probably dead person in the far, dark corner of the room, he thought he heard the words, "Blood on the moon." 'But then,' he thought, 'perhaps not.'

"I am not a successful Italian motion picture producer," Mario was saying. "The thing is, I refuse to prostitute my concept of what a film should be. There was a time when I filmed dreams like everyone else, fantasies filled with beautiful people in pursuit of happy endings. But the world is filled with so many dreams and illusions that no one can tell any longer what is real and what is not. That's why I devote myself to the documentary."

"How long have you lived in this country?" Wally asked.

"All my life," Mario answered. "I was born in New Jersey."

Augustus seemed surprised. "How, then, can you be an Italian movie producer?"

"I am just as much an Italian movie producer as you are a Mexican revolutionary. My father was Italian; yours was Mexican. We select the label that serves us best. An American movie producer could be a decadent tyrant. An Italian movie producer can only be a gifted artist. A Texas revolutionary would be a malcontent bum. A Mexican revolutionary can only be a sensitive hero."

As suddenly as she had appeared and then disappeared, the ravishing girl reappeared from the shadows. She moved to the table, and with a smile as dreamlike and beautiful as on the faces of those movie stars that Mario didn't film any more, she settled down into a plastic chair, next to where Wally was peeling the label off his Lone Star Longneck. Without a word, she took his hand in hers and put it in her lap. Augustus introduced her as Penelope Segura, daughter and apprentice of the famous *curandera,* Little Dove Segura. The younger Segura had night-black hair woven into two long braids and electric blue eyes and she wore jeans and a loose white shirt. Her complexion was dark, yet light, the color of maple sugar; her fine, high cheekbones were gifts from her distant Aztec forebearers. Her manner was at once sensual and heartbreakingly innocent. At first, she reminded Wally of Sophia Loren. Then, on second glance, she resembled the first girl he had ever kissed. It was a mesmerizing juxtaposition of images, and Wally was too entranced to say hello or to move his hand from her lap.

Gesturing to Penelope, Mario asked Augustus, "Does she know about... you know?"

"You mean Popeye," she said. "Of course I know." Her voice was deep, mellow and melodic. She squeezed Wally's hand and smiled up at him, her lips full and moist, her teeth white as the snow she had probably never seen. They ordered more beer and Wally felt very close to them all, especially Penelope, whose thigh occasionally brushed his. He feared, each time it did, that his jeans might catch fire. It also felt as if her blood flowed through their clothing and into his veins and his returned into hers. He had never fallen in love with someone so quickly and completely. It was not only that she was beautiful beyond measure, but also he sensed depths of mystery within her , mysteries that he would eagerly spend the rest of his life to solve.

Augustus was explaining that Little Dove Segura was well known all along the river for her miraculous cures. "Soon Penelope will be equally respected for her magic. She is as gifted as her mother in the arts of healing."

Wally looked to where Little Dove was sleeping against the old refrigerator. No two women, much less mother and daughter, could look so different. "So you work with your mother, curing the sick?" Wally asked, wishing he had a more intelligent thing to ask or say. "What, with herbs?"

"And other things. Mother heals the body; I heal the soul." She opened Wally's hand and pressed it against her thigh, and he felt all the residual guilt and anger and darkness flying from his body like bats from a cave. 'Who or what is this magical creature?' he wondered, gazing into the blue depths of her eyes.

"Perhaps our revolution will be remembered," Augustus was saying. "I remember my father telling how he fought in the Madero Revolution with Poncho Villa and then traveled a thousand miles on a burro to fight beside Zapata. Those were powerful days; the cause was so just. But this is the United States. Revolution is more difficult here. When a country is known as the embodiment of good, a just cause has no voice. During the Mexican Revolution, everyone knew Mexico was a place of tyranny. So, any cause, regardless of its motives, was a move toward social justice. In the United States, it is not so. In the United States, social justice is far more difficult to obtain than in countries less free. But tomorrow, if we win and tear down Popeye, people will take a look at what is going on down here. And they can't help but come to our support."

"My film will give the voice of your cause a fantastic volume," Mario insisted. "All the anger, the fear, the passion. It will all be there." Then he glanced at Wally and Penelope, who were now obviously holding hands beneath the table. "And then, there is the love angle," he said. "The American ballad singer and the wayward illegitimate daughter of the evil landowner who has joined her lover to storm the ramparts."

"Blood on the moon." The croaking voice now came unmistakably from the shadows in the far corner of the bar.

Wally searched for the source of the voice. "Who keeps saying that?" he asked.

"It's the prophet," Penelope said, the words flowing gracefully from her lips, soft and low. Although she had spoken less than a dozen words in his presence, Wally felt he could spend the rest of his life listening to this enchanting girl talk. Her voice had the deep, rich quality of a cello. The shadows at the rear of the room began to shift and then, from them emerged the most incredible figure Wally had ever seen. He moved in a malevolent vapor that seemed to swirl about him and it smelled of urine and decay. He seemed very old and bent like a small rotten tree covered with an awful, ancient beard of tangled Spanish moss. He seemed to be wearing many layers of clothing, each layer in ragged ruin, and on his head was some sort of burlap cap topped with an olive branch and a small American flag. In his hand, he carried a hoe, and as he moved toward their table he raised his terrible face to the ceiling and again cried, "Blood on the moon!"

"It's our prophet," Augustus said. "He roams up and down the Rio Grande searching for his lost prophecy." The prophet remained still, a few feet from the table, and he mumbled some deep catechism in a strange language. "They say he was born in Turkey and that he spoke out against sin and praised God in many languages. He was much like the great prophets of the Old Testament, but the years have made him silent, except for that one phrase."

"What does he want here?" Mario asked. "A meal? A beer?"

"He will never take charity. He works for what he gets. Mostly he gets his food from garbage cans. Sometimes he will hoe weeds for food." As if Augustus's words had pushed through some hideously tortuous avenue to his understanding, the prophet began to scratch his hoe against the wooden floor. Wally could see the prophet's eyes peering through his matted thatch of hair and beard and they seemed kind and sad, and Wally felt an overwhelming compassion for the awful old man. 'The poor, poor, old guy,' he thought. 'Trying all these years to tell us something.' He reached for the prophet's hand and the old man snarled and retreated, stirring a fog of corruption like a wind in an open grave.

"He's just hungry," Augustus said, and they motioned to Little Dove behind the bar to bring him some tacos and beer.

As the old man ate, squatting there on the floor by the table, his tired, milky-red eyes swept back and forth across the revolutionaries. He ate with one hand; the other hand clasped his hoe. "He's just got to go with us tomorrow," Mario said, risking a brief close-up of their ghastly companion. "It would be great! He would be the ancient river prophet bringing the wisdom and mysticism of the East to the movement. Great symbolism!"

"What wisdom?" Augustus laughed. "He doesn't say anything."

"He says 'blood on the moon,'" Wally said. "And look at his eyes. He has a great deal to say, if we could only understand."

"I believe he is much more than he seems," Penelope said, glancing at the prophet with apparent affection.

"We'll need Penelope when we film the march into town," Mario said, "leading the charge on the square. Right there with her men. It will probably be best to have one of her breasts hanging out like the women in the old French war paintings. Maybe she could even carry a child and a sword."

"Realism!" Augustus sneered. "So this is your realism? Old mad prophets and bare bosoms?" He sighed, rose, and said he was going home. He shook hands with Mario and then Wally, took Penelope's hand and lifted it to his lips and kissed her fingers. Then Augustus Salizar nodded to the prophet and walked out into the night.

"I thought documentaries were supposed to be objective," Wally said after Augustus was gone.

"They are," Mario said. "But that doesn't mean they shouldn't have a point of view. Every documentarian manipulates his subject to reflect his point of view. His choice of shots, his camera angles, the way the footage is edited, his choice of music—they all shape the story and what the viewer believes about the story. And in this documentary, we want the viewer to believe in the righteousness of the farm workers' cause. My documentary will seek truth, but truth sometimes takes a little teasing to reveal itself."

Soon it grew late, and they went into the back room where they were to sleep, and where Mario planned to shoot scenes of the American balladeer and the wayward daughter of the rich Texas landowner spending their last night together before storming the ramparts. In order to get the prophet into the bedroom they had to snatch up his food from the floor and walk backward, beckoning constantly as he skittered crabwise in pursuit. Although there was an electric light in the room, Mario had Little Dove replace it with an oil lantern he had seen behind the bar. When the lantern filled the room with a soft golden glow, Mario set up his camera. "You don't have to take off your clothes," he said. "That's for a later scene. For now, just climb onto the bed and sort of kiss and hold each other and look longingly into each other's eyes. Maybe feel each other up a little."

"Do you mind, Wally?" Penelope asked. "It would just be acting."

"If it's all right with you." Wally's heart was beating like a wild bird in a cage.

"I'd like to," she said, and she reached over and kissed him. Her lips were soft and her breath sweet and her touch was electricity and velvet. After a long while they parted and Penelope whispered, "I liked that, Wally."

"I did, too."

"I know, I felt that you did."

"I'm sorry," Wally said, terribly embarrassed.

"Oh, Wally, it's just good nature." Then she whispered, "You can touch me, if you want to, like lovers do. It will be good for the film."

She unbuttoned her white shirt and slipped his hand inside. Her breasts were full and soft, yet firm, her skin smooth as dark ivory. Wally felt his heart rushing blood to all the capillaries in his hand, all his nerve ends gathering into his fingertips. She placed her hand over his and guided him to her nipple and Wally thought he might faint or even possibly die with pleasure as they continued to kiss and touch each other, so filled with the joy of the moment they were unaware of Mario's camera.

After he had filmed Wally and Penelope's love scene from many angles and with different exposures, a half-hour that might have been the happiest of Wally's entire life, Mario called it a wrap, and he, too, climbed into the bed. They lay there, the three of them, awake, unspeaking, listening to the barking of coyotes in the South Texas night. Wally, his head overflowing with love, desire, and sorrow, was nearly asleep when the prophet climbed up and crouched at the foot of the bed and scratched the covers with his hoe.

The morning was a breathless thing. The sun rose clear and thrilling as a high heartbeat, and the sound of children and roosters sang hallelujahs to the new and golden day. Penelope was still sleeping, curled on her side, her almond eyes closed, her lips slightly parted. His heart seemed to flip over in his breast as he remembered kissing those lips the night before. Wally rose, feeling the buoyant freedom of a Saturday child, quickly dressed, gathered up his guitar, and rushed to the orange grove behind the theater where he was to meet Augustus. The Chief of SLAY was there, spitting out orange pips.

"I am glad you are here early, my friend," Augustus said. He offered Wally an orange. "It's good to live in a land where you can pick your breakfast from a tree." Wally paused a moment to pull great quantities of fragrant air into his lungs.

"Are you ready to play our small game?" Augustus asked.

"Game?"

"We are playing a game today. You know that, don't you, my friend--my friend with the sad guitar?" It was to Wally as if the sun had crept behind a cloud; but it was there still, in the center of the sky.

Wally sat down beneath an orange tree, next to where Augustus stood, and he struck that chord he liked best, the one that announces the lyric, "There is a house in New Orleans." As he played the minor chords, he thought about Penelope and the "House of the Rising Sun", and he wondered if it was possible that he and this amazing girl could be in love. It was surprising that she had been so forward, so open to his intimacies, and for a fleet moment, the thought came that she might be a prostitute; but that was impossible, and even if she were, he couldn't care less.

"Augustus," he said after a while, "I don't want you to tell me about games. I am trying to live life as best I can. That's all I know. I don't know about games." He wondered how long it would be before they found the deadly chocolate Holloway's Milk Duds in the wreckage of the *F-111*s and if they had already begun to hunt him down. "There was a time," he continued, "when we could have lived our lives with both sobriety and dignity. But now the two are totally incompatible with the times, these crazy times."

"You are more thoughtful now," Augustus said, "like the man I saw dreaming in the spinach field."

Wally wondered if Augustus would understand why he sabotaged the fighter-bombers and if he would consider it the act of a madman. "One day, if you care to listen, I will tell you about my thoughts, Augustus, as you have told me yours. Maybe tonight. I think you'd understand."

There were some last-minute details for Augustus to organize before the revolutionaries arrived, so Wally decided to walk downtown where he could watch the initial reactions of the people there, and then he would join the march to the statue of Popeye.

As he walked along the cracked cement sidewalks of Crystal City, the new sun pushed down promises of a punishing noon. Even now the dust had begun to rise on windless wings as if cast from beneath the earth by some evil will, hot and dry. The street held people passing, going here and there to where they went yesterday and would always go until they died, walking here and there to their grave. He felt a touch of guilt then, as he always did when he viewed people as a large and plural thing, the kind of thing seen from tall buildings or airplanes in old war movies. And so he began to look closely at the faces and say to himself, 'There goes a man unlike any other, who dreams and is afraid and is the center of the universe. He is totally unique. Yet, he and I are doomed. And that is our bond and our salvation. If only there was some way we could share this great odyssey to our grave, and find comfort in our mutual tragedy.'

There was a story he had once read by Leonid Andreyev called "The Seven Who Were Hanged". It told the story of seven comrades facing certain death and it told of their initial horror and loneliness. But on the morning they were to be hanged, when they were led two by two out through the snow to the gallows, they became exhilarated, almost joyful. He remembered one had said in those last few moments of life, as he stood with his comrade: "The shores of life cannot contain my love, which is as boundless as the sea." But there were seven to be hanged, an unequal number, and the last one had to go alone. And this was the greatest horror and loneliness of all.

The colorful fronts of the little shops along the main street reminded him that he needed a pitch pipe to tune his guitar. He looked for a music store and then realized there wouldn't be one. Across the street was the unemployment office and already a long line stretched around the block and out of sight.

"Poor souls," he heard a man say. He turned and there was a stocky, rather handsome man shaking his head sorrowfully. He indicated the unemployment line and again said, "Poor Mexican son-of-a-guns."

"No jobs, huh?" Wally said, realizing the man expected an answer of some kind.

"Nope," the stocky man said. His face was shaded by a broad white cowboy hat, but Wally could tell it had suffered many summers beneath the cruel border sun. He was a native here. Wally knew this by the way his boots grew from the pavement and by the way he breathed—loud and with a rattle, as if through layers of dust. "And what jobs there is don't pay nuthin'. And it's all gonna come to a head, Lord knows. I feel it in my bones." He shifted his bulk, squeezed his forehead with his hand and flicked off sweat. "Is that a guitar?" he asked, looking directly at the guitar.

Wally nodded, resisting the impulse to say it was a walrus.

"Folk singer?"

Wally said "Yes."

"Well if you're looking for soul, you'll find plenty of it over there in that line. Believe me, Buddy. Cause I've been trying to save those souls for many a year. Me and a few others around here believe their souls is just like any other in the eyes of our Lord Jesus."

"You're a minister?"

"First Blue-Eyed Baptist. Yonder behind the drug store. If you're not doing anything in particular, lemme show you our little church. I like to talk to young men of the world. Folks around here just don't always tap a feller's intellectual horizons, so to speak. And most of 'em don't talk English." His smile was so warm and his manner so comfortable that Wally grinned, said he'd be glad to, and introduced himself.

"Asa Pain. Reverend Asa Pain," the man said. "Friends call me Ace. They all laugh about that here. A preacher with a name like Ace."

As they moved through the gathering heat toward the church, Wally asked about life in Crystal City.

"Oh, this place has got its good and its bad, so to speak. But it's done right proud for itself, especially because it sits right where no city should be. Worst land in Texas. Wouldn't even grow weeds if we didn't dump thousands of dollars' worth of water onto the fields, and all that fertilizer. The Lord holds the rain back here so we gotta dig down toward Hell to water our fields."

They reached the church, a bright-white frame structure nestled beneath a grove of some kind of tree Wally wished he knew. He did recognize the magnificent bougainvillea and the poinsettias splashing small glories of color against the outer walls. 'It's a beautiful church,' Wally thought. 'A place where peace seems to be.' From the church, he could see the statue of Popeye and the route the marchers would soon be taking.

"So that's the Crystal City Popeye," Wally said, pointing at the big blue and white figure.

"And we're mighty proud of old Popeye here. Some folks think it's peculiar to build a great big old Popeye in the center of the town square. But it sort of represents our struggle and our achievement. Built somethin' out of nothin'. This is the spinach capital of the world. More vegetables are grown in this bad old land than anywhere else."

"Isn't this also called the migrant labor capital?"

"Got five thousand Mexican stooped laborers. More than anybody else. They make their winter home here and then fan out all over the country. But they always come back. Like swallows to the white cliffs of Dover, so to speak."

They sat down on the church steps and watched the morning spend itself on the dry brittle streets. A man passed selling snow-cones from a cart.

"But you know somethin'," the preacher reflected, "I guess when you add it all up, my ministry here has been a failure. My main mission was to narrow the gulf between the races."

"Races?" Wally asked, rather surprised.

"The white man and the Mexican," the minister continued. "I haven't been able to bring about a common understanding. Can't get' em to come to my church."

"Do you think it might have something to do with the fact that they're Catholic?" Wally asked.

Asa Pain waved the question away as if shooing a fly. "Kids filthy all the time. Fall asleep with your mouth open and they'll steal your teeth. Just somethin' about them like that. I thought in the beginning, the answer would be Christ. A brotherhood under Jesus Christ. That's why I built them their own church."

"Their own church!" Wally was beginning to see where this was going. "I suppose you call it the Brown-Eyed Baptist Church."

"Well, Buddy, don't be too quick to criticize. It's the first Protestant church they ever had. But, you see, I figured they needed to hear the message of our Lord. They are creatures of God just like the rest of us. Give 'em time and they'll be well near equal. So I built them a little church over there where they all live. And, Buddy, I was almost run out of town, so to speak. Folks called me a Mexican lover. Said I spent so much time with them I neglected my own congregation. So, I trained this fine Mexican I know and I gave him the church. Turned the whole thing over to him, lock stock, and barrel." He paused for a moment and took in great deep breaths of air and grace. "Ah, Buddy, it does my old heart good to see those people cast off their witchcraft ways and accept Jesus as their Lord."

"Why didn't you just ask them into your church? Why a separate church?" Wally asked the question with downcast eyes. It was one of those incredibly obvious questions that he had long ago learned people don't ask. Questions like: If the population of the earth is rapidly outstripping its capacity to produce food, why do you resist birth control? Or: If the Japanese were already defeated and negotiating for surrender, why did we slaughter a civilian population with an atomic bomb? Or: Why do our politicians create national forests to protect the trees and then allow private lumber companies to come in and cut them down? Questions like that. Questions so fundamental that to ask them is to be something more than a boor and something less than civilized. Then he asked: "Did you consider this, asking them into your church?"

"Well, yes, it was considered. But it wouldn't do."

"Why? Wally asked, eyes still downcast, fingers feeling the polish of his guitar. "They built your city, maybe they could help you build your church."

"You've got to understand the people down here, Buddy. As soon as a child is born, he's taught to hate the Mexicans, and vice versa. After all, they been killing each other along the border since time began, the races have. Buddy, they just don't trust us. That's why they're so deceitful. And why they steal the way they do."

"I just wonder," Wally said. "If the church can't do something about all that hate, who can?"

"We can only pray, each of us, that the Lord will take hate from our hearts. We can only pray."

Wally let a dissonant chord ineffectually express the anger he felt. And so the good people of Christ pass another opportunity to do what Jesus asked them to do. His mind searched for a severe enough action to jar the complacency of this good and peaceful sanctuary. Maybe he could scrawl obscenities on the altar or piss in the collection plate. Then he realized those were the thoughts of a madman. 'Well, if it waddles like a duck and quacks like a duck it must be a...' His thoughts were interrupted by what he saw coming down the street.

It was like a mirage, at first, something imagined in the heat. But then they swept around a corner, scattering children and dogs, and there was the prophet holding his hoe above his head and howling his strange vocabulary. And then there was Mario, galloping ahead like a retreating infantryman, his tape recorder strapped to his stomach, pausing occasionally to fire back at his pursuers with his camera. There were cardboard signs swaying above the marchers. One read: "I cannot live on

80 cents an hour." Another read, "Death to Popeye!" Augustus was also in the front ranks, his face calm, his eyes sad.

Crowds followed on either side of the marchers and it was evident the ranks had increased in number as the march progressed. There was a great deal of shouting and noise and honking of horns and Wally waved his guitar at Augustus and began walking across the street to join the revolution. He was almost across the street when he simultaneously saw Penelope and heard the police whistle.

"Hey, that lady has her tit out!" someone shouted, and the number of young men marching increased appreciably. Mario, wielding his recorder and camera, seemed everywhere at once. The crowd pushed Wally against Penelope, whose eyes burned with the righteousness of their cause and whose left breast swung free and brown and magnificent at the head of SLAY. Apparently, Mario had persuaded her to play the role of the woman in the old French paintings. In her arms, there was no child, yet she did carry a small stuffed bear and in her other hand she held a highly decorative Order of the Oddfellows ceremonial sword. Wally gave her arm a squeeze, and she leaned over and kissed him on his lips.

The policeman, who was shouting something about indecent exposure, was swept away by the crowd, his whistle drowning. "Your guitar!" someone shouted. "Play your guitar!" Wally nodded and tried, but he had no carrying strap and the guitar kept sliding down his side. So Penelope handed her stuffed bear to Augustus and she helped Wally hold the guitar. He began to play, in cadence to the moving, marching mass, the simple staccato chords to "When Johnny Comes Marching Home Again." And as before, as the marchers took up the song, there was a great booming "Hoorah! Hoorah!" at the end of the first and second lines. It was almost unbearable. 'A banquet for the soul,' he thought.

"The shores of life cannot contain my love, which is as boundless as the sea." He had never felt so involved before. The warmth of the pressing bodies, the timbre of the blending of their voices, filled him with a sense of joy beyond description. He sang until his throat hurt, and he thrashed at the strings of his guitar, unmindful of the sound. There was only the rhythm and the love. Out of the corner of his eye, he saw the prophet, still waving his hoe, and Mario was there, now here, now there again, his camera recording it all. The tide moved on.

It swept by the Baptist Church and Asa Pain and the Shell station and the bank and the corner drugstore, where old men with hickory faces regarded the marchers with dull eyes. There were the sounds of sandals scuffling and the roar of voices like one might hear at a poorly officiated prizefight.

And there was Popeye, pressing his pipe between concrete lips, his tiny eyes watching the approach of the marchers. Wally saw the wall of deputies waiting on the other side of the square, and then a sound truck exploded to life and a huge mechanical voice boomed out: "ALL RIGHT! ALL RIGHT! ALL YOU PEOPLE DON'T COME NO FURTHER!" It was a physical thing, this voice, filling the square completely like sand in a mold. The marchers paused, intimidated, moved to the base of the statue, and then stopped. The dust their feet had made swept on and away. No one sang. No one breathed. Wally could hear the distant purr of an airplane dusting the earth and he thought for a moment of the twelfth *F-111*. Without looking, he could tell the prophet was quite near.

"SPEAK YOUR SAY!" the great voice boomed with bored intolerance. The eyes of the deputies stirred within their paper-white faces.

Wally saw Augustus step forward, slowly, until he stood alone before the voice and the deputies, his shadow black as blindness, like a hole into which he might fall. He said nothing. He did not move.

"WHAT DO YOU PEOLE WANT?" Eloquent. Simple. Thunderous. Silence. Horrible. Tragic.

"SPEAK YOUR SAY!" the robot voice demanded.

Augustus's shoulders moved almost imperceptibly down and forward, and Wally was suddenly dreadfully afraid for the outcome of the revolution. He handed the prophet his guitar and moved to Augustus's side.

He could see there were tears in the eyes of the Chief of SLAY. "Augustus," he whispered. "Tell them what you want."

"Tell them what we want?" Augustus repeated, his voice as old and sad as a Tolkien tree. "So very much and so very little. Who can tell them if they don't already know?"

"But they are waiting. All our people are waiting."

"Do what you will," the voice inside Augustus said, and he turned to old wood and a soft moss began to grow on his shoulders.

Then, from the massed revolutionaries, there came a sound of incredible urgency. A sound like a harp from hell, hurling dissonance at the great rock sailor towering over the square. Wally whirled and there was the prophet howling some half-forgotten malediction at Popeye, his black awful fingers moving fast upon the guitar. Soon the crowd began to feel the prophet's rage and they began to chant to the rhythm of his guitar. Soon there came from the rejuvenated assemblage the cry: "DEATH TO POPEYE! The cry became a chorus and the crowd became, again, something beside itself. Wally felt that thing enter his will, and it was warm and weeping and imperative. As the prophet continued to punish the guitar, Wally rushed to the man who held a coil of rope, threw the coil over his shoulder, and began to climb the statue. He shinnied up its calf and pulled himself up upon the concrete blue knee.

"HEY YOU!" boomed the loudspeaker, "GET THE HELL OFF FROM UP THERE!"

Wally scrambled on, the end of the rope held beneath his chin, his knees and fingers abused by the rough cement. He gripped the extended stone elbow, swung himself up to the great tattooed forearms, rested there for a moment and then began to form a noose. The sound truck belched chains of thunder threats, and as he worked on the knot, he could see the deputies break ranks and rush to the base of the statue. A bar of fire flashed as Penelope drew her Oddfellow's sword, and from the marchers came a sound as if they had seen a shooting star. Wally slipped the noose over Popeye's head, and as Penelope held off the deputies, he slid down the rope and ran back to the front ranks of the marchers.

Now was the moment. He looked around him at the faces of the revolutionaries. 'They are beautiful,' he thought. There was on their faces an aura of profound innocence, as sometimes seen in portraits of the mother of Jesus and in the smiles of Oriental prostitutes. He smiled at them, and it seemed that each one of them returned his smile, and there flowed between them an emotion as powerful as eternity and as personal as a breath. Brown hands joined his on the rope and Popeye began to sway.

The stone expression did not change with the world rocking below like that. Popeye just continued to puff his pipe, perhaps dreaming of Olive Oil or Sweetpea or his next can of spinach. First back on his heels, then forward, the arc ever widening, an outlandish dance to the crescendo of sound exploding at the extremes of imbalance. Back. Forward. Back. Hanging. Forward. And then, as if filmed in slow motion by Mario, the Crystal City Popeye began to follow his pipe to the earth.

Augustus probably saw the statue falling toward him in the instant before he was crushed, and he might have called out, but he died instead.

"Give him air!" someone shouted.

"Screw air! Give him light!" Mario called as he pushed the crowd back and took a reading on the fallen revolutionary.

The sun fell into some tacky clouds and dusk fell onto the spinach fields. Soon it would be dark, thank God, and Wally wouldn't have to look into the faces of the people who passed on their way nowhere. In the distance, not really too far away, Wally could see a small boy, alone, clasping tightly to the remainder of the day. He was chasing something Wally could not see, perhaps a butterfly or something dreamed. He remembered when he was that boy, riding his bicycle in the ghost light of dusk, gliding silently on the dirt paths of a place called Signal Point. It was high on an Illinois bluff, and if the sun set just right, you could see its colors caught in the great Mississippi River, far away. He would lie in the grass, his bicycle by his side, and listen for night to come. All the familiar things had a different voice at night. Muted, softer, as if the night itself were a sleeping thing that should not be wakened. They were new sounds, night sounds, things not heard in the day. The distant conversation of invisible trains and dogs and dishes and screen doors slamming and mothers calling their children home. He listened now. The sounds were much the same, but his bicycle and Augustus were dead, as were the trains.

Mario approached, looking naked without his gear. "Where are you headed from here, Comrade?"

Wally was annoyed at the abrupt question, disturbing his reveries. And his voice quivered as it always did, maddeningly, whenever he felt his words might offend. "Why should you care? You didn't seem to care about anything else today. 'Give him light!' For Christ's sake, Mario!"

"I care, you bastard!" he replied, low and hard. "I feel terrible about Augustus. But I had to keep filming. Chances are that footage will bring him to life again. He will be remembered long after you and I are forgotten." He said nothing for a moment, then, softly, again, "I do care." He put his hand on Wally's shoulder. "Come on, let's go visit Little Dove."

They walked through the gathering darkness to the bar where Wally had first met Mario, Penelope, and the prophet, and he was shocked by the thought that it had been less than twenty-four hours since they had been there with Augustus. Poor Augustus. When they entered, Wally could tell, the prophet lurked somewhere near, and Penelope glowed, soft red and green, in the light of the Lone Star Beer display. His guitar was in her lap and her moving fingers spun random melancholy. 'How beautiful she is,' he thought. 'She looks a part of everything and probably is. She and I are constellations of neighboring atoms swimming in the totality of the universe, organisms with significance only to ourselves, with only an instant to share between nothings.' She looked up and smiled.

"He was a good man, our Augustus," she said, and she joined them at a table. Little Dove served them each a beer and they drank silently, a kind of prayer for the absent friend. The prayer extended into a third round of beer.

"You didn't answer me about where you're headed now." Mario said.

"I didn't know where I was going when I came here, and I don't know where I'm going when I leave."

"Home?" Penelope asked.

"Can't go home."

"Why?"

Wally shifted in his chair. "I'm sort of a fugitive. If I went back, I'd be arrested and probably executed."

"Righteous!" Mario said.

"You'd probably want to film it."

Penelope reached for his hand. "What did you do, Wally?"

Wally felt his face tightening and his tongue loosening as always happened halfway through his third beer. "I worked in this defense plant where they make supersonic bombers—real sophisticated planes designed to carry atomic bombs. I sabotaged eleven of them; fixed them so they'd crash."

Mario whistled, astonished. "How in the hell did you do that?"

"I put Holloway's Milk Duds in the air intakes of the jet engines."

"What are Holloway's Milk Duds?" Penelope asked. "Some kind of explosive?"

"No. It's chocolate. I packed Milk Duds in Reynolds Wrap so when the engines got hot the packages split open; all that chocolate gummed up the engines and the planes crashed."

"Son-of-a-bitch!" Mario said. "Best thing for you is to high-tail it across the border. But if they catch you here, make sure it's outdoors in cross lighting. About F8." He winked and Wally smiled.

"What about the pilots? Penelope asked.

"I'm sure they bailed out. I'm sure they're okay. I should know; I designed the ejection systems. I only wanted to kill the bombers."

"They won't catch you, will they Wally?"

"They'll try."

"The police, do they know where you are? Penelope asked, concern written in her amazing blue eyes."

"I don't think so. But I've got to keep moving."

"Why don't we all go to Mexico?" Penelope offered.

"Mazatlan!" Mario cried. "The greatest, wildest fiesta in Mexico! El Cordobes will be there this year, and I've never filmed a bullfight."

"What about money?" Wally asked.

"Hell, Wally, I got that all worked out. We'll go into the mail-order pornographic jigsaw puzzle business."

Wally laughed. Penelope leaned forward with intense interest.

"Here's how it works," Mario said, as they asked for another beer. "It's a natural, and we could pull it off. First thing we do is take a series of pictures, people making it in all sorts of positions. Hell, you and Penelope would be great. We wouldn't have to use freelance talent."

Penelope clapped her hands. "It would be fun, Wally. I could help Mario direct the photography, help him select one of the 729 different love-making positions that have been actually recorded, and that doesn't count oral sex or bestiality."

Mario was amazed; Wally was more than shocked. "Where the hell did you learn all that technical stuff?" Mario asked. Wally was not sure he wanted to know.

"Well, when I was a little girl and decided I wanted to become a prostitute, I figured I'd go all the way, be the best. So I studied and improved my mind. Did you know the Queen of Sheba had pubic hair that hung to her knees and that Solomon made her shave it off before he would make love with her?"

"You are not a prostitute!" Wally insisted. "Just look at you. You are an angel."

"Oh, Wally. It's all right. Maybe I'm not a prostitute in the traditional sense. I guess it depends on your definition."

Wally looked down at his hands.

"Don't be sad, Wally. I still love you. And you're a dangerous fugitive."

"Anyway," Mario continued, "you put advertisements in the horny magazines like *Nugget* and *Gent* and the sun worshipper's rags and you offer dirty pictures for five dollars."

"But you can't send them through the mail," Wally reminded him.

"Ah, that's the secret. You don't. You mount the dirty pictures on heavy cardboard and cut them into jigsaw puzzles. When they're in pieces, they are not pornography. You can't tell what the hell they are. Then, when the purchaser gets it, he puts it together in the privacy of his home. Great? Pure genius!"

"Will they come after you, Wally?" Penelope asked.

"I can't imagine they'd let me get away with what I've done."

"Oh, Wally," Penelope sighed.

"We better leave tonight," Mario said.

There was a scuffling sound, and from the gloom, emerged the awful presence of the prophet. He stood in the half-light, his mad, sorrowful eyes barely discernible.

"What about him?" Wally asked.

"He smells something awful," Mario said.

"He seems to like us," Wally said. "And he's been a real trooper. Did you see him swinging his hoe at the deputies?"

"I vote we take him," Mario said. Besides, he makes wild footage."

"I wonder who he is?" Wally asked, thoughtfully. "There was a time long ago when he had something to tell us. I guess he's forgotten what it was."

Penelope went behind the bar, picked up her Oddfellows sword and kissed her mother, Little Dove, on the cheek. Wally and Mario rose and after retrieving his guitar, Wally held out his hand to the prophet, who moaned and backed away, yet followed them out of the bar and through the silent street to the waiting Morris Minor.

CHAPTER 3
THE RESTAURANT OF GASPAR LOPEZ

They raced west across the vegetable fields to the tiny town of Cometa, and then south to the Eagle Pass Highway. The little Morris Minor purred contentedly and the wind tugged at the flag on the prophet's cap. The land was now dry, flat and empty as a skeleton's dream, and the car seemed earth's only living thing. And then, suddenly, the road dipped down into a small valley and Penelope said there was a place nearby that she wanted Wally to see. She directed him off the highway onto a narrow road that may have once been paved and it led into a small canyon cut by a free-flowing stream, lined with willows and cottonwoods. As they drove slowly along the bank of the creek, it seemed the temperature dropped at least ten degrees. The sun that had been so punishing a few moments before now offered a gentle golden light in the willows and on the canyon walls and on the riffles in the stream. Filigreed patterns of light and shadow danced all around them.

"What is this place?" Wally asked. "It's beautiful."

"The stream is fed by underwater springs," Penelope said. "In the old days, people used to come here for the healing waters. But in recent times, they are too sophisticated and too cynical for their own good and nobody comes here for healing any more. My mother brought me here when I was a little girl. I watched her heal a child with polio, just over there. But now there is modern medicine. Who's to say which is best? I haven't been here in years."

Penelope asked if they could stop for a while and maybe cool off before continuing on to the border.

They climbed out of the car and Penelope showed them the places where the springs bubbled up out of the creek and out of the rocks along the canyon wall. Some of the springs fed pools of warm water; others were ice cold. Wally took off his shoes, hung his guitar over one shoulder and waded out into the stream. He picked up a smooth, flat stone and skipped it off the water and into the willows, A cloud of butterflies rose and flitted in the sunlight like orange and black kites. "Monarch butterflies," Penelope said. "They are on their spring migration north from Mexico. In the old days there were black bears and bobcats here. My mother taught me how to make them tame so I could pet them."

Mario got out his camera and began filming the natural beauty of the canyon. The prophet seemed content to remain in the car, staring out into the middle distance. Penelope and Wally walked barefoot along the stream, holding hands. A shadow cut clean across the canyon wall, and Penelope said it was a peregrine falcon, "the fastest and most beautiful of all hawks."

Wally sensed that Penelope moved in absolute harmony with the life forms in the canyon. It was as if she and the butterflies and falcons and willows, even the black bears and bobcats, were notes in the same scale. How he envied her knowledge, her awareness and appreciation of the natural world around her. And he realized how much he could learn from this amazing person, who revealed more of herself each day. She squeezed his hand and smiled, as if she had heard his thoughts. It occurred to him that they might be a normal boy and girl, enjoying each other's company and the beauty of the day, and that he wasn't a fugitive and she wasn't an angel. He wasn't sure if the thought gave him pleasure or pain. They were what they were and he could envision no outcome where they could live happily ever after, holding hands like this, walking barefoot in a crystal stream. 'Maybe this moment is the ever after,' he thought, and he realized, feeling her hand in his, the close magical presence of her body and spirit, that he had never been happier, and if this moment was the ever after, maybe it was enough. Penelope squeezed his hand again and he knew for certain she had been listening to his thoughts.

They were approaching a place where the stream rounded a bend in the canyon when they heard the mandolin. It seemed, at first, a part of the magic of the morning, a melody performed by the wind. And then they saw the people. Some were playing in the stream or lounging naked in the shade of the willows or reading or simply listening to the music. Those who were clothed wore loose-fitting, tie-dyed shirts or shifts of extravagant color and design. Wally thought they looked like exotic flowers in a garden. Then a harmonica joined the mandolin, and the sound, interwoven with the laughter of the people in the water, was as enchanting and transcendent as any music Wally had ever heard.

When the girl with the mandolin noticed Wally and Penelope, she stopped playing, and all the others stopped what they were doing and stared, not unkindly, at the intruders. It was as if time had stopped, and the morning waited to see what would happen. The girl with the mandolin got up and walked toward them. She wore only a kind of brightly colored loincloth around her hips. Her breasts were small and only partially concealed by her long hair, very near the color of marigolds. Wally didn't know where to look or what to say and when he glanced at Penelope she was smiling, whether at him or the girl, he couldn't tell.

"I'm sorry," the girl said, noticing Wally's embarrassment. "I forget sometimes we might offend. But few of us wear clothes here." The man with the harmonica handed her a tie-dyed shift and as she slipped it on, the others returned to what they had been doing and the music and laughter resumed.

Wally felt he should apologize for something, but he didn't know exactly for what, maybe for intruding or staring or for seeming so conventional. Then Penelope said," What do you mean about people not wearing clothes? Is this a nudist colony?"

"Oh, no, nothing like that. We just believe in being free. You know, unrestricted. Come on, I'll show you." She led them through her community, a cluster of small, but beautifully constructed adobe huts. Some of the young people were working in vegetable gardens, others were sewing or tie-dying their loose garments, others were working at crafts or cleaning the huts. One young woman was imprinting the design of a butterfly on a clay pot.

When the girl paused to speak to a man making adobe bricks, Penelope turned to Wally and said, "Don't you think she's beautiful?"

"I guess so."

"I saw you staring," she teased. "She is the opposite of me. We are dark and light. Do you like her?"

"I don't know, Penelope," he answered, exasperated that she would ask such a thing. But he did know, and he knew he did.

"Are you a folk singer?" the girl asked.

"Well, sort of," Wally said.

"He only knows minor chords," Penelope said.

Wally felt humiliated, foolish, and wished he hadn't brought his guitar. And he wondered if maybe Penelope could be jealous. She had probably never met a woman who might be considered as beautiful as she. He gave her a hard look and she took his hand again.

"What is this place?" Wally asked.

"The Mexicans call it the Place of Butterflies. But we don't have a name for it. And we don't have a name for me."

"No names?"

"To name a place or a person is to attach an importance to it above the importance of a place or person that has no name, or whose name you don't know. That would be unlovely."

"I think everything should have a name," Wally said. "Otherwise how can you tell things apart? If people didn't have names how would we know who was who? What if God didn't have a name? People wouldn't know who to pray to."

"The ancient Greeks worshiped at an altar to an unknown god, Agnostos Theos," the girl said. "To be unknown and nameless is the same thing."

Wally said that in Hindu scripture God is referred to by a thousand different names. He knew he was showing off, but it seemed supremely important to impress this beautiful girl, especially after Penelope said he could only play minor chords. "In Tibet, the monks speak of the nine billion names of God."

The girl laughed and Wally thrilled to the sound of it. "To be called by nine billion names would be the same as being called by no name at all, don't you think?"

Wally supposed it would. Penelope just rolled her eyes.

"I know it must be difficult to understand. But the naming of something is an act of love. You name a child or a mountain or a lagoon because of the love you feel for it. But there are things you do not know that you can't name and you can't love. But love should be total. It should transcend the knowable."

Wally stole a glance at Penelope to see how she was taking this lovely, but bewildering, philosophy. To his surprise, she was gazing at the blonde girl with a pleasant intensity, as if seeking to know who this beautiful person was beneath her strange ideas.

"That's what we believe here," the girl said. "We are devoted to loving the world and freedom and each other."

"I have always believed in free love myself," Penelope offered, with a sideways glance at Wally.

"So, we live here communally. We make our own clothes, grow our own food, build our own homes. We live in harmony with nature and are totally independent and free."

They moved back to the creek, where some women were washing clothes and others were bathing. "But where did you come from?" Wally asked.

"Oh, from all over. From universities, mostly. From the city and the country. Everywhere. But we all have one thing in common. We were all, at one time, nearly destroyed by our devotion to a cause." They passed a boy and a girl playing a duet on reed flutes, then another couple making love in a bed of ferns. "Many were in various civil rights groups. Others were pacifists or were in efforts to alter legislation on capital punishment. But all, in our own way, discovered that love for an idea, in order to flourish, had to create a corresponding hate, or at least un-love for the opposing idea. In order to love the Negro children in Birmingham, you have to un-love the redneck who bombed their school. To a truly sensitive and compassionate person, such directionalized love can produce some pretty severe emotional hang-ups. For instance, when you love your country, you must, by definition, un-love those forces that oppose it."

"So, they came here to escape their causes."

"Not really. We came here to begin a new cause. The cause of total, undirectionalized love."

The girl led them to where a man was laying adobe bricks for a new hut and she made introductions in the strange way that people who don't have names do. "This is a boy with a guitar and this is a very beautiful girl with long black hair and blue eyes." Then she pointed to the man laying bricks. "And this is a man who makes fine bricks and is sweating." They sat down on a portion of the adobe wall the man was building. "The man who makes fine bricks and is sweating has an interesting story that illustrates why most of us are here."

The man was bare to the waist; his body glistened from his exertion with the bricks. He seemed slightly older than the others in the commune. He smiled warmly and began his story.

"In college, I was a lab assistant to a famous psycho-chemist. One day, he made a remarkable discovery. But first, let me give you a little background. The field of psycho-chemistry is the study of behavior patterns as they are related to chemical stimuli. Early experiments with drugs of the LSD class proved the existence of a chemical cure for schizophrenia. Then we discovered that chemotherapy could be a consistently effective treatment for a wide range of neurotic and psychotic behavior patterns. So what this famous psycho-chemist did was to blend a combination of chemicals that affect only those portions of the brain that deal with the antithesis of love, virtue and compassion. In short, he learned how to neutralize such emotional factors as hate, rage and greed. He put in a single pill, well, what all the great religions over time have tried vainly to instill in the human heart. It seemed then, if the drug could be administered to everybody, a true brotherhood of man would be the result."

"A love pill?" Wally asked.

"Exactly, a sort of aphrodisiac for the soul."

As Wally listened to the man who makes bricks and is sweating, he was aware of the amazing contrast between Penelope and the girl with the mandolin. While Penelope was dark and exotic and voluptuous, the girl with the mandolin was blonde and fair and slim. But they were both beautiful, as Penelope observed, they were opposites of each other. They might have been from two different planets. Penelope had never been far from her beloved desert arroyos, had never seen the sea. The girl with the mandolin was of the wider world, had been to university, knew about psycho-chemistry and Greek temples. Yet, he noticed that something was passing between them, lingering glances, not as if they were taking measure of each other, but more like two beautiful women admiring each other, not unlike they might find pleasure in looking at a magnificent painting in a museum.

"What happened with the pill?" Wally asked. "Did it work?"

"Because of the discovery's magnitude, the President called a meeting of some of the greatest minds in the country. The leading authorities in various fields that comprise our culture. There were economists, sociologists, religious leaders, military experts, legal types and all sorts of political figures. And to sort of sum it all up, they decided that love would put an end to all that's best in mankind."

Wally who had only been half listening because he had noticed that the girl with the mandolin and Penelope were holding hands, said: "Wait! That's absurd." Apparently, the man who makes fine bricks and is sweating was pulling his leg.

"Tell him about the general," the girl with the mandolin said. Wally was not sure what he thought about Penelope holding hands with the girl with a mandolin. It was as if neither one realized it was anything out of the ordinary. And he supposed it wasn't; but still....

"The general thought the love pill was a great idea. But he saw it as a military weapon. The general thought we should smuggle the love pills behind enemy lines and infest their food supply. They'd become totally vulnerable, and we could wipe them out in a matter of hours."

Penelope was now braiding the girl with a mandolin's hair. Wally wondered if maybe Penelope had never really known a girl, sort of like she had never known the sea. 'How happy she seems,' he thought, 'how beautiful they are together!'

The man who makes fine bricks and is sweating continued his story. "When the idea of a love pill was taken to the Attorney General he claimed that there was nothing unconstitutional about it, because there was no mention of love in the constitution. He did feel that it might make a shambles of our legal system, and if it were to be allowed in the jury box, everyone would go free. Religious leaders rejected the love pill outright. They claimed love was a gift from God, not man. We already had access to love, through Jesus, and there was no need for a synthetic man-made substitute. They ended up claiming that the love pill was blasphemy."

The girl with the mandolin stood, took Wally's hand, and helped him to his feet. Then she did the same for Penelope and hand-in-hand, the three of them moved into the shade of the willows. "So you see, we have all given our love, in one way or another, and we have had our love rejected. We have marched and we have suffered and cared. But the world calls us hippies and radicals and outcasts."

"So you came here," Penelope said.

"We needed a way to spend all the love we felt. Here we love each other and all things both knowable and unknowable."

"That's beautiful," Penelope said.

"You should stay with us," the girl said. "The three of us could spend our love on each other."

Then to Wally's astonishment, the girl with the mandolin kissed Penelope on the lips, a soft, lingering kiss, that seemed to Wally the most beautiful and erotic thing he had ever seen. He wondered, for a moment, if he was dreaming, and if he was dreaming, he wanted the dream to go on forever.

"Oh, Wally, could we stay? Just for a little while? I know you really like her, too. We could learn how to build adobe houses. I could learn to play the mandolin."

"If you are sure, Penelope. Only if you are sure."

"Are you sure, Wally?"

"Yes, I'm sure." Visions of their lovemaking nearly took his breath away.

Later the girl with the mandolin spread the good news that Wally and Penelope would stay with them in their canyon retreat. She introduced them to the others, a task that takes some time when introducing people with no names. It went something like this: "This is the beautiful girl with the long black hair and blue eyes, and this is the man with the guitar who plays only minor chords. This is the Oriental woman who has a samurai warrior tattooed on her abdomen and the man who makes good love but snores." It went on like that for some time.

Then, as if from a nightmare, the prophet emerged from the creek like something awful dredged from a cesspool. Soaking wet, he was even more disgusting than usual and he was striking out with his hoe at the crowd of flies that followed him like the tail of a comet. He was followed by Mario who had been documenting the prophet's attempt to do the breaststroke in the shallow water. When they saw the prophet, a few of the women screamed and all the people drew back in revulsion and fear. The Oriental girl with the Samurai warrior tattooed on her abdomen vomited into the grass. Wally felt the need to introduce the prophet in the manner of those who don't have names.

"This is the old prophet who is seeking his lost prophecy and stinks and is our companion." The prophet slithered up to Penelope and squatted at her feet. Then Wally introduced Mario. "And this is an Italian movie producer with a camera."

After a moment of stunned and extremely uncomfortable silence, the girl with the mandolin said, "Your companion?"

"Yes," Penelope said. "I have known him since I was a little girl. He is traveling with us."

"He can't stay here!" the beautiful girl with the mandolin said, and she backed away, her hand held to her nose.

"But he is our friend," Penelope said. "Please let him stay. Even horrible old river prophets need love."

"Not my love," said the girl with the mandolin. "Mine either," said the Oriental woman with the Samurai warrior tattooed on her abdomen. And one by one the butterfly people took their love back into the adobe huts and slammed shut the doors.

They moved back through the canyon to the Morris Minor and returned to the Eagle Pass Highway. For a long while, they drove in silence. Penelope was sitting by his side, her hand on his thigh. "Are you sorry?" Wally asked.

"I don't know. I liked kissing her. It was very strange. I have never touched a girl before." Then she asked, "How about you?"

Actually, Wally was devastated that the prophet had spoiled everything, but he said, "I don't know. It's probably for the best. Those people were nuts."

"Crazy as loons. But she sure was beautiful."

"Yes. She was."

"I wonder what it would have been like."

"Probably would have been something." Then a silence descended between them as they both considered the mysteries and delights of what might have been. Then Penelope snuggled close, laid her head on his shoulder, and slipped her hand into his shirt, and toyed with the hair on his chest. "Oh, Wally," she said and then seemed to fall asleep.

Too soon, the lights and service stations and neon and litter and incomparable ugliness of the border town engulfed them. How incredible, Wally thought, that mankind can so thoroughly and consistently screw up its environment. They approached Customs. For a moment, Wally feared that the combined forces of the FBI and CIA and maybe even the Texas Rangers, Border Patrol and Interpol might have sealed off the border. But everything looked as loose and lazy as it always had. An agent stood in the road, another stood at a window in the Custom's House. Wally geared down, then stopped.

"Where y'all going?" the agent drawled mechanically.

"Just over to Piedras Negras to look around, get some booze," Mario said. "Be right back."

The agent looked suspiciously at Penelope, his eyes darting to the hilt of her Oddfellows sword and then to the prophet who glared back evilly.

"What's that?" The agent said, nodded at the prophet, his voice full of disgust.

"It's a prophet," Wally said.

"Man, I can't let you take no prophet across the border."

"You have no right to stop him," Penelope said, and Wally was surprised to see her move toward the prophet protectively.

"I got a right to detain all suspicious-looking people and that's the most suspicious-looking people I ever saw." The prophet had begun to growl, the guttural sound coming from somewhere deep within.

"Where you've got this wrong, sir," Mario said, "is that this is obviously not a person. If you examine it closely, I'm sure you'll agree. It's a thing, not a human. So, unless you have a rule that says you must detain inhuman things, sir, I beg you let us pass."

The agent pushed back his hat and scratched his head. "It sure stinks bad," he said.

"You never knew a human smelled like that, did you?" Mario added. The prophet continued to growl, and the agent searched his mind for a serviceable regulation.

"If it ain't a person and it is a thing, then you gotta declare it." He seemed pleased with his logic. "And if you don't declare it, you'll have to pay duty on it when you come back, because they don't make them here." He reached behind him for a declaration form and before he could turn around, the little Morris Minor was gone, screaming across the Rio Grande, past the sleeping Mexican guards and into the city. Wally half expected gunshots, but soon they were swallowed up in a dark world of adobe and shadows. "I know every back street and alley in Piedras Negras," Penelope said. "They'll never be able to follow us." She guided them through the gnarled, winding urban canyons, the Morris Minor often laboring in low gear over the ruts and potholes. Beyond the windows of the little car, nothing moved. No one was in the streets. Although Wally knew people slept and dreamed and loved behind these walls, it was as if they were traveling through a parallel dimension, unseen and untouched by those they passed. Perhaps, sensing his mood, Penelope laid her hand on his knee.

The labyrinth of the city began to loosen, and they soon reached the highway west of the city. "There are two Federal police checkpoints ahead," she said. "They probably have a description of your car by now. We'll have to take to the arroyos to get around them." The first checkpoint was about fifteen miles southwest of the city. Just before they got to where Penelope knew the checkpoint would be, she guided Wally off the highway into a dry streambed. The Morris Minor danced wildly, following its drunken lights, and a flood of mid-eastern gibberish was shaken loose from the sleeping prophet's dream.

"Now, turn off the lights," Penelope said. Night socked in and Wally stopped to let his eyes get used to the darkness. Soon the moon touched the edge of things with a pale silver light and Wally urged the car forward, slowly, through the coiled arroyo.

"Welcome to the Chihuahuan Desert," Penelope said. "This is where I was born. It was my cradle, probably will be my grave."

"It looks like the surface of the moon, so dry, so lifeless."

"Sometimes, after a sudden rain, these arroyos can become raging rivers. One of the most frequent ways to die in the desert is by drowning."

"How can anything live out here?"

"I think you would be surprised how much life is out there in the darkness. When I was a girl I used to help my mother gather mesquite flowers for the brewing of tea. Sometimes I would help my father gather ocotillo stalks for firewood. Everything that we had was given to us free, by the desert. It provided our home, our clothing, our food and, sometimes, our pleasure. When I was older, my friends and I would experiment with the liquor fermented from the agave leaves and the moments of paradise found in the buds of the peyote. I found pleasure in arroyos like this. And I always gave much pleasure." She glanced at Wally. "But you don't want to hear about that."

"Who are you, then?" Wally asked, his eyes seeking a clear pass through the stone arroyo and the darkness.

"You won't believe me," but I will tell you anyway, because I love you." Then she began. "I was a prostitute for a while when I was very young. I did it because of the money it provided for things I never dreamed I would ever have. For a girl of fourteen, who quite often found pleasure and was pleasured by the boys in the village, sleeping with rich tourists in town was no different than what I was already doing. It was natural, and a new dress or a first pair of real shoes was a wonderful thing."

"But you stopped. "

"I found I did not like these men. I did not like the smell of their deodorant and their cologne. I did not like that they disrespected me. I didn't like that they were often drunk. What they were doing was not making love. It was something else, something that had little to do with pleasure. I realized by this time that I was beautiful and knew I was a good person. I began to realize they didn't deserve me. Forgive me if I seem boastful, but I was better than these men."

"And that was the end of it?"

"Well, not exactly. I stopped taking money, but I began making love for free, to the poor in the villages who couldn't afford a woman like me. I'd come down here to the arroyos and here would be this poor farmer out cutting cactus in the middle of nowhere, all filled with misery, the hot sun sucking all the life out of him. I'd talk with him awhile and then hold him and take off my clothes, let him touch me. Oh my God, the look in his eyes! I'd treat him gently and love him and give him an hour to dream about until he died. I guess his life would never be the same. The sun would keep beating down and there would never be enough water and he'd know his life would never get better, but he'd always have that hour to remember." She paused, her eyes catching a glint of moonlight. "And so that's my story. That's who I am."

"Thank you," Wally said, wondering how many of the poor she had pleasured.

"Oh, hundreds, Wally. Maybe many hundreds."

"I didn't ask, Penelope."

"But you did; I felt it. You don't have to speak, Wally. I hear your heart perfectly well. I know you love me, and it must be hard to hear these things." She leaned her head on his shoulder and squeezed his arm.

In the two days that he had known her, he had never loved her more. She was absolutely unique in the world, a force of nature, both transparent and unknowable, and for some reason that he couldn't understand, she seemed to love him back. They drove on. Penelope guided them back onto the highway and they raced through Allende and on through Monclova. The car lights raked along the cactus and yucca and mesquite struggling the grow by the highway and occasionally flushed an armadillo or a squadron of bats or a gaunt cow with soft, inscrutable eyes. Away the dry hills rolled, and to the south and west there was the ghost suggestion of mountains. As they passed the squat earth hovels in the villages, Wally wondered how many within were dreaming their magic dream of an encounter with an angel. 'How can I not love this woman?' he thought, and he drove on.

Dawn found them leaving Saltillo behind and racing west through a narrow canyon. Penelope had turned on the radio releasing the maniacal sermon of a border preacher. She turned, the dial and then they all heard it, and later, none could deny it and claim that it had been some strange anomaly of the radio waves. They all heard it; probably even the prophet. And what they heard was this:

"PENTAGON SOURCES REPORT THAT SABOTAGE IS DEFINITELY SUSPECTED. IN FORT WORTH, A HIGH-LEVEL CONFERENCE OF OFFICIALS FROM THE AIR FORCE, FBI, CIA, GENERAL DYNAMICS CORPORATION AND THE HOLLOWAY'S MILK DUDS COMPANY ARE EXAMINING THE REMAINS OF THE ELEVEN *F-111* AIRCRAFT. THE REASON FOR THE PRESENCE OF THE HOLLOWAY'S MILK DUDS PEOPLE HAS NOT BEEN REVEALED, HOWEVER, INFORMED OBSERVERS SPECULATE A MERGER BETWEEN HOLLOWAY'S MILK DUDS AND GENERAL DYNAMICS HAD BEEN IMMINENT AT THE TIME OF THE CRASHES. THE CONTROVERSIAL *F-111*, THE FIRST VARIABLE SWEEP WING FIGHTER-BOMBER, IS THE MOST ADVANCED WEAPON SYSTEM IN AMERICA'S DEFENSE ARSENAL. A FORT WORTH FARMER, WHO WITNESSED THE MASS CRASH, TOLD REPORTERS, "THEM THANGS CAME A FLAPPIN' OUTA THE AIR LIKE DYIN' BATS.'" IT IS REPORTED THAT ALL TWENTY-TWO PILOTS AND CO-PILOTS EJECTED AND PARACHUTED SAFELY TO EARTH. MORE DEVELOPMENTS AS DETAILS ARE AVAILABLE."

"Christ!" Mario whistled from the back seat. "I swear, I didn't believe you! That's the most incredible thing I have ever heard."

"Sometimes I don't believe it, either." Wally said. He felt suddenly both sad and exhilarated, as if he were watching a funeral from a roller coaster.

"I'm glad about the pilots," Penelope said. "You said you designed the device that ejected them. So I guess you could say it was you who saved their lives."

"I guess you could say that," Mario offered. "But don't count on that saving you from the firing squad." Mario then resigned himself to a series of diminishing exclamatory whistles. And then: "It's just crazy!"

Wally supposed it was, but felt a need to explain, just as Penelope had felt a need to explain making love to so many hundreds of impoverished Mexican farm workers. "You would have to know that place, General Dynamics. I guess it's not that different from many other defense plants. It has one product and that product is death. Every act of every man and woman in that place is specifically directed to dispense it with a maximum degree of efficiency. But they go about it as if they were building tinker-toys. Now *that's* insane!" Wally remembered thinking, one time, that maybe General Dynamics was a massive insane asylum. The guards at the gates were not to keep people out but to keep people in, and all the thousands of workers were engaged in some kind of high-tech therapy.

The sun was directly overhead, as if the earth hung from it. The highway stretching straight and true through the parched landscape. A goat suddenly appeared in the middle of the road. Wally swerved the car to avoid the goat and the car careened into a ditch and burrowed into a warren of brush and creosote bushes. It happened so fast that Wally could only sit for a moment in the new stillness and try to gather his thoughts. Everyone seemed to be all right; Penelope was gazing in the rearview mirror, apparently concerned about the goat; Mario was loading his camera to document the damage and the prophet was still sleeping, the little flag on his cap now limp.

Without the wind stream to chase the heat away, the sun pressed down like an anvil, oppressive and unrelenting. It had an actual presence, the heat did, containing a touch of panic, like a lost alarm clock ringing. Penelope managed to push her door open, and with her Oddfellows sword flashing in the sunlight, began to cut away the brush that had the car entrapped. Then, upon the low, wasted surrounding hills, white figures appeared. They stood silently watching and there was no sound. One of the figures began to scramble through the rock and dust, down into the ditch. He approached slowly, smiling.

"Welcome to the restaurant of Gaspar Lopez," he said, and he held out his hand to be shaken. He did not look like a bandit. His eyes, clear and kind, gazed steadily from a brown face, creased like wadded paper. Wally shook the man's hand.

"Surely an act of God," the man said, indicating the entrapped car. "Come," he said, as he turned from the ditch and led them along the highway toward a small adobe structure. As they moved from the car, they saw the goat they had so narrowly missed.

"What the holy hell," Mario said, as he examined the goat. It was a cardboard facsimile of a goat, attached to some kind of a spring device, which was in turn attached to a rope leading to the adobe structure on the side of the road.

"A pop-up goat," Wally observed. "It lies flat on the road, then when a car approaches, they apparently pull the rope, and the goat pops up in front of the car."

"But why?" Penelope asked.

"A mystery. An act of God."

Wally pulled his guitar from the Morris Minor and Mario got his camera and a battery from the trunk. The prophet was still asleep, so they covered him with a towel to protect him from the sun. Penelope lifted the camera tripod to her shoulder and they followed the native through the noon.

The figures upon the hills, perhaps fifty of them, men, women and children, moved in parallel. "Look at them," Mario said. "How can they live out here in this wilderness? Nothing but sun and stone."

"Those poor men," Penelope said. She gazed out at the men silhouetted against the burning sky and Wally saw her eyes go misty. He rolled his eyes.

The Restaurant of Gaspar Lopez was as melancholy a place as Wally had ever seen. It was merely a rectangle of mud cast up from the earth. A small, hand-lettered board above the door announced its name. 'So sad, so futile,' he thought. Within the walls, the abject simplicity nearly brought tears to Wally's eyes. The mud walls were painted white, as were the few simple tables and chairs, and on the walls were pasted old Norman Rockwell illustrations and religious posters. There was a sign announcing the management's right to refuse service if it wished. 'It is a pretending,' Wally thought.

"Is it not beautiful?" the man called Gaspar Ruiz asked. Wally noticed how the sunlight, leaning through the single door, lighted the enclosure like a small chapel.

"It's one of the most beautiful things I have ever seen," Penelope said, her eyes still misty.

"Please sit down," Gaspar invited. "This is a great occasion. You are the first guests at the restaurant of our village." Villagers began to squeeze into the doorway. "As you refresh yourselves, I will tell you the story of our restaurant." After he brought them warm Coca Cola and beer nuts, this is the story Gaspar told:

"For as long as anyone can remember," Gaspar began, "this village has never had enough corn. The land is tired and the rain falls on the other side of the mountains." He paused for a moment, and except for the breathing of the villagers, it was very still. Wally sipped his Coke. "One day, I was working my land and I looked down at the automobiles going to and from the big cities. But they never stopped at our village. It seemed to me that they were like birds. Birds do not stop where there is nothing to eat or drink. They flock where they can find nourishment. It is the same with automobiles. I decided that we must build a place to nourish these machines of the rich. A fine restaurant to draw them from the highway to our village."

"Well, you've built a fine restaurant," Wally said. "When was it finished?"

There was a suggestion of uneasiness in the room, the whisper of bare feet shifting and a subtle difference in the meter of the villagers' breathing. Gaspar Lopez looked down at his calloused hands. "The restaurant has been finished for three months."

"And we're your first customers?" Mario asked, incredulously.

"No one has stopped. We wait, and the automobiles pass on by."

"Not a single car stopped?"

"That is the truth, but it is not justice. We have nothing. The rich people in the automobiles have everything. We have fought a dozen revolutions to win social justice and still we have no corn." He was angry now and his voice bounded around the small room like a trapped animal; the villagers rumbled affirmation.

"And so, you thought of the pop-up goat to stop the cars."

"We tried other things. We tried signs by the side of the road. We had our prettiest girls wave at them. But they would not stop."

"So, you tricked them."

"Yes, it was a trick, as you say, but it is a just trick, and as you see, it works. You were the first, and now you are here in our restaurant refreshing yourselves."

Wally could think of nothing more to say. He looked at the expectant faces of the villagers in the doorway, and in the tight, hot room he felt a great avalanche of accumulated accusation rumbling down around him. It was true, had always been true that he was guilty of horrible crimes for which he could no longer hold himself unaccountable. This, the cars passing by, not stopping at the Restaurant of Gaspar Lopez, was just another of his crimes. Their weight was too great, the evidence far too damning. 'I did not stand in the schoolhouse door to block James Meredith's way,' he thought. 'I did not wear the executioner's hood during the Spanish Inquisition. I did not gas the Jews or subvert the Dominican Republic or burn the bus in Alabama or pour napalm on the children of Vietnam. I did not slaughter the American Indians or extinguish Hiroshima.' But he knew now, and he had known for a long time, that he must share the responsibility and, therefore, the guilt. He was a member of the tribe that did these things. It was in his blood, his DNA. These are the things he thought as he sipped his Coca Cola. But he said nothing.

Mario tossed a rumpled American dollar on the table. "That should cover it," he said, beginning to rise.

Gaspar smoothed out the bill on the table, studied it for a moment, then said, "No, I do not believe this is enough."

"How much then?"

"You had three Coca Cola's and three packages of nuts. That will be fifty U.S. dollars."

Mario sank back in his chair. Outside, a burro made a lonesome sound, and on the highway, trucks passed like giants breathing. "Is that fair?" Mario asked.

"Is it fair that hundreds of cars have passed this restaurant without stopping? Who pays for all the Coca Cola's they would have bought if they had stopped? Who pays for the building of the restaurant and the making of the trick goat? Who pays for this table and these chairs? Who pays for my pain?"

Wally was deciding that the answers to Gaspar's questions would never be found anywhere in this universe or any neighboring universe when a remarkable thing happened.

There was a series of distant shouts and then the sound of many people running toward the restaurant. Suddenly, a wiry old man burst through the door, his face filled half with rapture, half with pain. Gasping for breath, he announced in a rattling whisper: "The Promised One... the Promised One has returned!" And then he fell unconscious to the floor. There was a clamorous eruption of activity outside and everyone rushed from the restaurant. When Wally reached the door, the villagers stood immobile, all eyes turned toward, what? And then Wally saw him, a tiny form against the humbling immensity of the land, his ancient hoe signing circles in the air. As the prophet approached, the villagers parted like the Red Sea in biblical times. Some of the villagers dropped to their knees. Women tried to embrace him and there occasionally escaped from someone's lips a reckless, uncontrollable scream, as when a mother finds a child, long thought dead.

"It can't be him," Gaspar hissed.

"But the hoe," said another. "And the long beard and how he smells. And he is very, very old, as he should be."

"There are many old men with beards," Gaspar said, guardedly. "And there are many who carry a hoe. Let us not be deceived again. We have too often been deceived."

The prophet hobbled toward them, through the fields, like some ghastly apparition. He seemed to move in a loathsome green vapor, and although the sun was high, he cast an enormously long shadow, an obscene blackness that made children cringe in icy fear when it touched them. All the animals fell silent. As he came closer, Wally noticed something different about the old man, a certain alertness. His mad old eyes darted here and there as if searching for something lost.

"Perhaps it is the Promised One," Gaspar breathed.

Penelope moved to where Gaspar stood and touched his shoulder. "He is our friend," she said. "I do not think he is the one that is promised."

"He has been traveling with you?"

"Yes. I have known him for a long time. Ever since I was a little girl."

The prophet shuffled into the Restaurant of Gaspar Lopez. The crowd began to follow, but Gaspar held up his hand. He motioned for Wally, Penelope, Mario to enter and he followed them into the restaurant and propped the pop-up goat across the door. The prophet was crouched in a corner, beneath a calendar portrait of the Pope, murmuring, his eyes closed. "Now, my friends," Gaspar said, tell me about this man with the hoe."

"He's just a friend," Wally said. "We found him in a bar up on the river."

"What has he told you about himself?"

"Nothing. He doesn't speak any language we know. Every once in a while, he says, 'Blood on the moon,' but that's all. Penelope says there's a story along the Rio Grande that he came from somewhere in the Middle East." Gaspar raised an eyebrow and the prophet licked his awful lips with a blackened tongue and Wally wondered in what exotic places all that filth and stink could have been accumulated. "Who do you people think he is?" Wally asked. "What is this 'Promised One' thing?"

"Many years ago," Gaspar said, "a holy man came to our village. It was in a time before our grandfathers, a time before the oldest living memory. When we were children, they told us about the old man who always carried a hoe. A man with a beard such as this one you call the prophet. He came walking from the mountains above Durango, from the land of the wild ones, the Yaqui. He was a sorcerer. He stayed in the village many months and seemed very sad and tired. He told stories to the children about animals and mountains and life. He was very gentle. But it is told that sometimes he became so very sad that he would sit beneath the mesquite for days and his eyes would never move. Our grandfathers and their grandfathers spent many hours discussing the holy man among themselves. But they never found out who he was. The stories the old man told are remembered and are still told to our children when the night is still."

"What kind of stories?" Penelope asked.

"Many stories. Some are very simple, yet not easy to understand. He told of a land where a great buffalo lived, a great beast with long horns that loved to roll in the water. And he said that, as these beasts roamed the fields, beautiful white birds would ride on their shoulders. He said the buffalo and the white bird lived in peace and were good friends." Gaspar paused and looked long into the eyes of the prophet.

"Why did he leave?" Penelope asked.

"It is said they always knew he would someday leave. He had the look of one who must travel. One day he gathered the children around him and told them he was going away. But he said he had left them a great treasure. And if they could not find the treasure themselves, he would return and help them find it. He asked the children not to forget him and then he was gone."

The prophet began to moan softly. It was a sound as mournful as all the world's sorrow.

"This cannot be that man," Gaspar said. "He is too changed. He is more beast than man."

"There have been times," Penelope said, "when he seemed to remember, for a moment, who he was, when something hidden beneath the ruin comes close to the surface. Remember, Wally? The night before Augustus died? That night, he slept at the foot of our bed."

At that moment, someone knocked on the pop-up goat, moved it aside, and entered. It was three women. "We have gifts for the holy man," one woman said. They laid before him a roasted goat, an old gold railroad watch and a new pair of huaraches. Then they knelt before him. "We wish to welcome your return to our village," another of the women said. The prophet snatched up the watch and the huaraches and stuffed them into his ruined garments. And, then, snarling and belching, he tore at the goat with his black gums, the juices absorbed into his hideous beard.

"Did you find the treasure?" Mario asked.

"No. Through all the generations, the promise of a treasure became simply a story to amuse the children. But there have been times when our elders remembered that the old man had come from the mountains, where it is said, the Yaqui have caves full of silver. In those times, they have searched for the treasure. But our village is small. It does not have many hiding places."

"Maybe he buried it."

"That is what many believe. Every few years someone will dig a hole, but the treasure is never there."

In the late afternoon, the prophet grew restless, left the restaurant and he began to wander about the village. He did not move aimlessly, as usual, but there seemed to be a sense of purpose in his wandering and this was soon reflected in the excitement of the villagers.

"He is trying to remember!" Wally heard one woman say. The entire village followed closely at his heels, and every time he would pause, an excited murmuring would escape from the crowd and they would rush forward and ask, "Is it here? Is the treasure here?" The prophet would then turn and snarl and the crowd would fall back and follow him to a new site at a respectful distance. Several men in the crowd carried shovels. Occasionally, someone would place a gift at the prophet's feet, a dead chicken, a trinket, a piece of clothing. And he would turn the gifts over with his hoe, glower at the giver and return to his wandering. At one hovel, a woman brought her young ripe daughter to him. With one hand she pushed the cringing girl forward, in the other hand she carried a spade. The prophet's shadow fell upon the young thing's offered breast and she fainted dead away. Once, when the prophet paused, examined the earth, turned around three times and scratched a hole in the ground with his hoe, the crowd threw itself into a rapture of anticipation. But he squatted and relieved his bowels, and for a moment, a swirl of purple fog hid him from view. There was a peel of thunder in the cloudless air. When he skittered away, three men and a woman dug a four-foot hole where he had squatted.

The shadows lengthened. The sun slumped behind a veil of dust, and the west burned brown. The prophet approached a row of adobe huts and as he walked around the first, scratching the walls with his hoe, the villagers crowded around. The prophet disappeared into the door. The villagers held their breath. He crept out, walked a few paces and then squatted down, facing the door through which he had just come. For a moment, the villagers were suspended, motionless, and then, at an unsaid signal, they charged the hut and destroyed it. Systematically, they tore down the walls and then attacked the foundation with their shovels. There was no treasure. About the time they gave up on the first adobe hovel, the prophet entered the second.

Wally watched the search with a profound and eerie fascination. "It's incredible!" he said. "They'll destroy the entire village." He could see Mario out there, scrambling around with his camera.

"I cannot watch this," Penelope said. She walked off into the encroaching darkness. Wally followed.

They walked in silence for a while. The sounds from the village had a dreamlike quality as they moved to the top of a small hill overlooking the highway. The little Morris Minor looked lost and forlorn in its ditch. To the west, the sun had slipped beneath the horizon, leaving only a hint of itself, deep red, on the rim of the earth. It was a sorcerer's world of shadows and things unseen.

"Do you believe in goblins?" Wally asked.

"Goblins? Do you mean fairies? We call them *hadas*."

"When I was little, I used to lie in my bed on nights like this and listen for goblins. I didn't know exactly what they were, but they were small and friendly and had great adventures. There were elves and all sorts of creatures that ruled the night. And there were evil things, black-winged flying monsters that always threatened the little people. I used to whisper to the elves, 'Let me help you. Let me be on your side.' I imagined myself their good friend. The one human they accepted into their world."

"Do you think they would accept me?" Penelope asked.

"Of course they would."

Penelope laughed softly; her hand found his. The sky had blackened and it was very dark. "Do you think your friends are out there now? Your goblins?"

"I hope so. I would still join them if they asked. And you could come, too, and be their queen. We could ride white horses across the sky and look down on this pitiful old earth and all its stupid gyrations."

Penelope squeezed his hand. "And when little boys and girls asked us if they could join us, we would pull them up and carry them along."

In the distance, a tiny star proved to be the coming of a car along the highway. They watched the headlights carve a tunnel through the night. As Penelope watched the approaching car, she asked, "Do you think we are real?"

Wally smiled. It was such a terribly relevant question. "I don't know."

"What if we were just a story someone is writing?"

"It would be a love story," Wally said.

Penelope kissed his hand, then his lips. "I know I love you," she said. "That's real. Even if everything else is a fiction."

They became aware of a change in the sounds from the village. There was an escalation in the anger and frustration and the voices rose enraged above the general clamor of destruction.

"There's trouble," Wally said, and they moved quickly through the night toward the sound.

It was like something from a nightmare. A hundred torches and lanterns spit staccato light upon the ruins of what had been the village. Where homes had been, now gaped great holes. The small fields where corn had grown so imperfectly were trenched and a few men still probed the rows with their shovels. And the crowd! It reminded Wally of the night mobs that searched for the Wolf Man in old Frankenstein movies. Now they were moving slowly, threateningly, advancing toward the prophet who backed away, his hoe held ready. Now a voice was raised above the others. "You son of a she dog! Where is the treasure? Give us the treasure!" Wally noticed Mario on the fringes of the crowd waving his microphone in front of screaming faces.

When they reached the restaurant, Gaspar was there. "We must act quickly," he said, or they will kill him!" Together, Wally and Gaspar ran to where the prophet was fighting off the crowd with his hoe. They snatched him up, and as Mario joined them, they raced back with the prophet to the restaurant. Wally was amazed at how light the old man was. Beneath his rags there seemed to be only air and bone. They set him down in a corner where he slumped down like an old pile of sleeping tarantulas. Then they barricaded the door with the pop-up goat, the table, chairs and the long board that had served as a counter. "He will be safe here," Gaspar said. "The walls are very strong." Penelope moved to where the prophet lay and she comforted him. He lay quite still, accepting her attention.

"I wonder what's going on in his mind," she said, and she brushed a clot of hair from his eyes. Outside, the villagers howled, and some beat metallic objects with sticks.

"Why aren't you out howling with the others?" Mario asked Gaspar. "You're the one that wants fifty dollars for a Coca Cola."

"You had fifty dollars to give," he replied. "The holy man no longer has what they seek." Gaspar lighted an oil lantern and set it on the floor; it cast trembling fingers of light around the room. Suddenly, Wally noticed the prophet's eyes were locked on Gaspar and his lips were moving beneath his beard. The old man stiffened and trembled; his arm rose and his awful finger pointed at Gaspar. And then they heard the words, as if rattling from the depths of hell. "FER...NAN...DO LO...PEZZZ."

"My God!" Gaspar cried, and tears welled up in his eyes. "Fernando Lopez. That was my great grandfather!"

"Holy cow!" Mario exclaimed, whipping out his camera and recorder. "If he knew your grandfather, then he *was* here in the village! It could be true about the treasure!"

The prophet stood now and began to scratch the earthen floor of the restaurant with his hoe. He trembled still. Wally thought he must be struggling to recover some fragment of memory from his past. He mumbled Gaspar's ancestor's name again and again.

"He lived right here," Gaspar said, falling to his knees. "I built the restaurant over the spot where he lived."

"Then the treasure is buried right here," Wally whispered, so no one outside could possibly hear him.

As the villagers outside shouted blasphemies at the night, those in the restaurant began to dig, the prophet with his hoe, Penelope with her Oddfellows ceremonial sword, Mario with the pointed leg of his tripod, and Gaspar with an old iron hinge from the door. Wally held the lantern high, his heart beating almost out loud. The pile of loose earth grew and soon the hole they had dug was large enough to stand in. They loosened more earth and scooped it out. The air grew warm and close. The hole grew deeper. Penelope put her arm around Wally's waist and pulled him to her, and from the feel of her, he knew it was quite possible that she, at least, was real. And then the prophet's hoe screamed against metal. With their hands, they cleared the dirt away from a small, old trunk and they pulled it up and set it on the dirt floor. They all pressed close. No one made a move to open it. They stood with polite patience, as one regards a rescued stranger with a wild and wonderful tale to tell. Outside, the villagers were still shouting their grief and anger and they could hear it through the thick walls of the restaurant. Wally looked up at the prophet and noticed his eyes had died. The day had been too much for his frail and ancient constitution. "He's gone again," Penelope said. "Back to wherever he goes."

'Gaspar," Wally said. "It was left for your village. You open it."

The trunk was wooden with heavy iron bands to protect it from the abuse of the ages, but it was not locked. Borrowing Penelope's Oddfellow's sword, Gaspar inserted the blade between the trunk and its lid, twisted, and with an almost human sigh of resignation, the lid groaned open. The lantern's light crept in and Gaspar began to laugh. It was a laugh very near crying. The trunk was empty. But then, Wally saw the parchment. It lay like a lining, folded and old in the very bottom of the trunk. Carefully, Gaspar brought it out and spread it beneath the light of the lantern.

"What is it? Mario asked, taking a close-up of the parchment.

"It's all sorts of notes and sketches," Wally answered. "Looks like some kind of old flying machine. The notes are all in Italian, I think."

"Yeah, that's Italian," Mario said. Now they were all poring over the document.

"What does it say?" Gaspar asked.

"Hell, I don't know," Mario said, and shrugged.

"A fine Italian you are," Penelope said.

"I know what this is!" Wally said. "I've seen it in books on aviation history. This is Leonardo da Vinci's original plans for a flying machine. It's a sort of helicopter. I'm sure of it. It was probably brought over to the New World on an old ship and found its way here."

"What would the prophet be doing with it?" Mario asked. Wally looked over at the prophet, but he was lost in his unreachable world.

"I don't know."

"It must have meaning!" Gaspar said. "If this is the treasure, it must have meaning."

"If it is an original Leonardo da Vinci drawing of a flying machine," Wally said, "it would be worth a fortune."

"No," Gaspar said. "The meaning is more, deeper."

Suddenly, there was a tremendous pounding at the barricaded door and an increased intensity in the shouting of the villagers.

"Sounds like they're coming in after him," Mario said. "It's just a matter of time before they break down the door!" The pounding was more feverish now, and the whole restaurant shook and groaned from the onslaught. Penelope moved protectively toward the prophet and there was a quick, clean singing in the air as she drew her Oddfellows sword.

"Isn't there something we can do?" Wally asked Gaspar, who was still intent on da Vinci's sketches. The villagers were on the roof now, tearing at the tiles.

"There must be some meaning," Gaspar repeated, apparently unmindful of the tumult.

And then, just as the pop-up goat began to splinter and the furious faces of the villagers could be seen peering into the lantern light, another more terrifying sound ripped and tore at the fabric of the night. It sounded at first like Chinese firecrackers and then like a dragon belching and then the restaurant walls, up high, were flying apart in places.

"Holy Jesus!" Mario screamed above the din. "They've got machine guns!" Some instinct swept Wally to the floor and he crawled through the raining debris to the prophet's corner, pulled Penelope down beside him and he held her as close as he could. They covered each other with their bodies, their arms and legs pulling each to each, and the rain of broken tiles and powdered adobe half buried them. Then, after what seemed a hundred years, Wally was aware that the shooting had stopped. Slowly, he raised his head and there, in the rubble, stood a thin man in a dark blue suit, striped tie and enormous horn-rimmed glasses. He was lighting a cigarette from the hot barrel of his submachine gun. The man looked up and regarded Wally with calm curiosity.

"It appears," the man said, with what, under the circumstance, was amazing nonchalance, "that I arrived just in time. But then, that is merely appearances." He handed the weapon to an associate and then helped Wally to his feet.

"Who did you think would come after you?" he asked, as he gallantly helped Penelope from the floor.

Wally was still shaken up, his ears ringing from the sound of machine-gun fire. "I don't know what you're talking about."

"What I can't understand, Mr. Pillow, as if that was really your name, is why you wanted to be captured. Why did you let me catch you?" There was a stirring in the rubble and the prophet raised his awful head. "What's that?" the suited stranger asked, holding a handkerchief to his nose.

"It's our friend, the holy man," Penelope said.

The stranger's eyebrows arched way above his horn-rimmed eyewear. "Ah yes. The one they call The Prophet." He made a motion to extend his hand, but apparently, delicacy forced him back. "Now who could that be behind that beard?" he mused. Richter? Maelish? Ching Tao?" For a moment, he considered another possibility, but then seemed suddenly impatient. "It will all come out soon enough," he said.

"What'll come out of what?" Wally asked.

"All right, Mr. Pillow, if you want to play it innocent, let's tally up the score." He placed one foot on the trunk and leaned forward, elbow on knee, chin on back of hand. "First, the Soviets plant you at General Dynamics. You get forged clearance and all that. You sabotage eleven *F-111*s. And I must say, Mr. Pillow, your technique was brilliant. Yet, a plan so brilliantly executed wouldn't include leaving chocolate fingerprints on the fuselages. Nor would it include leaving a trail any common operative could follow. When I was assigned by the CIA to apprehend you, I knew it wouldn't be easy. But it *has* been easy. And I ask myself, 'Why?'" He began to pace, his chin still in his hand.

Outside, Wally could see a number of other men in dark suits with machine-guns holding the still smoldering villagers at bay. "And then, there's your connection to SLAY, hiding communist motives behind what appears to be an ordinary struggle for human rights. And, by the way, it was right to kill the man, Salizar. I gather he was becoming a hindrance. But why did you join forces with the one operating under deep cover as The Prophet? There is another question that I keep asking myself. Why is it that the two top agents of the two most powerful nations on earth have let me, a man of lesser reputation, apprehend them? And what was this ruse in the village? Why did you have the people act as if they would kill you?"

"You're full of a lot of long-winded shit," Mario said. "By the way, what's your name?" He had been cleaning his camera lens with a cue tip. "Just your name. Try to be brief."

"They call me The Lynx."

"Look, Mr. Lynx," Mario said, "If you think the prophet is this guy Ching Tao or whatever, why don't you go over and pull off his beard."

"The Lynx does not go around pulling on beards. I'm satisfied with my information and my deductions. What remains unanswered will become clear in time." He snapped his fingers and one of the dark-suited gunmen approached. "Now, my esteemed friends, I have made my move. I have eight armed men who will take you to the airport for a flight to Mexico City, where extradition papers will be served. It is now your move, Mr. Pillow, or whatever your name may be, and I await it with no small degree of professional interest."

Wally was surprised that he could so intensely dislike a person who may well have saved his life. But how can you like someone so wrong? Never in his life had he heard such an intricate chain of misinformation. The Lynx! What stupidity! 'The most incredible thing,' he thought, 'was that he was probably a very competent agent. They just get caught up in the intrigue syndrome. They live a life based on double-cross and deception and become incapable of recognizing simple motives. No wonder we always find ourselves aligned on the wrong side, all over the world.' As he watched The Lynx sweep his attention around the ruin of the restaurant, adding up evidence on his tilted computer, he began to feel quite superior and not a little angry. As a communist spy of great reputation, he could win the respect of those who accused him. As a nobody acting purely on the dictates of his conscience, he would probably be hanged or locked away forever.

"Okay, Mister The Lynx, you've got me. I give up."

"Now we're all going to leave quietly and calmly," The Lynx said crisply. He allowed Mario to leave the restaurant first, so that he could set up his camera and document the capture. Wally took a last long look at what had been the beautiful Restaurant of Gaspar Lopez. It was no longer masquerading; it was what it was—a badly battered old ruin in the middle of nowhere. Tomorrow cars would pass and if, by chance, anyone noticed the broken down derelict restaurant beside the road, they would probably think, "How timeless is rural Mexico. It remains empty and sad and without passion." And they would drive on without being aware that the Restaurant of Gaspar Lopez ever existed. Wally found his guitar beneath the rubble, Penelope sheathed her Oddfellows sword, Gaspar folded the sketches of the flying machine beneath his shirt, and they all passed by the pop-up goat into the night.

"Wait, for Christ sake!" Mario shouted, stepping from behind the camera. "We gotta do this right. We need more light!"

"We're more than willing to cooperate," The Lynx offered. "I understand the demands of professionalism." He ordered his men to bring more torches, a generator and electric lights.

"Now," Mario directed, "I want The Lynx and his men to bring up the rear. And, Wally, I want you guys in front of them with your hands in the air."

With much awkward shuffling, they arranged themselves as Mario instructed. He stepped back to the camera, looked in the viewfinder, then looked up again.

"One more thing," he said. "I'm striving for realism. When I start the camera and recorder, I want lots of sound. Just say what you would normally say. Wally can say, 'Don't shoot! Don't shoot!' or something like that." Wally smiled at Penelope and decided to ham it up; why not?

"Another thing," Mario demanded, "there's a trunk in the restaurant. Lynx, have one of your men bring it out. It could be full of atomic secrets or something. It will be a great effect." The Lynx sent one of his men for the trunk and Mario stepped back behind the camera and shouted, "Action!"

It was a magnificent portrayal. Wally and Penelope staggered forward, the torches casting a macabre dervish of light and shadow on their faces. The prophet loomed from the blackness of the restaurant like something vomited and his old eyes rolled with malevolent madness. Wally shouted: "McNamara is a sorehead!" and then burst into a falsetto version of "The Volga Boatman." Then came The Lynx, a little embarrassed, but not enough, Wally thought. And behind him came the phalanx of black-suited agents: two with submachine guns, five holding high lanterns and torches, and one bringing up the rear with the ancient treasure trunk. It was then, swift and terrible, that the capture of the saboteur went terribly wrong.

When the light fell upon the treasure chest, the villagers whooped like a home run had been hit and they rushed toward their precious treasure. The black-suited agents were overwhelmed. "Run like hell!" Mario shouted. And they did. Half-carrying the prophet, the master spies scrambled over the rocky fields where no corn now grew and away from where the village had been. Wally glanced back once and saw The Lynx silhouetted against the horizon, loping across a hill, just ahead of the pursuing torches.

CHAPTER 4.
SWAMP SWEENEY'S ROAD

"I've never seen a mountain before," Penelope said, her face radiant and excited as a child's. She leaned her head way back and looked up at the rugged peaks of the Sierra Madre rising into silver mist. The little Morris Minor convertible rose in gentle swells, higher and higher, toward the Continental Divide. "I thought I'd be afraid of the mountain," she said, "but it's friendly, the mountain. And more beautiful than I ever imagined."

"I've found it's a rule of thumb," Mario said. "In Mexico, the sad people are in the flatlands and the desert. In the mountains, people are able to find more happiness."

They passed small isolated villages where children played beneath fruit trees and sheep wandered like contented clouds and people waved to them as they went by. Higher and higher they climbed, along wet, fragrant cliffs painted by nature with rainbow hues. Occasionally, far above, they could hear the lonely rumbling of a truck and then, perhaps ten minutes later, it would come hurtling down, its brakes sneezing and grinding, its engine casting echoes into the valleys. As the huge trucks approached it seemed there was absolutely not room enough to pass, and they would all be hurled out over the abyss looming just inches away. And then the truck would pass in a violent rush of wind.

Soon the air became cool and crisp and light, and it was so silent that, if you listened carefully, you might hear words not spoken until tomorrow. They reached what seemed the very top of the earth and Wally urged the Morris Minor off the road. Ahead, the blue-green mountains formed soldier rows as far as they could see. Below was the emerald cloud forest through which they had climbed. They listened for a moment to the symphonic silence of the mountain, the hush of a stream caressing stone, the low wind song in the pines, the deep thunder of emptiness. While Mario was setting up his camera to film scenes of the mountains and Gaspar Lopez was seeking to uncover the mystery of the ancient parchment, Wally and Penelope walked away from the road, into the pines. They moved to a shelf of volcanic rock. At its edge was a sheer drop into a valley, where a silver river coiled through the forest. After a moment, Wally said, "Way over there, halfway around the earth, there is a man standing in Nepal looking this way. And there is nothing and nobody in between. We are just one person away from the other side of the world."

"I am certain I could fly," Penelope said, looking out over the abyss. He was also certain she could fly. After all, it was a skill angels possessed, but he reached for her hand just in case he was wrong about her aeronautical skills.

"I feel light," she said. "A sister to the wind." Wally was suddenly overcome with the beauty of this exotic, dark, unknowable woman at his side. He wondered if he really loved her, could love her, or maybe he just loved the idea of loving her, this Angel of the Arroyos, who seemed to love everyone in equal measure, but especially those who were lonely and unloved. As if to answer his question, she stepped into his arms, pulled his head down and touched her lips to his. "I love you," she whispered into his mouth. "Do you remember that night when Mario filmed us pretending to make love?"

"How could I ever forget?"

"Maybe one day we won't have to pretend. When we get where we are going." She paused, moved her finger along his lips. "By the way, do you know where we're going?"

"Somewhere we won't have to hide. A place where justice is not a myth."

Penelope grew pensive, her head resting upon his shoulder. "That drawing in Gaspar's trunk—the airplane—could that have flown?"

"No. It was close, but he had a few things wrong."

"You are a designer of aircraft. Could you get it right?"

"I think so, with a few modifications."

"You could build it, fly it?

"Sure."

"Would you take me along?"

"To the ends of the skies."

"Who needs white horses when we can fly away in Leonardo's flying machine? We could go where The Lynx could never find us."

"He will come after us, you know."

"But isn't he just a silly man? Not really real?"

The Glass Guitar

Before Wally could think of an answer, a black helicopter came, low and fast, its rotor whipping pinecones from the trees and scattering birds nesting in the hardwoods. What looked like a hand grenade came twisting down from the helicopter and it burst open at their feet, releasing a fountain of amazingly fragrant white powder. Wally thought the powder smelled like a combination of all the world's most pleasant aromas; pipe tobacco, apple pie, bacon, gunpowder, vanilla, gasoline. Before he could think of another good-smelling thing, the world began to spin, and as he lost consciousness, a net fell over them. Before Penelope could draw her Oddfellows sword, they were hoisted off the mountain and into the helicopter and away.

When Wally regained consciousness, he and Penelope were lying on a bed of condor feathers, her right arm around him, her head tucked against his shoulder. They were in what appeared to be some kind of laboratory, filled with vials of colorful liquid, elaborately curved glass tubes, several Bunsen burners, and an electrical apparatus similar to the one that brought Frankenstein to life. It occurred to Wally that they were destined to be subjects in some kind of experiment, or that they were dreaming.

"This is nice," Penelope whispered, snuggling closer.

"I guess we were drugged," Wally said, rising on an elbow, looking around.

"What a wonderful smell," Penelope said. "I've never known an aroma so pleasant."

"Like a rose?"

"I never smelled a rose," she said. "I have never even seen a rose. No, this is more like the desert air after a rain. Fresh and new and intoxicating."

Wally had a vague recollection of a helicopter and a net and a wild ride down the mountain. "I wonder where we are?"

"Maybe in heaven. But I don't remember dying."

That's when the man came through the door. He was a tall man with sharp, angular features. Sunlight through a window proved that it was no longer night and a golden sunrise was reflected in the wire-rim glasses the man wore. He pulled up a chair and regarded his guests with benign disinterest. "I see you are awake," he said. "You will feel disoriented for a while, but it will pass."

"We were drugged?" Wally asked.

"A derivation of Moonwort. In this form, Moonwort is an anesthetic. I created the formula myself. You were knocked out by olfactory overload. The Moonwort powder stimulated all ten million of your olfactory receptors simultaneously, causing loss of consciousness. A stronger dose can cause an olfactory receptor disturbance so severe you can literally smell to death."

Wally was speechless. Penelope looked at Wally with an expression that said, "This is one mucho wacky hombre."

"Where is The Lynx?" Wally asked.

Their captor seemed confused. "What is this Lynx?"

"CIA. The guys with the helicopter. The guys that brought us here."

"I don't understand," the man said. "That was our helicopter. We brought you here."

"Why?"

"We were told you were spies."

As Wally tried to understand this new, unexpected intelligence, he thought to ask: "Where are our friends?"

"We don't know. We went back for them, but they were gone. There was only the little English car. We believe they were taken by The People of the Mountain."

"What people?"

"An ancient race, the only people not defeated by the Aztecs. They have lived in these mountains since time began. They are a primitive people, very fierce. I would not want to be your friends."

Penelope sat up, concerned for Mario, Gaspar and the prophet. "Will you help us find them?"

"It would be difficult. The People of the Mountain are everywhere and nowhere. They seem to be invisible. No one has ever seen one."

"How do you know they are there?"

"Because everyone knows they are. They are our bitter enemy. They are totally against progress of any kind. They have opposed Swamp Sweeney's Road from the beginning."

"What's Swamp Sweeney's Road?"

"That's where you are. This is our base camp. We are building a road from the Pacific Ocean through the lands of The People of the Mountain. They just don't understand that we're doing it for them, that the road is in their best interest."

"So, you are working on the road?"

"I'm the chief demolition officer here. Without my explosives we could never blast our way through the mountains." He gestured to his laboratory. "As you can see, this is where I experiment with various forms of Moonwort explosives. Some mixtures are tailored for cutting down trees, others for clearing a passage through the mountain. It depends on how much sacred yeast I add to the Moonwort."

"So, we're on Swamp Sweeney's Road?"

"Indeed."

"And where is that?"

"Well, Swamp Sweeney's Road goes from the Pacific coast, across the Sierra Madre Mountains to somewhere in the interior of Mexico."

"Where in Mexico?"

"We don't know. We haven't gotten there yet."

Now Wally heard the unmistakable clarion call of a bugle, playing reveille. "That's Swamp Sweeney's bugler, second call. The men will be mounting up on their bulldozers and heading out into the mountains." As if on cue, Wally heard the rumble of what sounded like tank treads and the grumble of powerful diesel engines.

"Could we start over? Wally asked. "Who the hell are you and where the hell are we and what the hell is Swamp Sweeney's Road?"

"Of course, you must be confused, and it is complicated. By the way, my name is Billy Bucket. You will be staying here with me for a while."

"Are we prisoners, Mr. Bucket?" Penelope asked.

"In a sense. But you are free to go. The problem is, of course, there's nowhere to go."

"We could go where the road goes."

"But where is that, my friends? It's obvious you haven't read about Swamp Sweeney's Road. Come," Billy Bucket said, offering his hand to Penelope. "I have something that will answer all your questions." He led them past all the laboratory equipment and what, he explained, were barrels of Moonwort extract, to a table containing a tall stack of magazines. He handed one magazine to Penelope and one to Wally. "It's the bible of our industry, *Progressive Earthmover Magazine.*"

On the cover of the magazine was a dramatic color photograph of an enormous bulldozer pushing over what appeared to be a grove of flowering fruit trees. On the side of the huge machine was a cartoon drawing of a naked woman riding a lightning bolt. It reminded Wally of the logos World War II bomber pilots painted on their planes. In the background was a magnificent mountain vista framed in clouds white as magazine paper. A caption below the photograph read: *Pictured above is The Ace Earthmover Corporation's newest model D-12 Adonis bulldozer. Last week, the corporation reported a net profit of 6 billion dollars, a 100-percent increase over the previous year's profits. It has been estimated in excess of 11 trillion cubic yards of earth have been moved by the Adonis D-12 since the model's introduction. According to the company's president, Ace Glover, this is tantamount to moving New Zealand. He didn't say where or how far.*

Wally thumbed through the pages of the magazines. The D-12 Adonis was only one of the featured machines. Here were huge cranes and scrapers and what used to be called steam shovels, and plows and augers and monster bushwhackers and other great bladed leviathans. They were all busily at work digging and gutting and tearing away at prairie and forest and hillside.

This is what Wally and Penelope read on an editorial page of *Progressive Earthmover Magazine:*

Those who oppose the construction of Swamp Sweeney's Road base their objection on the matter of its destination. We agree, at this point in time, the road leads essentially nowhere. But it won't always be nowhere. Already, thriving communities are blooming like gardens along the road to take advantage of the commerce that roads always bring. Where once there was only trackless jungle, there will soon be shops, and perhaps malls and salons where women can get their nails done. Our hope is that Congress continues to provide funds so that the road can become longer and longer, thus making room for more and more thriving communities along its way. When interviewed on the subject, Swamp Sweeney explained that he was carving a nation in the wilderness. "This nation, our research shows, is approximately 100 feet wide and 900 miles long, so far making it the thinnest yet fastest growing nation on earth."

"This is absolutely the nuttiest thing I've ever read," Wally said.

"A road to nowhere may sound nutty to the uninitiated," Billy Bucket said, not a little offended. "But tell that to the wives of the good men buried in graves along the shoulder, who gave their lives for it to get there."

"You really are serious?" Penelope asked, having a difficulty keeping a straight face. "You mean you're actually building a road to nowhere?"

"Nowhere is nowhere," Billy Bucket said. "Everywhere is somewhere," he added and he led them out into the morning sunlight. Swamp Sweeney's base camp squatted where the road tumbled into a cul-de-sac of stone and rubble. It lay at the foot of the mountain like something thrown away. The bulldozers had leveled a plateau large enough to embrace the tons of machines man uses in his campaign against the earth. Billy Bucket pointed out the great D-12 Adonis bulldozers and the cranes and ditching machines and huge steel rollers and graders and the mammoth new 816 Jungle Converter that could consume great swaths of the planet in its steel jaws. As Wally looked out at the camp, it seemed everything existed to tend the machines, as if they were idols to a crass and noisy god somewhere. Even now, denim-clad worshippers knelt at the machines, urging from them more noise for the gods. Around the machines, arranged like wagons circled against Indian attack were the little portable campers where the road workers lived. Billy Bucket pointed out the Domino Palace, the social center of the base camp where the workers gambled their wages on such domino games as Blind Hughie, Chicken-foot and Mexican Train. At the center of the camp was the great ornate tent where Swamp Sweeney lived and issued orders to move the road each day a little further toward its non-existent destination. The tent was made of goatskin, dyed blue like an old dead person, and was fringed with soft balls of yarn. The effect was not unlike something out of an old Genghis Khan movie. To the west of the camp was the horrible scar that the Adonis D-12s and the 816 Jungle Converter had savaged through the living green. To the east was a towering peak, rising Lord knows how far, maybe to heaven, for it was rarely revealed without its cloak of grey and silver mists.

"It's beautiful," Penelope said of the peak, still quietly celebrating the first mountains she had ever known.

"It is called Reventador, a volcano, like the one in Ecuador. I grant you it's beautiful," Billy Bucket said. "But it's also a big problem. First, it is standing right in the way of where the road must go through. And second, the peak is the ancestral home of The People of the Mountain. They command the high ground with their bows and poisoned arrows."

"So, what will you do?"

"I will create an explosive so powerful that it will blow the mountain to Kingdom Come."

"And The People?" Penelope asked. "And what of our friends? They must be up there with them."

"I don't know that I have any choice."

After a breakfast of scrambled condor eggs and fried iguana, Billy Bucket ushered the others back to his laboratory.

"There's always a choice," Wally said. It reminded him of what Augustus Salizar had said about hope—that only people who had hope, had hope. Maybe the same could be said about choice.

"You just don't understand how important it is for the road to get through. It is my destiny." He showed them another issue of *Progressive Earthmover Magazine*. Here is what they read: "Moonwort X9, a substance recently developed by the dynamiter William Bucket, will be the explosive used in the demolition of Reventador Volcano, the last obstacle blocking the progress of Swamp Sweeney's Road. Mr. Bucket refuses to reveal the chemical makeup of Moonwort X9. However, *Progressive Earthmover Magazine* has learned that it contains quantities of condor down and puss from the terrible wounds on the arms and chests of mountain dwelling condor pluckers. Baba Bubba, former Hindu weightlifter and spiritual leader of Swamp Sweeney's Road, said, 'The People of the Mountain cannot survive in this brave new world—not without what the road can bring them. So, we have to blow away their volcano.' When asked if that wouldn't also blow away their home and their culture, Baba Bubba replied, 'They shouldn't have shot at us with those poisoned arrows.'"

"Baba Bubba?" Wally asked, exchanging an incredulous look with Penelope. Is he a Hindu, or a Christian, or what?"

"Well, actually," Billy said. "None of those ordinary religions. Our spiritual leader practices a faith based on the worship of yeast."

Although he knew it was wrong to ridicule someone's religion, Wally could not suppress a burst of laughter. "You believe this nonsense?"

"Fervently. But it's complicated." Then Billy Bucket explained why Swamp Sweeney had chosen him as Chief Demolition Expert. "I didn't always want to be a dynamiter," he began, "but when I was a sophomore in high school, my vocational guidance counselor gave me a battery of tests to determine if there were any areas in which I might excel. The tests were conducted in an atmosphere of acute negativism, because my guidance counselor suspected I had no aptitude at all. But to the complete surprise of everyone, including myself, I received the highest score ever received in the field of demolition. I was encouraged to pursue a college curriculum in this field, but since no college courses were offered, I embarked on an extensive course of self-study."

Billy then told them how he read all the existing literature on explosives, beginning with the early Chinese experiments in firecracker design and extending through the firebombs dropped on Dresden during World War II. Before graduating from high school, Billy had apparently astounded experts in the demolition field by grasping the very essence of the demolition art. It was a philosophy Billy expressed in his senior thesis, entitled *Ethics and the Firecracker*. "It goes like this," Billy said. "Explosions occur when growth is more rapid than the ability of time to contain it. It holds true for a firecracker, a bomb or anything that explodes. The same is true with the Big Bang Theory of the origin of the universe. A tiny core, no larger than a pinhead, expanded in a blink of an eye so much faster than time could contain it and bam, welcome to the Cosmos."

Billy Bucket went on to explain other observations he had made in his thesis, *Ethics and the Firecracker*. He told, for instance, how man has always received enormous aesthetic and sensual stimulation from explosive displays. Children have been trained from infancy to view fireworks as beautiful and they receive great joy in blowing up tin cans and small boxes and an occasional bird. The human animal just seems to find joy in blowing up things. It's in our DNA. And the degree of this joy is in direct proportion to the magnitude of the explosion. A child claps his hands when his tiny Yankee Boy Assortment ladyfinger firecracker blows the wing off a butterfly. When airmen observe the results of a bombing run over enemy cities, they quite frequently refer to the resulting fires and explosions as 'beautiful.' These same airmen also report having erections in proportion to the power of the explosions unleashed."

Wally remembered the erection testing he had performed in the *F-111* with the Human Factors Engineer, the need for which was actual proof that at least this part of Billy Bucket's nutty theory was correct. In fact, he was beginning to find much of what Billy had published in his *Ethics and the Firecracker* was not absolutely bonkers. Surely, it was no less believable and reasonable than sabotaging supersonic fighter-bombers with Holloway's Milk Duds or assassinating Popeye.

"I'm not a philosopher," Penelope said, "but it seems to me your strategy is to save the People of the Mountain by destroying them."

"Billy," Wally said, "don't you see how preposterous all this is? A road to nowhere? Moonwart? *Ethics and the Firecracker? Progressive Earthmover Magazine?* Baba Bubba? The worship of yeast? It's all absurd!"

"You think so?" Billy said, staring into Wally's eyes, then he turned his head and gazed into the deep, blue mystery of Penelope's soul.

"Of course, Billy," she said. "Think about it. And think of the injustice of it all. Think of the People of the Mountain."

Billy's shoulders slumped, the light seemed to leave his eyes, he turned away, spoke softly over his shoulder. "I think about it all the time. Sometimes I wonder if I am a monster. I am tormented by doubt. But, then, Swamp Sweeney and Baba Bubba teach us that there is joy in the building of the road. That it is not only the right thing to do, but the only thing." Billy Bucket seemed so beat-down blue that Penelope reached for his hand and slipped it into her shirt where her good and generous heart was. "You poor, poor man," she said, tears pooling in her eyes.

Just then the camp's bugler bugled that the noon meal was being served, the tune a lip-numbing variation of "Flight of the Bumblebee," which was Swamp Sweeney's favorite song. After composing himself, Billy Bucket led his captive guests toward the Domino Palace, where they joined a phalanx of booted and denim clad heavy equipment operators pouring from their bulldozers and other earth-marauding machines. They settled down at tables, sweeping the scattered dominoes aside or to the floor. From a riser before the group, Baba Bubba, the former Hindu weight lifter, asked that they bow their heads for a benediction. He was a remarkably large and obviously powerful man with a full beard that reached almost to his waist. Wally wondered if the beard wasn't a safety hazard for one who operated dangerous road-building machines.

Here is what Baba Bubba said: "It has come to my attention that there are among us those who do not believe in building a road to nowhere and who do not believe in a religion based on the worship of yeast. Yet, I assure you that everything there is, and everything that was, contains a seed of cosmic yeast and the universe is most like a great loaf of raisin bread rising." At this point, there were shouts of "Praise Yeast!" from the gathered faithful. Wally was reminded of the born-again Christians gathered to pray in the bomber factory.

Baba Bubba continued, "There is nothing in nature that does not grow larger in time. The Universe itself grows larger. The lotus opens. The mind expands. And so, it is only logical that God is Yeast." There came an affirmative staccato clatter of dominoes on the wood tables, a sound not unlike that of skeletons dancing.

"And now," he continued, "I would like you all to turn to *Progressive Earth Mover Magazine*, volume 16, page 12, paragraph 2, for the text of today's message." Throughout the Domino Palace came the slap of magazines, the whispery turning of thumb-soiled pages, and the renewed timpani of dominoes. Then the spiritual leader of Swamp Sweeney's Road read the following: "'Dispatches from the field indicate there is a probability of open hostilities breaking out between Swamp Sweeney's Road and the band of terrorist headhunters defending their homes in the Reventador Volcano. Noted theologian-engineer Baba Bubba has sent crews to attach eviction notices to the walls of the high passes. Since the crater and, in fact, the entire mountain is slated to be destroyed by Moonwort blast, Swamp Sweeney has vowed to drive the terrorists from the mountain, in order to prevent bloodshed. Attempts to contact the terrorist organization have failed. However *Progressive Earthmover* has learned that the danger from these terrorists is clear and present and growing each and every day. The savage People of the Mountain are not only a danger to Swamp Sweeney's Road but to roads in other countries, even those that lead to homes and schools in our own neighborhoods. It is for this reason that we urge everyone to support the brave men and women who are risking their lives to protect our way of life.' This, according to the holy book." Then the former Hindu weight lifter raised both massive arms and shouted: "There is joy in the building of the road!"

Lunch was served by the widows of martyred bulldozer drivers who were killed when their machines tumbled off the high, precipitous mountains into the turbulent Great Enema River, a stream that flowed roughly parallel to Swamp

Sweeney's Road. They were assisted by the ladies of the community of whores—camp followers, who had joined the construction crews as they came ashore on the Pacific coast and who now lived in a large wooden structure on the perimeter of the camp. From large wheel-mounted kettles, they heaped ladles of minced condor thigh and grits. "Which one is Swamp Sweeney?" Wally asked.

"Oh, he's not here. He's rather reclusive. He keeps to himself in his tent. He leaves the building of the road to his chief engineer, Benjamin Put."

"What's he like?"

"Swamp Sweeney? He's wonderful," Billy Bucket said, a faraway look in his eyes. "A truly great American. He has built roads all over the world, through some of the most difficult terrain imaginable, across deserts, Arctic ice, jungles and mountains. His men love him. I love him, I think. He and his road give my life meaning."

"Do you think Baba Bubba was referring to you when he mentioned there were doubters among those building the road?"

Billy Bucket stiffened, the color drained from his face. Sensing his discomfort, Penelope took his hand and put it in her lap. "Oh, God!" he said. "Don't even think that."

"What would he do to a doubter? A blasphemer? What could he do to you?"

"He demands loyalty. Absolute loyalty."

"He wouldn't kill you, surely," Penelope said.

"I don't know. For him, building the road is everything."

"By the way, Billy. What's going to happen to us? Penelope and me? I guess you realize we're your number one doubters and blasphemers. Yeast sucks! A road to nowhere is just plain fruitcake!"

"Please keep your voice down!" Billy Bucket hissed through clenched teeth. "I don't know what will happen."

"Will you help us escape?" Penelope asked. "Why don't we, all three, leave. I know the camp has a helicopter. It's probably the one that brought us here. I could distract the guard; Wally can fly us out of here."

"I can't fly a helicopter," Wally said.

"You said you could. You said you could fly me to the end of the skies."

"If there's a helicopter, there's got to be a helicopter pilot. Maybe he's even sane. Hates yeast."

Billy Bucket was obviously becoming more and more uncomfortable.

"Billy, you could help us. See if you can find the pilot."

"Come with us, Billy. To the end of the skies. We'll find a place that's not ruled by maniacs."

Before Billy Bucket could answer, there suddenly came the treble brass bleating of the camp bugle. Abandoning their roast condor breast and grits, the workers rushed from the Domino Palace and formed up ranks outside. Billy Bucket explained that it was the call to assemble and that something momentous must have happened. Wally and Penelope and Billy followed the crowd of heavy equipment operators who all seemed intent on something happening at the very top of the Reventador crater. "It's Benjamin Put," someone cried, pointing to the crater's rim. "He's way too high!" Someone else said that he was attacking the savage enemy alone, moving into the belly of the beast.

How vast and silent the mountain was. And way off and alone, an Adonis D-12 moved against the mountain. The sound its motor made came very faint to Wally's ears, a sort of purr upon the wind. He watched the machine moving, now forward, now back, so very tiny against the mountain. And he felt a welling up inside, a sort of admiration for Benjamin Put. There was something noble about the little machine working alone against all that stone, moving closer and closer to the top of the world. How lovely was the ballet of the lonely, purring Adonis D-12 and the majestic volcano they called Reventador. Maybe, just maybe, after all, maybe, there was joy in the building of the road.

And then, as everyone watched in horror, the old volcano trembled ever so slightly and the little bulldozer began to fall from the heights, Benjamin Put still at the controls, fighting gravity and a gathering avalanche of stone. It happened slowly, like an event remembered. The bulldozer bounded softly down the mountain, tumbling, sliding, falling, graceful as only the death of something so noble could be. And then it disappeared into the raging Great Enema River down below.

Because of the humidity and tropic heat in the Great Enema River bottoms, Benjamin's Put's body began to decompose the instant it stopped rolling. The funeral was set for the evening of the day he died. The haste reminded Wally of the horrible B. Traven story of the boy who died beneath *The Bridge in the Jungle* and decomposed before his funeral could be arranged. Wally's mother, aware of his severe instability, had hidden the book when he was fifteen, probably fearing a depression would interfere with his chores. Benjamin Put's casket was to be closed during his service because he had somehow arrived at the foot of Reventador without his head. Swamp Sweeney immediately dispatched a work party to search for it. When they returned empty-handed, a strange and thrilling mood settled down upon Swamp Sweeney's Road. It was part mourning and part that kind of closeness only felt when brave men are afraid. It was not whispered exactly, but just simply known, that Benjamin Put's death had been no accident and neither had been his awful decapitation. Just as everyone had always known, something or someone lurked in the crater of Reventador. It was obvious that the People of the Mountain were the savage headhunters they were reputed to be. Here and there, about the camp, the heavy-equipment operators began to arm themselves.

Swamp Sweeney assigned the construction of the casket to the ladies of the community of whores, who had done such a great job building their whorehouse and had stolen all the hand tools, anyway. All afternoon orders were issued, willy-nilly, by messengers coming and going through the fringed flap of the blue goatskin tent in the center of the camp. Benjamin's battalion of bulldozer operators guarded the camp's perimeter against attack by headhunters and, occasionally, the sound of small arms fire could he heard as the guards spun off wild shots toward the slopes of Reventador. The machines themselves were strangely quiet. Only a few welders worked, constructing what appeared to be a great, corrugated, iron pan in the center of camp. Once the pan was finished, just before dusk, great quantities of holy dough were brought from the camp kitchen and were reverently placed in the gargantuan pan. Then, just before dark, they brought Benjamin's body in. They opened the nice casket the ladies of the community of whores had made and several pallbearers lifted out the body. It appeared to be all covered with paprika. And then, with the kind of shock one feels when confronted with something unbelievable that one suspected all the time, Wally realized they were about to bake Benjamin Put in a biscuit.

The service began with a chorus of "Flight of the Bumble-bee," played *adagio* in a minor key. The pallbearers attempted to sing along—a dreadful, chaotic blending of bass and bari-tone—a Russian male chorus on crack. Then the D-12 operators not standing guard against a possible intrusion of savage head-hunters gently lifted their headless leader and plopped him down in the bed of holy dough that lined the bottom of the gar-gantuan pan. One of the loveliest of the ladies from the com-munity of whores strutted forward with a sacred patty of cosmic yeast and placed it in the pan. A bulldozer engine exploded to life and the Adonis D-12 moved thunderously forward and pushed the great iron cover onto the pan and Benjamin Put dis-appeared from view. Now there was a fire and Benjamin Put began to become one with the universe.

As Wally watched the great funeral biscuit rise, he felt he was experiencing an out of body experience. Perhaps an out of mind experience, as well. Surely he was dreaming and soon he would wake to discover he had had far too much to drink the night before, and the world would assume it's true, familiar, yet imperfect self. He listened to the mourners and small arms fire directed toward the savages upon Reventador, watched the leaping flames and soon decided, all that was happening was an hallucination, perhaps brought on by another Moonwort-gen-erated olfactory overload. But then he caught a sweet, peppery whiff of paprika rising from the funeral biscuit and he was enveloped in a deep and abiding sorrow for the world, himself and everyone else who shared his journey through time and space. 'I am a part of all this,' he thought. 'I stand apart from it, yet I am a part of it. How can one live with dignity in an absurd world?' He thought about this for a while and decided he could only try and somehow get through it all without doing too much harm. Then he felt Penelope's hand reach for his own and he looked down into her blue expressive eyes and at her full, fine lips and the rise of her perfect breasts above her good and generous heart and he decided this was all the truth he needed to know.

Billy Bucket found the helicopter pilot the morning after the funeral. The demolition expert had been entangled in an epic struggle with his doubts ever since Benjamin Put had been laid to rest. It seemed that the absurdity of the funeral had finally broken through his blindness and he had begun to see how evil it would be to destroy the ancestral home of the People of the Mountain. He swore that he would forswear a belief in the sanctity of yeast, the building of the road to nowhere and that he would destroy the Moonwort formula that was so powerful it could destroy a whole mountain.

It seemed to Wally that Billy Bucket was almost ready to surrender to sanity, yet not ready to plunge full in. As Billy, Wally and Penelope talked late into the night, lying together upon a bed of condor down, Billy had admitted that he was not really convinced there were savage headhunters in the volcano. After all, no one had ever seen hide or hair of one. And then, who among them had been shot by poisoned arrows? Where were the bodies? Where were the arrows? Then, near dawn, he had tearfully admitted that he wasn't even sure there was a Swamp Sweeney.

"Who had really seen him? No one that I know of. He's always in that tent. What if he is some kind of construction of our collective imagination? Maybe we needed a symbol to explain all the harm we were doing in the interest of progress. Maybe none of this is real."

"But *Progressive Earthmover Magazine*," Wally reminded him. "I held those magazines in my hands."

"Maybe it's printed here," Billy said, "edited by Baba Bubba and his cronies. They are the only ones who enter Swamp Sweeney's tent. Maybe there's a printing press in there. Lord knows what goes on in there."

After she had told Wally once more that she loved him and would love him forever, Penelope turned to Billy Bucket and began to kiss his tears and his confusion and his madness away. As Billy had struggled to find his better angels, Wally was fairly sure he had found at least one of them in the expressive blue eyes, the fine full lips, the generous heart and the other heavenly parts God had bestowed on the Angel of the Arroyos.

Now, just as the first pale light of dawn touched the peaks to the east, Billy Bucket said he would take them to the helicopter pilot. He would help them escape, but he wanted to go along.

There was a tense and desperate sense of siege in the camp as Billy Bucket led Wally and Penelope through the shadows to where he was sure the pilot might be. The huge D-12 bulldozers were arranged in defensive formation, their great iron blades facing the distant volcano. They passed the Domino Palace and the huge 816 Jungle Converter, crept silently through the community of whores until they reached where the helicopter stood in the half-light, like an enormous, brooding insect. Because everyone's attention was on the dark slopes of Reventador, looking for the hordes of savage archers that might descend on them at any moment, little attention was paid to Billy Bucket and his new friends.

Behind the helicopter was a Quonset hut, and when they slipped in the door, they found two men playing dominoes by lantern light. One was introduced as the pilot, a one-armed man, with soft grey eyes and almost white hair. He was wearing Bermuda shorts and flip-flops, not exactly what Wally assumed helicopter pilots would wear. In spite of his white hair, he had a youthful body, like a surfer past his prime. The second man was Black, rotund, with a round, pleasant face and sad eyes that seemed to have seen all the suffering of the world. Billy Bucket introduced him as Papa Blue, the ubiquitous camp bugler.

The pilot's name was Major Tom. Billy Bucket said he was a former test pilot and astronaut.

"An astronaut?" Penelope exclaimed, looking at the helicopter pilot with bright, admiring eyes.

"It was years ago," Major Tom said.

"The Major is too humble for his own good," Papa Blue said. "He was one of the original astronauts, along with John Glenn and Gus Grissom and the rest. He's the one David Bowie wrote the song about."

"That was you?" Mario asked. "'Ground control to Major Tom'?"

Major Tom scuffed his flip-flops.

"You mean that was real?" Wally was amazed. "I thought you disappeared forever, went spinning off into the cosmos."

"Ground control had it wrong. They just lost me when I fell out of the Mercury capsule over New Jersey."

"That's when he lost his arm," Papa Blue said. "He caught his arm on the hatch. His arm went spinning off into the cosmos, but Major Tom was here on earth all the time. Just shows how you can't believe just about anything. NASA was so embarrassed about the whole thing that they claimed the flight had never happened and and struck his name from all their records. Since he didn't exist, and had only one arm, it seemed his flying days were over. But Swamp Sweeney gave him this job."

As Major Tom surveyed the intruders, especially Penelope, who was magnificent in the lantern light, Papa Blue played soft minor chords on what appeared to be a trumpet.

Billy Bucket explained what they wanted: a flight out before the People of the Mountain attacked.

Papa Blue laughed. "There ain't no People of the Mountain, son. That's all just a story." Then he played a riff, soft as a whisper.

Major Tom stood. "I went to all the trouble to fly you here and now you want me to fly you back?"

"So that was you who caught us in the net," Wally said. "What about The Lynx? The CIA?"

"No. It was just me." Major Tom stared at Penelope for a while, almost as if he were trying to memorize her—beauty stored away for an ugly day. Penelope seemed not to mind. She simply smiled back. Then Major Tom tore his eyes away from Penelope and spoke to Billy Bucket. "I thought you were a true believer. What got into you?"

"If you're so eager to go, why did you come here in the first place?"

"It was a great job. Travel, good pay. There was a sense of doing something worthwhile. And there's not so many jobs these days for dynamiters."

Major Tom pulled out a chair for Penelope and sat at the table beside her. "I know what you mean. When I heard about this position with Swamp Sweeney, I jumped at the chance."

"What about you, Mr. Papa Blue?" Penelope asked. "What brought you here?"

"Well, Darling, I been playing the blues all my life. Started playing the trumpet when I was a boy down in the Mississippi Delta. Then I made my way to Memphis, to Chicago; went on tour with Paul Butterfield. Man, how that white boy could play the blues. But one day in Chicago I was caught with a white woman and them boys beat me up and down good. Busted my lip so bad I could hardly play, at least not like before. I mean I could, but my heart wasn't in it anymore. The soul was gone. When I heard about this job, I thought, 'You don't have to have soul to play the bugle.' How hard could it be, there's only a couple of notes?"

For a while they were silent, listening to the soft melody from Papa Blue's horn.

After a while, Major Tom said, "Well maybe it's time to leave this crazy place, anyway. What do you say, Papa Blue? No more Swamp Sweeney, no more Baba Bubba, no more yeast."

Papa Blue smiled. "No more Flight of the Fucking Bumblebee." The two men rose, shook Wally's and Billy Bucket's hands and took turns hugging Penelope, then took another turn, and another.

"I don't mean to be an alarmist," Billy said. "But we better hurry before the People of the Mountain attack."

"Jesus Christ, man, I thought you saw the error of your thinking," Papa Blue said. "I've never seen a white boy so captive to a lie."

It was then they heard the raucous rallying cry of a bugle echo through the canyons. "How can that be?" Wally asked, eyes wide. "You're here, Papa Blue!"

"It's my day off. They've got a recording."

"What's the bugle call mean?" Penelope asked.

"It signals that the enemy has been sighted. Fire at will."

Then came the sound of sustained gunfire from the bulldozers and screams of panic from the community of whores. Wally and the others rushed out of the Quonset. Out beyond the perimeter, on the lower slopes of Reventador, dark shapes moved steadily forward. Then they could hear return fire, stone-tipped arrows hitting the metal blades of the bulldozers.

"It's true!" Billy Bucket shouted. "They're coming for our heads!"

Then it became apparent that they were not being attacked by poisoned arrows, but by automatic rifle fire. As the attackers drew nearer, Wally could see they were not naked savages, but men wearing dark business suits carrying AK47s.

"It's The Lynx!" Wally moaned.

A loud hailer blared Wally's name. "I'VE GOT YOU NOW, WALTER PILLOW! THE JIG IS UP. COME OUT WITH YOUR HANDS UP!"

"You must be some bad-assed dude," Papa Blue said. "You still want to go, we better make tracks."

Under a hail of gunfire, Wally, Billy Bucket, Penelope and Papa Blue clambered aboard the helicopter. Within minutes, Major Tom was aboard, and the rotors whined and whipped the air, whirling faster and faster; and then they were aloft and away.

"What now?" Major Tom called, as Swamp Sweeney's Road disappeared behind a curtain of mist. Wally looked down and thought it was almost as if it had never been there at all.

"Can you take us to where you found us before?"

"I can."

"We've got to find our friends. Since they obviously aren't prisoners of savage headhunters, maybe they're where we last saw them. At least that's a good place to start looking."

"And if you find them, what then?" Papa Blue asked.

"We'll drive on across the Sierra Madres to Mazatlan. It's carnival season and Penelope has never seen the sea."

"What about you, Papa Blue?"

"If you have room, I'd like to go along. I always wanted to play in a mariachi band."

"How about you, Billy? Will you come with us?"

"Isn't it the Mazatlan festival where they have such marvelous fireworks? I've got a Moonwort formula that would set the sky ablaze with color. So, if you don't mind me tagging along, I accept your invitation."

Where will you go?" Penelope asked Major Tom.

"I can't go back. So I think I'll borrow Swamp Smith's helicopter and head north, maybe California, get a job flying with my old boss. He's the only person besides Swamp Sweeney crazy enough to hire me."

"He doesn't talk about it," Papa Blue said, "but his old, crazy boss is Howard Hughes. He flew for Hughes Aviation. Flew in the *Spruce Goose*."

"You flew in the *Spruce Goose*?" Wally was astounded.

"Just once. It only flew once."

"What's the *Spruce Goose*?" Penelope asked.

"The largest airplane ever built, that's all!" Wally said, thrilled to the marrow of his bones to be sitting beside one of the few who had flown in the legendary flying boat. As an aircraft designer, Wally had studied every aspect of Howard Hughes's masterwork, had built miniature models of the several revolutionary designs leading up to the final design.

"What was it like?" Wally asked, seeking an answer in Major Tom's grey eyes.

"It wasn't a very long flight. Not more than a minute."

"But she flew! Nobody believed a 200 ton wooden aircraft could fly!" Wally thrilled again, as he had as a child, to the astonishing achievement. An airplane made almost entirely of wood, a wingspan longer than a football field, a tail assembly tall as an eight story building, eight Pratt and Whitney engines with the power of 24,000 horses. And she lifted off the water, graceful as a swan. And here was a man who had experienced that first and only flight.

"Why only a minute?" Mario asked.

"It was supposed to be a taxi run. We weren't supposed to fly that day at all. But as we reached 90 mph, she simply lifted up off the water. I think even Howard was surprised. But there we were, some eighty feet off the surface."

"Why didn't you keep flying?"

"There were twenty-eight people aboard. There were engineers, systems experts, a lot of news people. There weren't enough life jackets and most people weren't strapped in. I believe this might have been the most difficult decision Howard ever made and he had to make it in an instant. He put her back down. He had risked his own life in airplanes hundreds of times, but he wasn't willing to risk the lives of others."

"And the *Spruce Goose* never flew again" Wally said. "That was the first and last flight."

"Why?" Penelope asked.

"Howard had always been a little crazy. But after that flight he went downhill fast. I think he knew he was losing his skills and didn't want to risk the plane."

"Someone else could have been the pilot. How about you?"

"No. That would never happen. Howard would never relinquish the controls of anything, airplane or life."

"So, what happened to the plane?" Penelope asked.

"She's still there in Long Beach, in a huge hangar. Still being maintained in perfect condition after all these years."

"It's sad," Penelope said.

"Yes," Major Tom said. "I would have loved to have her fly again."

For a while they were silent, Wally wondering what it would have been like to feel the *Spruce Goose* lift from the sea.

"So, then you became an astronaut?" Penelope asked.

"Yes, on Howard's recommendation. I had flown just about every kind of plane there was, so why not a space ship? And the rest is history. Or a song, depending on your point of view."

"I love knowing you," Penelope said, leaning over and kissing Major Tom lightly on the lips. Then she turned to Wally, her blue eyes filled with love and wonder. "Until I met you I had never seen a mountain, never known an astronaut, never seen a man baked in a biscuit, and now I'm going to see the ocean. And I had never flown like this, above Mother Earth. Is this the end of the skies?"

"Maybe the beginning," Wally said, and Penelope snuggled close, her head on his shoulder, her hair smelling a little like Billy Bucket's most beguiling Moonwort fragrance.

And so, they flew on.

Soon they could see Wally's little Morris Minor, looking lost and lonely by the side of the road.

CHAPTER 5
LEONARDO'S DREAM

It was not difficult to find Mario, Gaspar and the prophet, because of the crowd of extras Mario had assembled for filming his documentary segment on Zog I, King of the Albanians. When they caught up with their friends they were filming a re-enactment of one of the fifty-five assassination attempts on the life of this imminently forgettable Royal. The *Alcalde* of a near-by village was playing King Zog I; his wife was performing the role of Sadije Toptani, Queen Mother of the Albanians. The prophet played one of the assassins and fifty-four villagers played the parts of the other fifty-four assassins. Later, Mario would explain that he was filming all fifty-five assassination attempts simultaneously, to save film. When Wally came upon the scene, the prophet and the fifty-four villagers had surrounded King Zog with the obvious intent to kill.

"Cut!" Mario cried when he saw his friends. Overjoyed that they were alive and safe, he rushed with open arms to their side. However, the reunion was forestalled because the villagers, not understanding the meaning of the word "cut," were beating the bejeebers out of King Zog I and the Queen Mother, and Mario and the others were only barely able to rescue the principle leads from their assassins. When order had been restored, Wally asked Mario why he would select such a little known historical figure as a subject.

"He was family. He was my illegitimate father."

"How can you have an illegitimate father?"

"My mother was Italian, one of Mussolini's mistresses. When Italy invaded Albania in 1939, King Zog, not at all pleased about the invasion, had his way with Mussolini's mistress before fleeing into exile."

"So, you are really an Albanian movie director?"

"Precisely. And what good Albanian movie director could pass up the opportunity to immortalize our country's greatest hero, Zog I, King of the Albanians?"

Wally looked to where the *alcalde* lay bleeding, surrounded by bit players who had apparently really gotten into the motivation of their characters and were still smoldering with rage and confusion. Finally, Penelope, with deft swings of the Ceremonial Order of the Oddfellows sword, drove the perplexed extras off the set and Mario set up his next scene. It was a close-up of King Zog I making his farewell speech to his people. Mario shouted "Action" and the faux king made what Wally thought was an impassioned performance, until Penelope told him the king was cursing his burro in language that made even a former prostitute blush. When Wally pointed this out to Mario he said it didn't matter. "It will be dubbed in Albanian, anyway."

"But how will this fit into our documentary? How can you tie this in with the footage shot in Crystal City? What does King

Zog I have to do with Gaspar Lopez's restaurant or the prophet's search for his lost prophesy or our lives as fugitives?"

"Wally," Mario began, seeming peeved that Wally was apparently so blind. "What is life but a series of disconnected events and miscellaneous encounters and surprises that somehow, in the end, just happen to make sense? I don't know how King Zog I fits into the pattern of our lives. This is not scripted, Wally. This is documentary. It just happens. It's not easy being a documentarian, especially one with an illegitimate father and a mother who dated Mussolini."

It took some time for Billy Bucket and Papa Blue to become comfortable with the prophet, or with Mario, for that matter. But soon, following the example of Wally and Penelope, they made an extra effort and became a part of the feckless assemblage. They all piled into the little Morris Minor convertible and headed for the Pacific coast.

The little car moved down the mountain like something from a circus—those comic automobiles into which an impossible number of clowns have been packed. Wally, Billy Bucket and Mario were crowded in the front seat with Penelope lying across them, her feet out the window and her head in Wally's lap. Papa Blue and his trumpet took up most of the back seat, leaving a small wedge of space for Gaspar Lopez on one side and the awful prophet on the other. Wally had rarely felt such a limitless happiness. He was surrounded by good friends, old and new, the day was fine and it seemed he had somehow left behind all the things in life that tormented and threatened his sanity. Papa Blue was playing "House of the Rising Sun" soft as a lullaby, and Wally wished someone else were driving so he could get his guitar out and play along. Soon Penelope's deep contralto began to add low velvet harmonies, a sound as sensual as any Wally had ever heard. But the enormous surprise was that the awful prophet rose up and began to howl gibberish in a rather decent tenor, the effect something between the sound of a European police siren and an Islamic call to prayer. And so, the little clown car drove on, filled with love and freedom and music.

Soon the road began to ride the mountain down, and Wally strained to catch sight of the sea. He began to feel the excitement he'd felt as a child, when the old family Chevrolet approached the coast. They would drive, each summer, from Illinois to the Alabama shore and his father would offer a prize to the first one to see the ocean. Wally and his sister would start shouting out false alarms just south of Jackson, Tennessee.

They moved through lofty green pines now, by the little villages of Palmito and Potrevillas, and passed through the Tropic of Cancer to Santa Lucia. The mountains seemed to grow weary here; their peaks pushed down to gently rolling foothills.

Wally slowed at an intersection and drove up a narrow road, to where a village nested on the brow of a hill. Instinct told him there would be a view of the sea across the broad valley below. He parked the car and awakened his sleeping passengers.

"Where are we?" Mario asked, as the others, with groans and sighs, unfolded their cramped limbs and climbed from the little convertible.

"I don't know the name of this place," Wally answered, "but I have a surprise for Penelope."

"What is it, Wally? I love surprises! Is it a rose? I'd love to see a rose."

"Just wait. You'll see."

They moved upward through an orchard of lemon and peach trees and then along a well-tended vegetable garden until they came to a grove of eucalyptus trees. Holding Penelope's hand, Wally led them into the grove. He looked back and saw the others were following along, the prophet taking up the rear, as strange an assembly of travelers as one might ever see. "Now, close your eyes, Penelope."

She clutched his hand, brought it to her eyes. She was almost dancing with excitement. 'Never has she looked so much like a child,' he thought.

When they came to the brow of the hill, they could see beyond the eucalyptus trees, beyond the diminishing hills, beyond the broad valley, the wide blue mystery of the sea. "Now you may open your eyes."

For a while, Penelope seemed confused. She looked out at the distant sea, then into Wally's eyes, then back to the sea again. "The sky has fallen," she said. "It is draped across the distance. It is blue but has no clouds. And there is another sky above this sky."What is it, Wally? What have you given me?"

"It is the sea."

Penelope fell to her knees. "How very wide. It goes forever, like the desert, but blue. How very beautiful. I see now; it is more than blue. It is golden where the sun touches it, and green and white, and I feel it is alive, has thoughts." Her eyes filled with tears and they streamed down her cheeks into the earth. "Thank you, Wally, for giving me the sea."

They continued their pilgrimage toward Mazatlan. They passed the sleeping village of Chupaderos and went on toward the sea. Wally saw a green parrot rise from the branches of a tree, the underside of his wings a magnificent blue. There were more people on the road now, all moving toward Mazatlan and the fiesta. They followed a rickety wooden bus, overflowing with potential celebrants and Wally breathed the smell he could identify from all other of the world's odors: the exhaust of a rural Mexican bus.

Soon their progress through the gathering crowd had become so slow, they decided to stop at a small café along the road. They extricated themselves and settled on plastic chairs at a plastic table that reminded Wally of the sad little restaurant of his friend and companion Gaspar Lopez. Gaspar looked about the café with an unknowable expression. This lively restaurant with its colorful beer advertisements, bullfight posters, robust menu and bustling business must have been what Gaspar envisioned for his restaurant in the desert. Gaspar sighed and removed from his shirt the ancient drawing by Leonardo da Vinci.

"Still looking for the meaning of the drawing?" Wally asked.

"It is there," Gaspar said. "Somewhere here is the answer to the riddle of my village."

Penelope was hand-feeding the prophet a plantain. Papa Blue was polishing his horn with a compound of Moonwort, hastily formulated by Billy Bucket from his seemingly endless stores.

"Maybe there is no answer," Wally said to Gaspar. "Maybe everything that happened was just a series of accidents. Sometimes I think people look for answers and meanings when there are no answers and meanings. Like a shooting star. I'd hate to think I'd have to find a meaning for that."

Gaspar looked up at Wally. His eyes contained either disappointment or anger. "This drawing caused my friends to go mad. It led to the destruction of my village. How can you say it has no meaning?"

"I'm sorry, Gaspar; I wasn't thinking."

Gaspar returned his eyes to the parchment and Wally could see his lips moving over the cryptic words. "Who is this man, Leonardo da Vinci?" he asked.

"He was a great man, an artist and inventor who lived many centuries ago in Italy."

"And this flying machine. Did he ever construct it?"

"No. He had the right idea, but they didn't have the technology. He was way ahead of his time; just not far enough ahead."

"Why would it not fly?"

"He didn't know how to power it. He had the principle. The Archimedes screw. It is what turns the rotor. But the ratio of power to weight was too low. One man cannot lift himself off the ground."

"And today?" Gaspar asked. "Do we have this knowledge today? Could the machine fly?"

"Sure. At least I think so. Instead of manpower, you put in a gasoline engine."

"Then, we shall construct the flying machine!" Gaspar announced, as if it had already been settled. "If a great man draws a plan for a thing, he means for that thing to be done. The meaning still lies ahead of us." He folded the parchment and returned it beneath his shirt."

Having heard the conversation between Wally and Gaspar, Mario turned to Wally and asked, "how far are you going to let this thing go? It won't fly. Never could. Gaspar will be devastated."

"I know," Wally said. "I feel bad. But I couldn't find a way to tell him. Besides, how do you know it won't fly? They said the *Spruce Goose* wouldn't fly."

"Because it's impossible, and it's wrong to lead Gaspar on like this."

"It's not a bad design. It just has a few flaws. Besides, designing airplanes is what I do. Or what I did.

"Before you destroyed the most advanced weapons system in the world.

"But still... maybe I can make this one fly. It would be poetic justice."

"I have to admit it would make a great documentary. An illiterate, lovable old guy in a desert village finds da Vinci's plan for a flying machine. Against all odds he builds the thing and flies it above the Mazatlan fiesta." Mario seemed to grow more and more excited. "I'd film the entire process in detail. Capture the creative process. Penelope can be Gaspar's beautiful daughter. You can be her American lover, or maybe Billy Bucket can be. Papa Blue can write the score."

"There's one problem, though," Wally said. "In the end, the thing has to fly. If it doesn't, you don't have a film."

"Maybe special effects. Smoke and mirrors."

"I thought you were a purist, Mario. A documentarian of the old school."

"Well, maybe it's still a good story, even if the thing doesn't fly. As they say, it's the journey, not the destination that counts. Gaspar's dreams are dashed, but he endures. Maybe we end the film with him starting to build a new plane, maybe from a drawing of Orville and Wilbur's *Wright Flyer*. In either case, I can film you and Penelope making love, or maybe Penelope and

Billy Bucket. At the moment either you or Billy Bucket achieve climax I can cut away to the fireworks over the old city."

Wally rolled his eyes.

Later that afternoon, they crossed Urias Bay and then, like a caricature out of Wonderland, the overloaded Morris Minor swept into the old port city. Penelope sat up high on the back seat as if she were queen of the prom, her raven hair floating in the wind like a black flame, her thin blouse, pressed by the breeze, clinging beautifully against her breasts. Papa Blue practiced Mariachi riffs on his Moonwort-polished coronet. The prophet knelt in the back seat, waving his hoe and casting malevolent oaths at a following Volkswagen. Mario ground away with his camera, capturing the scene for the ages.

Mazatlan sat like a small, aging lady upon a peninsula, her folded skirts falling into the sea. She seemed to Wally like a cubist painting gone wrong. A collection of colorful squares and boxes and angles dropped, willy-nilly, in a place too beautiful for them to be. It was not that he thought the city was unattractive, but it just seemed out of place—an old inland town suddenly finding itself by the sea. It was as if the sea and the city had never quite been properly introduced. They existed side by side, each fulfilling itself, yet somehow missing the harmony of New England or the Mediterranean Coast. There were flowers everywhere, and festively dressed people splashed brilliant color against the adobe walls. The people walked aimlessly, yet with a sense of purpose, born of tense expectation. Wally could feel the excitement in the air, for tonight the fiesta was to begin.

As they neared the city center along the coastal road, Penelope suddenly asked Wally to stop the car. "I want to go to the water," she pleaded. "I have to touch the sea."

"Mario can drive," Wally said, pulling to the side of the road and turning off the ignition. "I'll go with you."

"No, Wally. I will always be thankful that you gave me the sea. But this first time, I want to experience this thing alone. Do you mind?"

"Of course not. Just be careful. Don't swim out too far."

"And don't talk to strangers," Billy Bucket added.

Penelope smiled, kissed Wally, then slipped from the car and disappeared into the crowd toward the beach, the scabbard of her Oddfellow's sword gleaming in the sunlight.

Downtown, by the sea, the streets were alive with celebrants. Many had come in from distant villages, wearing the distinctive and traditional clothing of their region. There were the very old, the very young, the wealthy and the poor, all eager to experience the mysteries and delights of this last opportunity to find joy, and perhaps mischief, before the onset of the somber Lenten season. Here and there, Mariachi bands wove through the crowds, vying for space along the seawall, with children selling Chiclets and old men selling puppets of Pancho Villa and his *esposa*. One of the wandering street vendors had attracted an especially large crowd, including Wally and Gaspar. They were intrigued by what he called his *helicoptero*. It was a toy that bore a striking resemblance to da Vinci's flying machine. The toy was mounted atop a cylinder encircled by a string. When the vendor pulled the string, the cylinder revolved, turning a rotor, and the little helicopter leaped high into the air and hovered overhead, to the delight of the crowd. It occurred to Wally that the toy was much like a child's spinning top; but when the string was pulled, it did more than spin—the rotor lifted it into the air. Here was the Archimedes screw envisioned by da Vinci.

"Is this not the answer?" Gaspar asked. "If the small helicopter will fly, all we need to do is build one big enough to carry me into the clouds. I know it can be done. Together we can do this thing. You know all about airplanes, we have the plans drawn by the famous Italian, and I have a friend in Mazatlan who is the best carpenter in all of Mexico. We will go to his shop, and he will help us construct the flying machine."

It was difficult, even impossible, not to see Penelope returning from her pilgrimage to the sea. She was radiant, seemed at the heart of a new dimension of light, a luminescence that seemed to flow from somewhere within. Everyone around her seemed to fall away to grey. Even at a distance, Wally could see that her electric blue eyes glistened with tears. When she drew near, she threw herself into Wally's arms. "It was beautiful," she breathed. "It is the greatest thing I have ever seen: so old, so deep, so alive. As I watched it, I could feel its moods changing, sometimes sad, and sometimes filled with joy. The sea changes its color and shape according to the movement of the winds and the clouds."

"Did you go in the water?"

"At first I was afraid. I never liked swimming in the Rio Grande, especially in those few places where my feet couldn't touch the bottom. But as I walked into the shallows, and then deeper, I became calm. I swam way out and floated on the body of the ocean. When I came back to the beach, I saw that a group of fishermen had been watching me. I think it gave them pleasure to watch because of the way my wet clothes were clinging."

"So, you came back?"

"Not right away." There was on her lovely face the expression of one who has misbehaved, yet would be hurt if the misbehavior went unnoticed. She kissed him again and then stood by his side, fingering the buttons of his jacket, her eyes downcast.

"Don't tell me you stayed with them."

"They are so poor, Wally, and so sad, and they work so hard with the nets and the price of fish is so low. I let them take off my wet clothes so they could dry in the sun. And then I made some love with them."

"How many?" Wally asked, not really wanting to know.

"All of them. Oh, Wally, don't be mad at me. The sea was so beautiful, and the fishermen were so sad. And it was the sea that brought the fishermen and me together. The sea you gave me."

Wally looked into her eyes and then up to where heaven must be. "I'm not mad. Just insane to keep loving you."

"But you do still love me, right?"

"Me and half the men in the Western Hemisphere."

"There were really not that many fishermen," she said.

Wally rolled his eyes and turned away.

"Cleopatra once made love to two hundred men in a single night," she said defensively, "and Antony didn't ignore her."

Wally turned back and looked at her. She was so beautiful that it swept his heart, his logic and his good sense completely away. 'When you fall in love with an angel, a mythological creature,' he thought, 'I suppose you have to take the good with the bad. Besides, there weren't that many fishermen. Better fishermen than Roman Senators and Centurions.'

Gaspar guided them up a winding cobbled street until they were high above the sea. From here Wally and Penelope could see the vast, blue Pacific catch the first colors of what would be a beautiful sunset. Several lifeless islands rose offshore like drowned camels.

"There!" Gaspar pointed. "It is the *carpenteria* of my friend." A sound of hammering was heard, and they walked across the street into a shop where a man whom Gaspar introduced as José Buenaventura was driving nails into a coffin. It was cool inside and the scent of pine seemed fresh and clean.

"Gaspar, my friend!" José exclaimed. "So you are back again for the fiesta. It is good."

"For the fiesta and something else. A favor to ask."

José laid his hammer down and wiped his hands on his loose trousers. "How can I be of service to you, old friend? You do not look as if you need a casket." He was small and lithe with dancing eyes, and a jet-black mustache dominated his face. Wally saw in his manner a certain freewheeling sense of adventure, like the hero's best friend in Mexican movies. Gaspar introduced them all, except the prophet, who was raking sawdust on the floor into little piles and then scattering them with his hoe. The shop was filled with a great number of coffins. Some were quite ornate and all displayed obvious good workmanship. Wally's eyes were caught by a soft, slow movement in one of the coffins and there, in the satin-lined bottom, was a great yellow cat yawning, its mouth open like a small, dark cave. Wally shivered involuntarily and the cat closed its mouth and went back to sleep, where someone would eternally. Wally hoped that Gaspar would not see the cat, because he would probably attach great significance to it and puzzle over the meaning for days.

Gaspar spread Leonardo da Vinci's parchment out on a workbench. "We would like you to help us build a helicopter." Gaspar looked up at his friend and smiled, as if building a helicopter was the easiest thing in the world to ask.

"A helicopter?" José extended his fingers and drew little circles in the air above his head. "I have never constructed a helicopter." José appeared to become very thoughtful, perhaps considering the challenge. "These days, I work for the dead. The living cannot afford my skills. The dead are eligible for government money, so for them I work night and day. But a helicopter?" He caressed his mustache and looked down at the parchment. "Tell me more about this drawing."

"This is the plan to guide the construction," Gaspar said. "It was designed by a prominent Italian, using the principle of the Archimedes screw." José studied Gaspar's eyes, perhaps seeking sanity there, and then he returned his attention to the drawing. "This is how it will be," Gaspar continued. "Only it will be very large. Big enough that I might fly it over the city and the sea and the offshore islands."

As they talked about the drawings, Wally was shocked to find he was following the conversation with growing fascination. The hundreds of books about flight he had consumed as a youth all began with the tragedy of Icarus and then the dream of Leonardo da Vinci. And now, after so many centuries, that dream could at last be realized. He felt again that particular tight thrill he once felt when he painstakingly assembled the planes of his old heroes: the Wright Brothers, Bleriot, Lindberg and Wally Post, and all the other giants who first challenged gravity. Even later heroes, like Howard Hughes and his wonderful *Spruce Goose*, an airplane that fired his imagination as much as any other. He had lived their adventures by building exact models of the planes they flew, from the *Wright Flyer* to the *Spruce Goose*. And then General Dynamics came along. It seemed, at first, unbelievable serendipity that he was able to make a living building model aircraft, the small, exact models used in wind tunnel tests. He was spending his days doing what he loved best. But he soon found that the soaring romance of the fragile old aircraft did not exist in the jet age. The last of the flying things had been built. Now they just strap young engineers onto computers and rocket them skyward. They are more like projectiles than anything else. More like rocks thrown than things free to soar aloft. And at General Dynamics, he finally realized, to his horror, that he was assisting in the design of death machines. It was a bittersweet memory. The terrible guilt he had felt was the bitter. The sweet was the Holloway's Milk Duds he had placed in the air intakes of the supersonic *F11* fighter-bombers, which brought them down just as surely as would well-aimed heat-seeking missiles.

"Yes," Wally heard José say. "There is no doubt I can build this thing, but I could not promise it would fly."

"If it does not fly," Gaspar said, "it is not a helicopter. Just as a bird that does not fly is not a bird." His patience with his old friend seemed to be wearing thin. "I have told you about the Archimedes screw. This will make it fly!"

"Don't worry, Gaspar," Wally heard himself say. "I'll help. I'm pretty sure we can make it fly. "

"We'll call it *Leonardo's Dream*," Mario said, taking a reading with his light meter and then framing a few establishing shots of the *carpenteria* and then close-ups of Gaspar and Jose, the major stars of his next documentary.

"Of course, there is the matter of financing the project," Mario said. "Both the construction of the plane and the production of the documentary." Billy Bucket and Papa Blue said they had some money tucked away that might help. Wally wondered if he would be able to access his account, with the FBI and CIA hot on his trail. It would be a dead giveaway of his location. Penelope said she could easily raise some funds from rich American tourists. It had been some time since she had done tricks for money, but she thought she might remember the basics of how it was done.

"What we ought to do," Wally said, not wanting to hear details of Penelope's fund-raising strategy, "is to start a real company. Get regular financing. Sell stock. We could call it the Italian-Mexican Helicopter Cooperative."

"Who would be dumb enough to buy stock in a five-hundred-year-old helicopter?" Papa Blue wanted to know.

"The town is full of rich tourists," Billy Bucket said. "You never know. A little tequila and a low-grade Moonwort olfactory overload and you never know just how dumb rich tourists might get. And there's always Penelope. She could do some reconnaissance, check out who is spending big. Or who might spend big."

"But no tricks, Penelope!" Wally was adamant.

"Of course not! What do you think I am?"

Wally said nothing.

"I'll just do this. I'll search for rich Americans. It is not difficult to tell who they are. I'll proposition them, maybe let them have a little feel to get them excited, then I'll tell them I cost a thousand US dollars for the night. I don't mean to boast, but it is likely they will agree. Then I'll let them have another little feel and ask for a down payment of $100 US dollars. By this time, their desire for me will overcome their good sense. They give me the money, I let them have another little feel to let them know there are no hard feelings, and then I disappear into the crowd."

For the next hour, excitement danced high among the coffins in the Italian-Mexican Helicopter Cooperative as they discussed the building of the helicopter, the making of the documentary and their plans for financing the projects.

"But what about The Lynx?" Penelope asked, a question that seemed to come out of the blue. In all the excitement, Wally had completely forgotten that he and his companions were fugitives. "What if he's here?"

"We'll need some kind of disguise." They asked José to help them work out disguises and he leaped at the task, as if he had been appointed the company's security officer.

"I have the most ideal thing!" he cried, his eyes flashing. He rushed to a trunk in the back of the shop and returned with an armload of red, white and green uniforms, a battered bass guitar, a dented tuba and a snare drum with a broken head. "All this belonged to a Mariachi band that fell off the mountain. The bus fell and they were all killed. They had no money so I built them caskets in return for these things. It is sad, but they weren't a very good band anyway. They would have been shamed at the fiesta. It is better they fell off the mountain. Dressed like this, you will be just another of the hundreds of Mariachi bands entertaining the fiesta crowds."

"I love it!" Mario said, and he blew a goofy basso bleat on the tuba.

Chattering like children, they tried on the sad, old band uniforms. They were tattered and faded and mismatched and it seemed they were veterans of a thousand fiestas. They traded trousers and jackets and hats and boots until they each had the best possible fit. Wally was not surprised that Penelope was stunning in her costume. The white pants and jacket with gold trim, although showing signs that the bus had caught fire when it reached the bottom of the mountain, suggested that the band's departed female member had been very shapely. Penelope was delighted with her wide white sombrero and high-heeled boots. Mario looked like an Italian gaucho, caught too long in the rain and left too long in the sun to dry. The reds and greens were so faded they almost ceased to be colors at all. Only the silver buttons and the blood on the jacket reflected the light of the sun. It was fortunate that one of the dead musicians had been exceptionally rotund, and his uniform fit Papa Blue perfectly. Billy Bucket looked fabulous in his tight pants, red sash and enormous sombrero. As expected, the prophet objected strenuously to the disguise. When they approached him with the uniform, he skittered away through the sawdust, whining Sumerian curses. They finally trapped him behind a casket, and as gently as possible, pulled the uniform over his many layers of putrid, rotting burlap. Yet, no amount of persuasion could force him to wear boots. Wally draped the snare drum over the prophet's shoulder, stepped back, and decided the old man made one of the most remarkable caballeros the world had ever seen. He had the feeling that the uniform would immediately begin to rot from the inside out and turn brown like litmus paper. But there was no transformation—just a wisp of black vapor, rising as the prophet glowered and drooled dark spittle onto the head of his snare drum.

In all the excitement of establishing the helicopter corporation and trying on their disguises, Gaspar had disappeared. Wally looked for him among the coffins, but he was nowhere to be seen. Finally, Wally found the old man outside the *carpenteria,* sitting with his back against the wall, looking out over the city. It was strange that Gaspar seemed so melancholy when everyone else was bouncing off the walls with excitement. Wally sat down beside him.

"What's wrong, Gaspar? You seem sad."

"I believe you are making a mockery of what I'm trying to do. Wearing the clothes of the dead, pretending to be a Mariachi band when only Papa Blue can make music—it is disrespectful. Building and flying the helicopter is not a game for me. It is not something I do lightly. I thought, of all people, you would understand."

Wally felt terrible. "I'm sorry, Gaspar. We just got caught up in the spirit of the fiesta. All the happiness."

"Happiness is not the spirit of the fiesta. It is all very sad. Look around you and see if you don't see the sadness."

Wally looked down at the city again, but he saw only celebration. A magnificent rocket exploded high over the harbor.

"It is the earth," Gaspar said. "Look at all the things near the earth. Look at the peasants sitting on the seawall, the hovels at the foot of the hills, the people in the streets. There is little joy down close to the earth." He pointed toward the hotels and the nearby hills on which were the houses of the rich. "When you look high above the earth you see happiness."

"But the people in the streets are dancing, laughing, are celebrating the fiesta."

"No," Gaspar said. "Look deeper. That is a cry of pain you see, the pain of a prisoner eating a yearly piece of cake when he knows he will have only tortillas for the rest of the year. If he didn't have the cake he would forget how bad it was to have only tortillas. He paused and swept his eyes over the city. "I know only this," he said. "The earth brings sorrow. It is plain. One's mission in life should be to break free of the earth, from the hoe, from the shacks by the sea. Look at the church steeples, look at the clouds and the stars." A beautiful rocket, as if in punctuation, threw itself all over the sky. "Do you think this is the meaning of the promise of the holy man? That the machine of the prominent Italian is a way to break free from the earth?"

"Gaspar, my friend," Wally said, "I really don't know what to think." But he was disturbed by Gaspar's belief that he could somehow conquer sorrow. He thought how beautiful it would be to build the flying machine, purely because it would be good to do such a thing—a simple thing, a pure thing. No complicated motives or clouded meanings or crap like that. He knew now that he was frightened for Gaspar Lopez, the peasant who would rise above the earth on the wings of a myth.

When Wally returned inside, Billy Bucket was drawing up corporate papers, Mario was making a sign for the front door of their corporation, and the others were drawing up a list of materials they would need for construction of the helicopter. They worked until the sun was low upon the offshore islands. Wally was supremely happy. The only thing that seemed to cloud his mood was the nagging guilt he felt about enabling Gaspar's delusion, not putting a stop to this helicopter charade before it got out of hand. Yet he still felt the exhilaration of knowing that *Leonardo's Dream* just might fly. At last, the sign was finished, and Mario filmed Billy Bucket hanging it above the door. They all shook hands and high-fived and took turns kissing Penelope, and they sealed their partnership with a bottle of tequila that José had supplied. And then they marched militarily down the cobbled street toward the sea, where the opening festivities were in full swing.

Beyond the city, the sun slipped behind the sea, like a drop of falling dye, setting the west on fire. Overhead, rockets splashed glory and people moved and surged like lava in the streets. Everywhere was a frenzy of sound: the wailing brass of bands, the whoosh and boom and crack of exploding fireworks, the thousands of voices raised like a single strange and mindless song. In the confusion, Wally became separated from his friends and he pushed his way to the *Avenida del Mar* and across, and climbed up on the seawall from which there was a sweeping view of the sea, the waterfront street and the squat old Mazatlan hotels. High behind the hotels were the dry hills, one of them holding the highest lighthouse in the hemisphere. Its beacon had left the ships at sea to fend for themselves and the powerful light now played among the celebrants along the seawall. In the bay, two small ships fired rockets at each other in mock battle; occasionally a rocket would go astray and explode above the crowd. Wally was fascinated with the delirious scene. At his feet a line of wild-eyed dancers coiled along behind a group of drunken musicians. The city throbbed. Tequila bottles arced through the air and shattered on the seawall. The broken glass in the street winked like diamonds, or as Gaspar might say, like frozen tears.

After fighting the crowds for a while, Wally spotted the other members of his Mariachi band farther down the seawall. They seemed to be serenading an American couple, a middle-aged man and his bejeweled wife. Penelope was sitting between the man and his wife; the prophet was crouched under the table. When he reached them, Penelope winked and Mario made the introductions.

The gentleman was a retired florist from Peoria, Illinois. The man's name was Peter Cromwell; his wife's, Gladys. They were on the first leg of an odyssey that would take them around the world, "to see how the rest of the garden grows," as he put it. Mr. Cromwell was a pleasant, red-faced man who seemed delighted with the idea he would soon be swept into someone's confidence. It occurred to Wally that most people go through life without ever knowing any secrets. And to share secrets must be one of the basic needs of man. Gladys Cromwell was perhaps forty and quite attractive, in an intense sort of way. She revealed that she taught an anthropology class in the Peoria public library. Wally noticed she was concerned about the prophet's presence under the table.

"And so, Mr. Cromwell," Mario announced. "Now our entire musical aggregation is here."

Mr. Cromwell winked at Wally. "He told us about you people not really being a Mariachi band."

"Did he tell you why we're in disguise?"

"I told them everything, Wally. I hope you don't mind. But there are so few people you can trust in this town."

Cromwell beamed, his wife slapped at something beneath the table and Wally, knowing he would never be able to keep a straight face, signaled Mario to take charge of the meeting.

"Well, the thing is," Mario said, "our corporation has made the long-sought personal helicopter breakthrough. The government, the Air Force, even NASA, have failed in this quest. Trouble is, they've all been looking in the wrong places. They were looking to advanced technology to solve the problem. But our secret was to look backward. We found the answer in the drawings of Leonardo da Vinci."

"Fascinating," Cromwell breathed, and then he leaned conspiratorially across the table. "You know, I'm not exactly new to the aviation business myself. I just recently made a tidy sum on General Dynamics stock. You know, that recent thing when all those *F111* fighter-bombers were destroyed? Well, the morning after, when I heard about a possible merger between General Dynamics and Holloway's Milk Duds, I bought stock in both companies. I just had a hunch. Well, Milk Duds stock soared, but the funny thing is, what happened at General Dynamics. It turned out that there was no merger at all. What really happened was that the planes had been sabotaged by putting Milk Duds in the engines. And the Air Force didn't want to admit that such a silly thing would bring down their mighty bombers. So they planted the rumor to explain away the presence of the Holloway's people. I bought both stocks. Made quite a killing, I'll tell you."

"Well, I'm convinced you're on to another hot one," Mario said. "With Doctor Prophet at the helm, I'm convinced we have a glorious future ahead of us."

"Doctor Prophet?" Gladys asked.

"The executive under the table."

Everyone pushed away from the table where the prophet had cast aside his snare drum and was now drinking tequila from Penelope's boot.

Cromwell brought a handkerchief to his nose. Oddly enough, Gladys Cromwell seemed more curious than appalled at the bundle of bone and rag at her feet. "He's not from around here, is he?" Peter Cromwell asked.

"He came from a small village on the Ganges," Mario answered. "He came from a cult of highly gifted and intuitive holy men. As a young man, he broke from his heathen philosophy and devoted himself to science."

Gladys Cromwell suddenly lunged forward. "Was he a Shivite holy man?" she asked with obvious excitement. "He must have been!"

"Not necessarily," Penelope said. "The Ganges is a very long river. He could be a Veraugee." Wally was stunned that Penelope had such a grasp of geography and holy men.

Gladys Cromwell looked at Penelope with total disbelief. "How do you know about the Veraugee? Only the most learned sexologist would know that cult. They are known for their penises that hung all the way to the ground."

"The male sex organ is Gladys's field," Cromwell said proudly.

"Mine, too," Penelope said. "I'm not sure Doctor Prophet is a Veraugee. I'm almost certain that he's a Lingayut."

"Ah, the fabled Lingayut," Gladys responded, he eyes aglow. "Famed for their magnificent phallic amulets. They worshipped the Heavenly Root, and their penises were reputed to be too large for even the gods to reckon."

"But they couldn't get erections," Penelope added.

"How true, how utterly true. They tied heavy stones to their members and destroyed their erectile powers." Gladys clucked her tongue sadly in benediction to the Lingayuts.

"My wife's field is a rather lonely one," Cromwell said. "Most folks don't want to hear about such things. We used to have parties, but—"

"My favorite research," Gladys interrupted, her jewels sparkling in the light of the fireworks, "is into the practice of the Hoolee. The Hindu Hoolee men would strap three-foot long striped wooden phalli to their crotch, and they would go running around the village brandishing and clutching them and poking them at people while screaming obscene ballads."

"Wonderful!" Penelope cried, laughing and clapping her hands. Wally noticed a growing rapport between the Peoria sexologist and his Angel of the Arroyos. They were as delighted as schoolgirls in their discovery of each other and their common intellectual bond. Mr. Cromwell listened and smiled and nodded his head happily. Then their attention returned to the prophet.

"If he's a Lingayut," Gladys confided, "he's probably wearing a phallic amulet. Have you ever noticed?"

"He never takes his pants off," Penelope answered. Even when he goes to the bathroom he goes right into and through his clothes.

"I'll bet my reputation he's a Lingayut," Gladys insisted and she whipped a notebook from her purse, rose and moved around the prophet like a circling lady wrestler. She made notes on her pad, wetting the tip of her pencil with her blackening tongue. Then she was thoughtful for a moment, a thoughtfulness that seemed to grow in intensity until, in a crackling, unnatural voice, she blurted, "I must see his member!" She made a lunge at the horrible old man, and he skittered away howling what Penelope was sure, were Lingayut blasphemies.

Wally was shocked. "Mrs. Cromwell!" he shouted. "You are not dealing with an ordinary holy man! He's a corporation president. You wouldn't try to pull down Frank Davis or Jimmy Ling's pants."

"But he may be the last living Lingayut!" she cried, suddenly in tears. "His amulet would be priceless! Do you know how long the museums of the world have been waiting for an authentic Lingayut phallic amulet? God, don't hold me back now!" She made another lunge at the prophet.

"Gladys!" Cromwell admonished. "Sit the hell down!" Wally was surprised at the authority in the gentle florist's voice and at the rapidity with which Gladys Cromwell leaped back to her place at the table. She sat quietly, breathing hard, casting little sideways glances at the prophet. Then she attacked a fifth of tequila, and in a few moments, had drunk herself to insensibility.

The first night of the Mazatlan fiesta was reaching its climax. The elegant American ladies were in the street now, dancing with dusky young fishermen and imagined matadors. Young sailors from some fortunate freighter groped after young girls with such frenzied good humor and artlessness that it delighted all who watched. Confetti stormed down from high windows and the Mariachi music engulfed the city like the caress of crass and perfumed arms.

Wally, his Mariachi band and the Cromwells struggled through the heaving streets back toward the Italian-Mexican Cooperative's helicopter factory. Occasionally, over the sound of the celebrants, Wally could hear Penelope's tequila-soaked boots squeaking. Peter Cromwell carried his wife over his shoulder like a sack of cantaloupe. Sometimes she would open her mascara-splashed eyes and clutch with stiff fingers at the trousers of the prophet's band uniform. Riding the crest of the tequila, Wally asked Papa Blue if he could play "Folsom Prison Blues" on his trumpet.

"I can play anything," Papa Blues said, and he did so, in strange contraposition to the general festive atmosphere. The prophet joined in with his drums, and Wally, who had salvaged his guitar from the trunk of the Morris Minor, played along. It was one of the first songs he had learned to play without watching his hands. They all, even the semi-comatose Mrs. Cromwell, joined in the singing.

Soon, a serpentine following of drugged Mexicans and American tourists fell in behind them, to be led, they cared not where, by the otherworldly music and Penelope's otherworldly beauty. The undulating throng followed them up the hill, past the shops and bars, through alleys, over a schoolyard wall, and on toward the *carpenteria* of José Buenaventura. When Wally and the band would speed up, the crowd would speed up as well. When they would dodge around a corner, the crowd would dash after them in hot pursuit.

"How the hell are we going to get rid of them?" Mario yelled. Finally they tucked their instruments away and galloped full speed through the winding streets. The prophet was remarkably fast for a suspected Lingayut, probably weighed down by a heavy phallic amulet. Gladys Cromwell, on her feet again, ran with all the grace of certain animals, like birds whose feet are on backwards.

José saw them coming, pulled them hurriedly through the door and closed it before the crowd descended. The celebrants swept on by like an avalanche of idiots and then they were gone. When Wally caught his breath and turned around, he stood astounded by what José had done in their absence.

There in the center of the shop stood the frail skeletal beginnings of the flying machine. At first Wally thought it seemed like the dead remains of some prehistoric flying insect. But as he walked around it, he found in its design the aesthetic grace that da Vinci had breathed there. He remembered da Vinci's observation in his Codex Atlanticus that, "A bird is an instrument working according to mathematical law, which is within the capacity of man to reproduce in all its movements." Wally could almost feel da Vinci's presence in the room. He could hear his flamboyant, derisive voice say, "Yes, I'll admit the Sistine Chapel has a certain originality of style, Michaelangelo. But will it fly?"

"I used the fresh white pine of the mountain slopes," José said proudly. "It was for the coffins. But it is better to soar with the birds than to be buried with the dead."

"It's beautiful," Penelope said, her boots singing wet trebles as she walked around the framework. "But what about wings? Shouldn't the framework be covered with cloth or wood or something?"

Jose's eyes flashed. "I have the perfect thing!" he said. He brought from the workbench a stack of colorful posters announcing that Manuel Benitez, El Cordobes, would be in Mazatlan during the fiesta to fight the brave bulls.

Gaspar embraced his friend the carpenter. "Such posters will make a fine covering for the framework of our helicopter.

They will be displayed where the entire city will see them. The name of the greatest matador in the world will be written in the sky." With a small hammer he began to help José cover *Leonardo's Dream* with the brave and smiling face of El Cordobes, talking all the while about the glories of flight and the necessity to free one's self from the earth.

Wally checked the dimensions of the helicopter against da Vinci's drawing and found them to be perfectly accurate.

"You know," Cromwell said pensively, "maybe there's more here than meets the eye." He climbed up onto the pilot's seat and moved his hands in pantomime as if he were piloting the craft in flight. "I was just thinking," he continued. "Suppose we were to mount a machine gun up here. A light little plane like this could sneak around trees and tight places where big planes can't go—like in Vietnam or Laos."

Wally felt a growing disgust with both Cromwells. "Why don't we stick to the original plan, Mr. Cromwell," he said with as little emotion as possible.

"I'm just trying to be logical," Cromwell said. "Where we might sell ten to the civilian market, we could sell a thousand to the military. All we have to do is mount a little machine gun up here."

"Oh, I don't think so," Wally said. He noticed Gaspar was following the conversation with downcast eyes.

"I can't finance this thing too far," Cromwell said. "From the Government you can get all you want. They'll pay more than double what anybody else would pay."

Wally shook his head.

"Well, I'll tell you this," Cromwell said with the same surprising authority with which he had reprimanded Gladys. "If you don't at least consider it, I'm gonna withdraw my financing. It's just plain stupid to overlook a perfectly good market." He wrestled his bulk down from the pine framework and then spoke directly into Wally's face. "How bad do you want to build this thing anyway?"

"It's very important to Gaspar," he answered. And I think it's important, too." But he knew Cromwell wouldn't understand that this would be the culmination of da Vinci's dream. They would finally build and fly the first aircraft designed by man. And so he said nothing more.

"Well, then," Cromwell said. "You better damn well consider the military market! I mean it!" And he walked over to where Gladys was trying to corner the prophet behind a coffin, grabbed her by the arm and then dragged her out into the charged darkness.

Wally left further instructions for the construction of the flying machine and then walked down into the streets of Mazatlan. The voice of the fiesta was lower now, almost angry. The fireworks exploded less frequently yet the continued crystal crashing of tequila bottles upon the pavement proved the streets were becoming dangerous. It was a time of great physical friendships and quick, careless hatred. He had been amazed earlier that he had seen no fights among the crowds. If a crowd of similar size in a United States city had consumed a similar quantity of alcohol, half of them would now be dead. But still, he felt the threat of danger in the shadows and from the knots of men and boys roaming through the ankle-deep confetti, breaking bottles against adobe walls.

The Glass Guitar

As he walked toward the sea along the Avenida Del Mar, it seemed that he moved through a vast pasture of broken glass, overturned chairs, bits of colored paper, shattered shells of rockets and other carnage. It was like a battlefield, like pictures he had seen showing Civil War scenes, the dawn after battle, pastures filled with dead and dying horses and men. Maybe, he decided, the fiesta *is* a sad thing and the streets *are* paved in frozen tears.

A great moon lumbering through a tattered sky lighted his way toward the beach. He took off his shoes, and the feel of the loose warm sand gave him the immediate sense of returning to something beloved. The cool salt wind blew in from China, dragging the seas behind. The off-shore islands served as a breakwater and there was very little surf. He remembered reading that there was a place not too far to the south, where, at certain times of the year, the surf was twenty meters high. He wondered if surfers were ever challenged to ride this mightiest of all waves. In the moonlight he could see the turds of children and broken shells and bits of things washed ashore. He found a smooth stone, picked it up, saw that it was beautifully marked and was nearly translucent. It felt good and warm in his hand and he decided to worship it, place it in a leather pouch and wear it next to his body for evermore. Better to worship a stone than yeast. Perhaps it's all that remains of a planet. 'If I carry the stone with me', he thought, 'even when I make love or am very happy or sad, it will share my life, and something of me will enter the stone. When I die the stone will become my eternity. I will be dust, but somewhere on earth my stone will be.' It was a good thought, and he pressed the stone to his cheek so it might gather oils and begin the absorption of his soul.

Now he passed where Penelope had been with the fishermen and, as always, he tried not to envision her making love to other men, especially many other men, like the fishermen and the impoverished *campesinos* in the *arroyos*. But what right had he to censure her for making serial love when he was guilty of so many more inexcusable things? Still, what was he going to do about Penelope? He loved her, but he couldn't have her. She was an angel, a pure spirit, a creature like no other God made. But there was enough woman in this angel to drive him to distraction. He remembered the night Mario filmed them pretending to make love. He could still taste the intoxicating nectar of her lips, the firm softness of her breasts. They had not been so intimate since, but there had been love between them then, and there was still love now. But where was it going? he wondered. He had long realized that she really was an angel, a supreme soul made of love and light, and he was an inferior being fashioned from clay.

He began to feel the fatigue of too much tequila and far too much introspection and was weary of his continuing effort to safeguard his sanity. He decided to find a place along the sea to go to sleep and not think or dream. Then, down the beach, a lantern punctured the darkness. In its light, he could see the vague shapes of several men. As he drew closer, he could see that they wore the outfits of a Mariachi band. They probably had come across the mountains on a battered bus. He thought maybe he didn't want to be alone, after all. He decided to join them and share with them the lantern light and the music of the sea.

One of the musicians rose to greet him. "So we meet again, Mr. Pillow," The Lynx said, a sardonic smile beneath the brim of his sombrero.

Wally felt a deep disappointment, but no fear. Who could be afraid of a mere silly man in the presence of the sea? He rubbed his mystic stone between his fingers.

"The Mariachi band uniforms make a good cover, don't you think, Mr. Pillow?"

"All the spies are wearing them this year."

"But few spies make good music," The Lynx said. "Your group plays the worst I've ever heard. And I'll have to acknowledge, I've never heard a Mariachi band play 'Folsom Prison Blues.'" He paused and asked Wally to join the other Mariachi operatives around the lantern, as if it were a fire. Wally noticed they were all warming their hands over the illusion.

"How did you get away from the villagers, back in the desert?" Wally asked, actually quite curious. "Last I saw, you were in full retreat."

"I don't know what you did to stir them up so. They were quite insane. We had to kill a few."

"And how did you fare against Swamp Sweeney?"

"Tragically, the road to nowhere is no longer going nowhere; thanks to you, the road is closed. We suffered casualties, but here we are."

"Well, I'm glad to see you safe," Wally said.

"Why are you glad?"

Wally shrugged, not knowing.

"You have followed this pattern from the first, Mr. Pillow. It is as if you want to be caught and punished, but I doubt that is so. First, you left chocolate fingerprints on the bombers in Fort

Worth. And in Crystal City and in Mexico you invited capture. Nobody plays "Folsom River Blues" at a pre-Lenten fiesta. But you did! I ask myself, what is your game, Mr. Pillow? Where are you leading me?" The Lynx began to pace the sand.

"I don't know," Wally said, and he didn't.

"I do have some ideas about all this," said The Lynx. "Would you like to hear them?" He forged on, not waiting for an answer. Wally decided that The Lynx would look something like Sherlock Holmes if he had a pipe and wasn't wearing a sombrero. Such was the intensity of the counterspy's concentration.

"I've discovered that you have established the Italian-Mexican Helicopter Cooperative. I have learned the man you call The Prophet, alias Ching Tao, has been set up as president of the international corporation. With your connections in Russia and Mr. Tao's Red Chinese affiliations, I must ask myself: What do they want here in Mazatlan? And then, when I discovered your plan to manufacture a lightweight, vertical takeoff attack plane, I had part of the answer. Where are America's enemies? In Vietnam, in Cambodia, Russia and China. But who looks to the south? Nobody, sir. That's who. So you knock out the *F111*s and open up a southern front. Attack the vulnerable underbelly of America." The Lynx moved directly in front of Wally and pointed a thin finger at his nose. "What do you think of that reasoning, Mr. fancy-ass spy?"

"I'm sleepy and a little drunk," Wally said, and he really was. He yawned. "Would you shoot me if I went over by the seawall and went to sleep?"

The Lynx spun around and faced the sea. For a moment he seemed to pout and then he gathered himself. "You will learn not to trifle with me, Mr. Pillow. Reputation isn't everything.

Often, the hare is mightier than the elephant." He turned back to face Wally. "Tell me where the real aircraft factory is located."

"You've probably seen it.—in the *carpenteria*."

"Do you think me a fool? That bunch of sticks and that absurd little shop is a front? Where is the actual factory?"

"Look," Wally said. He was very tired. "I promise, scout's honor. There is no factory. All I want to do now is go to sleep. I respect you and think you are a fine fellow, but please leave me alone."

The Lynx looked into Wally's eyes. "You are a truly cool one, Mr. Pillow. I hope to learn a lot from you." A smile, almost warm, touched his lips and then was gone. "But in the end, I will probably have to kill you." He turned, motioned for his operatives to follow, and then disappeared into the night.

In the *carpenteria*, there was a storm of activity. José clamored over the near-completed flying machine, his hammer tapping and pounding here and there on pine, salvaged from the coffins. Gaspar paced back and forth, issuing orders in Spanish to a crew of additional workers he had recruited from the streets. When not filming the progress, Mario was leading a tour of tourists. "And here," he called, "is the city's leading industry, the Italian-Mexican Helicopter Cooperative." He gestured to the helicopter. "And this is *Leonardo's Dream*, the only aircraft designed by that creative genius, Leonardo da Vinci."

"Will it fly?" a voice asked.

"Of course it will fly! It will fly this very evening, above the fiesta. Five-hundred years in the making, but tonight it will soar like an eagle. And this is the pilot." He pointed to Gaspar, who smiled at the tourists and seemed quite proud.

"It looks like a crummy bunch of junk," a little boy said before being silenced by his parents.

Wally, who had not been able to sleep by the sea, had returned to the *carpenteria*. He pulled Gaspar aside. "What's this about tonight? We haven't even got a motor!"

Gaspar's eyes were blazing. "Come. I will show you our motor." They walked through the shop to the back door where a large truck was parked. It belonged to the local Coca-Cola bottler. On its top was a huge Coca-Cola bottle. Wally remembered seeing the truck the night before, leading the fiesta parade, the huge bottle spinning atop the old truck. "This is our motor," Gaspar said. To Wally's surprise, when he examined the drive mechanism, it seemed possible that it might transfer enough power to turn *Leonardo's Dream's* rotor.

"I'll be damned," Wally said. "I really think this would do it. But we have no rotor."

"Ah, my friend, but we have." Gaspar showed Wally the huge fan that had turned for the greater part of a century, high in the ceiling of the great old Belmar Hotel. "This will be our rotor. The entire city is excited about the flight. When they found out who designed the helicopter, and that it was powered by a principle discovered by a prominent Greek, and that it carried the endorsement of Manuel Benitez El Cordobes, all the city decided to help. The Coca-Cola people and the managers of the Belmar Hotel loaned us the motor and the rotor without cost. The flight will be an important moment in the history of the city and in the lives of all who are enslaved by the earth."

Soon the morning sun began to wake the city. The shops were opening and the tourists were beginning to drink in the bars and in the cool, hollow hotels by the sea. Wally, Gaspar and José worked to install the gasoline engine and to mate the Belmar Hotel fan to the drive mechanism. But Wally found no joy in the work, only a growing feeling that he was doing something terribly wrong. When he could no longer remain quiet about his concerns, he called Gaspar aside. "I know you won't understand this, but I don't want you to do this thing."

"But you know I must."

"I'm not trying to talk you out of anything. Hell, I want to see it fly, too. I just wish you'd re-examine your motives."

"You are right. I don't understand."

"I don't either, really," Wally said. "I just know, or at least I feel, that self-deception is the most terrible of all sins. Even being a hypocrite is not as bad as being self-deceived. To be false to others is bad enough. But to be false to yourself is the ultimate calamity."

"You don't believe there is meaning in the treasure of the holy man?"

"Yes, I think I do believe, but maybe not in such a literal sense. The flying machine could be a symbol for the spirituality of man, that part of man that is capable of rising above his environment."

Gaspar thought about this. The sound of Jose's hammer could be heard and the scent of burning corn was broadcast on the wind. A child complained about the world and then was comforted. Below, the city began to accept the first shy celebrants who tested the state of the fiesta, gingerly, cautiously, as a swimmer would test the temperature of the water with his toe.

The people spilled out into the streets, blinking into the sun, and they began to gather on the seawall around full, clear bottles of tequila.

"Tell me one thing, Wally," Gaspar finally said. "A symbol is a thing you use when you don't have the real thing. For instance, the ship out there in the bay has a flag because it is not possible to carry a country. Or, if you do not have a fish, you can draw a picture of a fish. This is a symbol, is it not?"

"Yes."

"Then a symbol is a second-best thing, less desirable than the thing it represents."

"Yes. I suppose so."

"Then it is clear, I should not accept a symbol when I can choose the real and true thing."

"Hell, I guess so, Gaspar."

"Then I have been chosen to do this thing! There is a necessity for me to rise into the air on the flying machine. Not as a symbol, but as a real and true thing."

"A miracle?" Wally asked, and he grew heartsick even as he said the words.

"Si. *Milagro*," Gaspar said and lowered his eyes.

It seemed everyone in Mazatlan had heard about the coming flight. Children pressed themselves against the window of the *carpenteria*, peering in with wide animal eyes at the strange mechanical bird. Groups of men, recently sobered, stood in groups watching and scratching their crotches, making small wagers that *Leonardo's Dream* would not fly. When Wally had first glanced at the sketches, he knew the design was basically sound. The aerodynamics were perfect. Now as he made a quick power-to-weight ratio analysis, he became convinced the craft had enough power to lift and support a load, more than four times that envisioned by da Vinci. So, in addition to the tiny pilot's platform, he had José construct a larger platform to accommodate either passengers or freight.

As Wally was making final adjustments on the controls and fuel system, the Cromwells pushed into the shop, followed by what could only be a group of touring diplomats. The diplomats were divided into two groups; one radiated around a handsome young Arab with a trim beard and flowing traditional dress, the other centered around a stern Israeli military officer, his breast covered with medals. Cromwell moved from one group to the other, obsequiously, and Wally could hear Gladys Cromwell regaling the women in the Arab party about the Moslem village where the boys manipulated their testicles until, at puberty, they reached the size of muskmelons. The reply to her comment was lost in the general confusion.

"Look sharp!" Cromwell whispered to Wally. "I think we have some potential investors." He winked, and as he was preparing to return to his guests, Wally grabbed his arm.

"Who the hell are these people?" he asked, wiping engine oil onto his trousers.

"They're delegates to a pre-Olympic planning conference in Mexico City. They're here for the fiesta. But they've expressed interest in a compact, light-weight anti-personnel helicopter."

"Who? The Arabs or the Israelis?"

"My goodness, Wally, both! It would hardly be fair to offer it to one without offering it to the other." He paused, looked around secretively, and climbed up next to Wally on the engine mount. "I just can't understand your attitude, Wally. Everybody knows we sell armaments to both sides. I've read up on it. It's not only historical fact, it's good business. If we had sold jets only to India, they'd have wiped out Pakistan in a matter of weeks. But by arming both sides, we maintain political stability and insure a continuing and expanding market for our war plants. My gracious, Wally, I thought anybody who had worked at General Dynamics as long as you had would understand the logic of all this."

Cromwell scurried back to his guests and Wally threw himself back into his work. For a few minutes he concentrated very hard on not thinking about what Cromwell had told him. He merely occupied his mind with the problem of mating the Belmont Hotel fan to the drive mechanism from the Coca-Cola truck. Then the absurdity of this proposed arms race between the Arabs and the Israelis crept into his mind and he recalled the Assassination of Popeye and the pop-up goat, and Swamp Sweeney's Road and he wondered how many absurdities you could stack one upon the other before this tower of the absurd becomes reasonable, rational and sane, in the same way that dreams can become real or pain can become pleasure. Everything, he decided, secretly wants to become the opposite of what it is.

By mid-afternoon the engine and rotor were mounted in place and a fuel system, consisting of a fifty gallon drum and an elaborate fuel-injection system of enema tubes and an aquarium pump, had been installed. José had attached the flight control cables to the control surfaces and Wally had briefed Gaspar on the rudiments of vertical takeoff. Gaspar was an eager and easy student and soon he was manipulating the controls with confidence and what seemed a natural flair for such things.

Wally only wished that Major Tom had been there to give the fledgling pilot pointers.

There was a spirit of keen optimism in the air. The workers seemed very proud to be part of the project and they strutted and grinned at their friends, who watched and discussed the progress with growing enthusiasm. Occasionally, a new group of spectators would join those already in the shop and a voice would shake loose from the others to exclaim: "There is Gaspar Lopez, the peasant from the desert! He is the one who will pilot the plane and fly above the fiesta!"

Another large group of spectators pressed into the shop. A concession stand materialized, and soon everyone was drinking tequila, sucking limes and waving paper birds on strings. Then, a bandstand was assembled by stacking coffins side by side, and a group of *caballeros* began singing love songs in close harmony. It was as if the fiesta itself had been compressed into the *carpenteria* of José Buenaventura. Wally was connecting the battery when Penelope swept into the already-teeming shop. She seemed magnificently alive and especially beautiful. She was followed by a crowd of rapturous-looking fishermen. Wally turned to look at her. She was so incomparably lovely that he could only smile and wish they were of the same species, either she human, or he an angel.

Then he pushed the helicopter's starter button and the motor made the sound of a small boy trying to sound like a motor starting. The great old Belmar Hotel fan began to turn, slowly, its blades groaning and creaking and casting thin, swift shadows across the tense, watching faces. All other sounds ceased except the little boy growling. Then, there was a hollow explosion, a frenzy of raucous coughs, a belching of blue smoke, and the motor caught, roaring angrily, the rotor flinging its wooden arms in wild and windy circles. A huge cheer escaped the crowd and there was much tilting of tequila bottles and shouting and singing. The turning rotor roared and sawdust rose from the floor and danced in the air. The flying machine trembled and strained as if anxious to rise, after its five-hundred-year sleep, and Wally throttled down, knowing all was ready now for the flight. He grinned when he noticed the noise had awakened the good, old, awful prophet, who had been sleeping in a coffin, to escape the intellectual pursuits of Gladys Cromwell.

The night of the flight of *Leonardo's Dream* fell like a fantasy upon the city and the sea. A great, foppish, old sun loafed for a while on the horizon and then flopped into the sea, splashing crimson and livid purples and lavender and deep, dark gold against the West. The sea led away, vast and brooding. Gulls swept like grey fears, low upon the horizon and the high lighthouse cast its Cyclops eye toward China. There was a light, chill wind from the sea and on it were broadcast the jubilant voices of the fiesta's second night.

Wally watched the great procession climb Ice Box Hill toward a high place where temporary bleachers had been built to accommodate those who would witness the historic flight. Leading the procession was the Coca-Cola truck, towing the flying machine that lumbered up the rocky slope with graceless docility, its wooden rotor turning slowly in the breeze. Gaspar, wearing World War I goggles beneath his sombrero, rode in the pilot's seat. After shooting a few scenes of the procession, Mario joined Wally, Penelope, the prophet and their new friends, Papa Blue and Billy Bucket, as they ascended the hill. Wally felt very close to his companions and they seemed to feel it, too. Even the prophet seemed to walk a little closer than was his usual habit.

Then Papa Blue noticed something strange about a mariachi band struggling up the hill about fifty yards away. "They're playing *Clair de Lune*," he said. "It's hardly a Mariachi favorite. And another odd thing, they're all carrying trombone cases, even the drummer."

"Oh, shit!" Wally said. "It's The Lynx and his agents." One of the violinists was having trouble with the catch on his trombone case and a machine gun clattered out onto the slope. "Listen guys," Wally said. "We've got to get out of Dodge!"

"But how?"

"We'll fly out with Gaspar."

"But what if it doesn't fly?" Mario asked.

"It will!" Penelope said. "You told me it would fly, Wally."

"It wasn't exactly a promise. Here's what will happen. When Gaspar gets *Leonardo's Dream* revved up, grab the prophet and jump on board. We'll fly right out from under their noses."

"Man," Mario warned, "they have those fucking guns."

"I think we can catch them by surprise," Wally answered, not altogether sure about that, or anything, anymore. Then Wally saw the fat figure of Peter Cromwell churning up the hill, the Arab and Israeli delegations in tow. Gladys was locked in intense and animated conversation with a tall, veiled Arab woman. The crowd moved on up the hill.

They arrived at the crest. Below, the city throbbed and surged, and exploding fireworks punctured the night sky. The people settled upon the hillsides in packed and random patterns. Many sang the traditional songs of their villages to the accompaniment of yellow guitars and others shouted praise and encouragement to the peasant from the desert, who would soon challenge gravity. Brass bands blared and bleated, tequila flowed like nectar and there was a scent of lemons and the sea in the air. The Coca-Cola truck ground to a stop and Jose's labor crew moved *Leonardo's Dream* into place before the wooden bleachers, which sagged beneath the weight of celebrants and dignitaries. The little aircraft that had looked so formidable in the crowded *carpenteria* now seemed frail as a dandelion. As Wally saw it there, perched timidly on the rocky hilltop, he felt suddenly terribly afraid. It was so small and silly. It danced gently in the wind and looked not unlike a small boy who has waited too long to go to the bathroom. 'There's no way such a crazy little thing could fly,' he thought. But it was too late to back out now. The bands were wailing, the crowd cheering, the speeches being made. The members of the Israeli and Arab delegations were introduced and applauded. Gaspar was cited as the most dynamic figure in the history of Mexican aviation and the prophet was awarded a medal by the wife of the Mayor of Mazatlan, who fainted dead away while trying to pin it to his awful robes. She had to be carried away. In the near distance, Wally could see The Lynx laughing derisively at *Leonardo's Dream,* and it was perhaps this that renewed his courage and resolve. Before he helped Gaspar into the pilot seat, he, Mario and Penelope said their goodbyes to Billy Bucket and Papa Blue. After Gaspar pushed the starter button, they all climbed aboard.

How the crowd cheered when the brave little machine leapt to life and began flinging its rotor 'round and 'round. Gaspar pulled the throttle back and there was a roaring and rushing of wind that made the very earth tremble and blew the sombreros from the heads of peasants and tax collectors and turned a tuba inside out. It blew Gladys Cromwell's skirt high over her head and rustled the beards of the Arab Olympic committeemen. Passing birds fell down dead from the sky and fish in the sea became skittish. Gaspar pulled the throttle further back and it began to rain mushrooms. The rotors pounded the air and *Leonardo's Dream* began to rise crazily above the cheering spectators. It lurched and spun and swayed, and then, to Wally's sublime relief, he realized that it was, at last, doing what a hawk can do. The dream of Leonardo da Vinci was flying!

In a flash, Mario and Penelope opened a wooden box near the center of the flying machine where they had hidden a large supply of Chinese firecrackers and rotten fruit filled with a non-lethal preparation of Moonwort from Billy Bucket's endless supply. They hurled the rotten fruit bombs down on The Lynx and his men. Wally could see them wrestling with the catches on their trombone cases as the Moonwort-laced fruit bombs began to stampede the crowd, many among them suffering mild to severe olfactory outrages. One of The Lynx's operatives managed to fire his machine gun before being trampled by the crowd. The bullets stitched an ugly chain of holes through the brave and smiling portraits of El Cordobes covering the wings. For a moment, the little plane shuddered from the impact, and then flew on. Gaspar flew like one possessed. He dove and swooped above the crowd like a barnstormer, scattering celebrants in every direction. It was as they made their last pass that the prophet squatted and released through his tattered trousers an object-concept-mystery so incomprehensibly awful that it caused the gods to weep. Down it fell, surrounded by swirling nebulae and gagging hellions and black fire, down toward the horrified faces of Peter and Gladys Cromwell, The Lynx and the Israeli and Arab diplomats. As Wally watched, they turned to stone, and the earth opened like an old boil and sucked them under.

Leonardo's Dream sailed out over the city and circled high above the dancing light of the aerial rockets. Suddenly, Wally was not aware of the engine's sound, only the rushing wind and the faraway silence of Mazatlan. They moved on wings of wind out to sea, the fiesta merely a firefly now. When Wally turned to congratulate Gaspar, it was obvious the old man was dead. One of the machine-gun shells had shot his throat away.

There was no conversation, no debate what to do. They couldn't carry Gaspar Lopez with them to the ends of the skies. And so, Wally helped Mario pry the peasant's brown hands from the controls and then let him tumble, tumble, tumble far down, down into the sea.

Wally was devastated. He wept without sound, without tears, without cease. He grieved for Gaspar, for himself, for angels and demons, and for the world and all its wandering pilgrims. He grieved for God and he grieved for Satan. He grieved that consciousness must end, that even the universe was uncoiling toward oblivion. Penelope held him close as Mario took the controls and they flew out over the dark and limitless sea toward China.

CHAPTER 6
THE LAST OF THE GREATER QUETZALS

The fog began to rise from the sea before dawn, like smoke from ancient fires. For a while the jewelry of the night sky was veiled by mist, each star surrounded by a diffused silver halo, a night sky, as envisioned by Vincent van Gogh. Yet there was sufficient starlight to reveal they were flying merely a few feet above the Pacific swells. No one had slept all night, each wrapped in a cocoon of solitude, each contemplating the fragility of mortality, each listening for the moment *Leonardo's Dream* would run out of fuel and they would be cast into the sea.

Wally felt Penelope's body warm against his side. "What's going to happen, Wally?"

"I don't know, Love."

"I don't suppose we can expect a miracle."

"I'm pretty sure *Leonardo's Dream* will float. It's made from Jose's pine coffins."

"Do you know where we are?"

"We can't be too far from Baja California."

"Too far to swim."

Wally said nothing, wrapped his arm more tightly around her, and he realized that it was probable he would soon die. He was more curious than afraid. In the next few hours all the questions mankind had asked would be answered. Is there a God? Is there something beyond? Had he been too hasty to dismiss the possibility that Jesus was the Son of God and had died for his sins, and maybe that seemingly-ridiculous born-again nonsense might have some modicum of truth buried within it somewhere? He listened to the drone of the little engine and decided he had never really come to grips with the matter of God, much less Jesus. He supposed he did believe in some sort of cosmic intelligence that had figured out how to put the universe together and set it spinning through Time. If the world exists, it must have been created. There had to be a first cause. And thought of the biblical account of the first five days of creation. He counted them off from his Sunday school memories. On the first day came light. On the second day came the firmament, whatever that was; something that separated above from below. On day three came the sea and dry land; day four brought the stars and the moon, and then on the morning and evening of the fifth day came the animals and birds and insects. Only problem was these weren't twenty-four-hour days; each of these days was actually millions of years. But the sixth day is where the Bible gets wacky, the idea of making man in His image, and then poor Eve out of Adam's rib. 'It is possible,' he now thought, 'that God looked very much like Penelope, if we were created in His image, and maybe that was why he worshipped her so.' But he rather supposed that she was made not of clay or a rib bone, but was a creation of starlight. He looked up to Penelope's parents, the stars, and he remembered the passage in *Huckleberry Finn* where Huck and Jim were rafting down the Mississippi discussing how the stars were made. Finally, Huck explained to Jim that the moon had laid them. Wally smiled to himself, thinking that was probably as good an explanation as there was.

Penelope stirred against him. Her blue eyes became a part of the star field.

"Are you okay?" he asked.

She nodded her head and touched his face and they watched the first fingers of dawn unfold a thin ribbon of white between the dark of the sky and the greater dark of the sea. Soon, the east began to show streaks of gold and a red, like spilled blood, along the horizon and above on soft rows of pillowed cloud. Then, as they watched in wonder, the great orb of the sun itself rolled up from the other side of the earth, setting the sea and sky ablaze with horizontal curtains of fire. The reflections made it difficult to know where the sea ended and the sky began. It was like two abstract paintings held edge to edge. Soon there were two suns—one rising, one falling—and they were so mesmerized by the grandeur of the morning that they would later claim not having been aware that the aircraft's engine had sputtered to a stop and they were dropped gently onto the sea.

Perhaps what happened next was a kind of miracle, because *Leonardo's Dream* not only floated like a goose, she rode the waves as if born to them, high and dry, easing up and down the Pacific swells with ease. As it grew light, they could see they were alone on the eternal sea, perhaps the only people on the planet. Once acclimated to the reality that drowning was not in their immediate future, they began to enjoy, even delight in their situation. "Who knew," Mario said, "that Leonardo designed his airplane to be amphibious?"

The day grew warm with a light, cool breeze from the west. The sky was an amazing cobalt blue and the sea as clear as tinted vodka. To Penelope's delight, a school of silver flying fish, maybe thousands, sailed past from one wave crest to another. It wasn't long before she discovered they were being followed by a pod of dolphins, some moving so close that Penelope could reach out and touch them. "We made eye contact," she said, tears of delight running down her cheeks. "They can read my thoughts and I can read theirs. They said not to worry. We will be fine."

In spite of the dolphins' promise, Wally and Mario began to take stock of their situation. They had a few gallons of water they could drain from the engine's radiator, and a half bottle of tequila, but that wouldn't last long at all. So Mario began making rain catchers from the fabric of their Mariachi costumes and their wide sombreros. Each rain catcher would hold at least two gallons of rainfall. Food was also a problem. They only had rotten fruit left over from bombing The Lynx and his cronies, so Wally busied himself putting together some sort of fishing gear. He made a hook from a nail holding the El Cordobes posters to the frame of the helicopter. Next, he made a fishing line by unraveling the braid of his Mariachi uniform jacket.

"What about bait?" Mario asked.

Wally explained his plan. "Instead of the usual bait, which we don't have, we will use some of Billy Bucket's supply of Moonwort. Maybe we won't even need a hook and line. We use a highly diluted formula of Moonwort, spread it here and there on the deck. If we mix it right, when the flying fish fly by, they will be attracted to the wonderful scent, have a mild olfactory outrage, become disoriented, and we will grab them when they flop unconscious onto *Leonardo's Dream*."

And so it was, for the first days of their survival. They all agreed that, if their situation wasn't so desperate, they would be magnificently content. On the second day, a pod of dolphins came to visit, playing and leaping and swimming up to the former helicopter, to be touched and petted.

"Wally, may I swim with the dolphins? Please?" Penelope asked.

"Just be careful and don't swim too far from the helicopter. This is a little deeper than the Rio Grande."

Penelope stripped down to her perfect self and slipped into the sea. Almost immediately, several dolphins swam up to her, nuzzling her, touching her with their bottle noses, then leaping into the air clicking and whistling with apparent joy. Penelope released her grip on the helicopter and floated several feet away, her hands held out to the circling dolphins. They gathered around her and under her and surged upward, lifting her gently half-out of the water, then releasing her again, obviously enjoying the game. 'It is probable,' Wally thought, 'they had never had a naked human woman for a playmate, much less a naked angel.' Penelope took a deep breath and slipped below the surface. For a while, she became a member of the pod, every bit as graceful as her playmates, swimming and cavorting by their side. Then she grasped one of the dolphin's dorsal fins and she was pulled along, slowly at first, then at greater speed, and the dolphin seemed to sense that she, like they, had to surface occasionally for air, although at more frequent intervals. Wally thought he could watch their play forever, especially when she climbed on a dolphin's back and rode him through the water like the boy on the ancient bronze Grecian statue. They circled the former helicopter for a while and then the dolphin delivered Penelope back to her human companions.

"That was the most magical thing that ever happened to me," she breathed, when she was back aboard, slippery and golden. "Except maybe kissing the girl with the mandolin. I could sense the dolphin's love, Wally. I think I could understand their language."

Later, Wally remembered ancient stories of dolphins rescuing drowning sailors. He recalled that there were even contemporary reports of dolphins protecting swimmers from sharks. "If we tied a line around your waist," he asked Penelope, "and you climbed aboard a dolphin, do you think that you and the dolphin could pull us through the water?"

"I don't know, Wally. I could ask them." She slipped back into the water to confer with the dolphins. There was a great deal of clicking and whistling. When she returned aboard, she said they had an even better idea. "If we had a lot of lines, many dolphins could pull us faster. They even suggested some of them could push."

And so they busied themselves cutting their Mariachi uniforms into strips to make traces for the dolphins. Soon Mario and Wally were just as naked as Penelope and the dolphins. They decided to reject the prophet's rotted clothing, for obvious reasons. When Wally saw his own pasty white body next to the bronzed Angel of the Arroyos, he was embarrassed. She had never seen him in his altogether and he cupped his privates in his hands.

"Don't be silly, Wally," Penelope said, laughing. "You have a fine body. In fact, I think you might have some Veraugee blood in your family. Just look at you," she added, playfully pinching his member. She turned to Mario. "And you are a handsome male, too, Mario. Maybe no suggestion of Veraugee blood, but a fine male of the species." Seeing she might have hurt Mario's feelings, she moved to him, gathered him in her arms, and kissed him to smithereens. When she came up for air, she said, "No sailor could have more beautiful shipmates."

Soon they had knotted together a number of traces for the dolphins to pull. Penelope returned to the water, distributed the knotted strips of Mariachi uniforms, and with a resumption of clicks and whistles, she discussed with them the art of pulling *Leonardo's Dream* through the water.

Back aboard, Penelope whistled, and the seaborne former helicopter began to move. Faster and faster she rushed through the sea, sheets of white spray flowing out to the side, an actual wake rising out behind. Hundreds of dolphins surged beneath the craft, lifting it partially out of the water so that it slipped easily across the swells. It was very nearly like flying, and soon they were skipping along the crests, accompanied by clouds of flying fish. Ahead, several dolphins pulled at their traces, while hundreds of others swam alongside, as if offering encouragement. Penelope clung to Wally, her blue eyes afire with excitement. Of course, Mario filmed the entire adventure, clamoring about the craft seeking the best prospective. Even the awful prophet seemed to take interest in their unlikely passage toward the east, his beard flowing out behind him like dirty laundry.

Penelope pointed out a grey whale, huge in the near distance, keeping pace with its cousins, the dolphins. As they watched, the monster rose into the air like a small mountain, regarded them with what seemed amused curiosity, then returned to the sea in a mammoth geyser of spray. Soon, hundreds of seabirds joined the chase. They were flying so close that Wally could almost reach out and touch their wings. He would not have been surprised if King Neptune himself and all his court would have emerged from the sea to join the passing parade. The air was filled with the chattering of gulls, the clicks and whistles of dolphins and the magical serenade of wind and sea.

Wally was not sure how much time passed before they saw the island rise from the horizon. As they drew closer, it seemed like a forlorn construction of soaring pillars and spectacular spires of rock, appearing much like an enormous Medieval castle set adrift. There were no other landforms or islands nearby. This one was absolutely alone in a vastness of the Pacific. Soon their forward motion slowed and the craft settled back into the sea. The dolphins circled as if waiting for instructions. The nearer they drew to the island, the more formidable it appeared to be. Where the surf hit the reef surrounding the island, a chaos of spray and foam rose high into the air, and Wally wondered aloud if it would even be possible to land on the island without being crushed by the surf. Penelope slipped once more into the sea to confer with the dolphins. When she returned, she said the dolphins knew a pass through the reefs into a small lagoon.

"Did they say if anyone lived on the island?"

"I asked them that, but they changed the subject."

Now, slowly, a few of the dolphins returned to their traces and pulled them almost into the teeth of the raging reef. But there was a small break where *Leonardo's Dream* slipped through, riding the crest of a wave like a sleigh through snow. And now they were in a quiet lagoon, the turquoise and silver water revealing myriad sand dollars and elegant shells on a sand bottom that led to a small beach. For a while, as Penelope said tearful goodbyes to their rescuers, Wally looked up at the towers of rock and wondered if he had ever seen a place quite so lifeless. Seabirds soared high on the cliffs, brightly colored tropical fish swam at his feet, yet nothing else moved. There were no tropical palms to bend in the wind and nothing green seemed to grow.

Soon, with a final aerial display, the dolphins departed, and they were left alone on the eerie isle. It was not until they were wading ashore, wearing only their boots to protect their feet from coral, and sombreros as protection from the sun, that the islanders emerged from caves in the stone. They, too, were stark naked and appeared to be the survivors of some cataclysmic disaster. There were both men and women, bronzed by the sun, terribly unkempt; the women's long, tangled hair would have put Medusa to shame, and the men wore beards that hung nearly to their waists. The islanders did not approach, nor did they display any threatening behavior, they merely squatted in place to study the intruders, as if they were examining some newly discovered species.

Wally imagined, in some distant epoch of human history, two clans of naked primates might have met like this, albeit minus boots and sombreros, and either fought or mated. Although he was not in a mood to fight, interbreeding with these women was not high on his agenda. For a while, the two groups stared at each other; then, it seemed the islanders grew bored and all but one returned to their caves.

The man who remained spoke English with a New England accent, and said his name was Montclair. "You have nothing to fear from these people," he said, as if to differentiate himself from the others. "I have been waiting for someone to help me escape this place. Perhaps together we can find a way."

He led them up a trail through the rock formations to a cave. "Welcome to my home," he said, motioning that they squat down beside him on the stone floor. Montclair was no less disreputable looking than the others. His red hair and beard were, perhaps, less tangled and his eyes were a startling emerald green. Wally imagined he might have been handsome in some earlier life. "I would offer you tea and some cakes, but we are not really prepared for guests here, so all I can offer you is the story of these people, among whom, sadly, I include myself."

Here is the story Montclair told.

"The islanders are a cult of people with members from Europe, the United States and Asia. In our former lives, we had been attorneys, politicians, social workers, people deeply committed to important causes. I was a diplomat devoted to securing peace between warring nations. And each of us, in time, became painfully aware that our causes were fraudulent, that the more committed we became, the more meaningless our efforts to effect change.

"I discovered that accord between nations was impossible, as long as their leaders were more concerned with power than peace. Somehow we became aware of each other, were drawn together by our pain and frustration and sense of betrayal. Separately, then together, we began to reject the trappings of so-called civilized society, like materialism, an interest in politics, religion, and all possessions, both material and spiritual. We came together in San Diego, and, recognizing our mutual angst, we found an old sailing ship and sailed away to dispossess ourselves of the world. By chance, we came upon this island. Once here, like Hernán Cortés or Alexander, we burned our ship, so that return would not be possible. We also burned our clothes and books and any materials we might have used to keep journals, because to keep a journal would suggest that our experience here was worth possessing.

"In short," Montclair summarized, "we possess nothing. We reject everything."

"Wally," Penelope said, "it's like the Butterfly People, but different." Wally had been thinking about the girl with the mandolin ever since Penelope mentioned her, earlier in the day "Both groups escaped the world. But these islanders became ugly and indifferent. The Butterfly People became beautiful and loving."

"Except for their bias against prophets, Wally said. "All that endless talk about love meant nothing when push came to shove."

"Damn hypocrites!" Penelope said, and they both smiled at the memory of the encounter in the canyon.

"There is a meaning in this," Wally said. "Why one group got ugly and selfish, and the other group became beautiful and loving. If only Gaspar were here, he would find the meaning for us." Wally felt the dull pain of grief as he thought about their old friend Gasper Lopez, the peasant who would conquer sorrow.

Wally noticed there was no fire pit in the cave, no smoke stain on the cave's ceiling. "Do you possess fire?" he asked.

"Certainly not," Montclair replied. "We survive on raw fish, seaweed and bird eggs, which, by the way, is an exceedingly more healthful diet than what we have rejected."

"Have you rejected sex? I see no children."

"We do not have sex. To have something is to possess it. And so, possessing sex must be rejected."

"Why do you want to leave?" Penelope asked.

"Because some of the things we have rejected are civility, hygiene and hope. We are detestable, cruel, filthy, thoughtless and rude."

"But..." Penelope said, making a quick survey of the primitive man squatting beside her.

"I know. You wonder what makes me different. You think I am the pot calling the kettle black. And I suppose you're right, except for one thing. I have rejected all these things, but there is one thing I have managed to cling to. And that's a belief that a person can change."

"Oh," Penelope said, "you poor man." She moved closer to him on the cold stone.

Montclair looked into her eyes and sighed. Then he stood and led them to another section of the cavern, where sunlight reached down through a hole in the roof revealing an astonishing gallery of primitive art. Here were depicted in brilliant color the daily lives of an ancient people. There were scenes of domesticity, of lovers, of mothers holding babies, children at play, of hunters and priests. Here were strange animals including one that looked much like a unicorn, and enormous exotic birds attending women at their baths.

"What is this?" Wally asked. "Who are these people?"

"I don't know," Montclair said. "I often spend hours here seeking the mystery of who they were and where they came from and how they happened to be here."

"These must be pictures of their memories," Penelope said, reaching for Montclair's hand. "Certainly they weren't recording their experience here on this desolate island."

"But the point is, they were here. They were living, breathing, dreaming, beautiful people. They stood right here where we stand. Maybe they were shipwrecked or maybe there was a land bridge to the Americas that was reclaimed by the sea. But even imprisoned in this awful place, they remembered who they were, and their humanity remained intact. And as I gaze at their memories, I remember, too. I remember who I am, or at least who I was, and maybe who I could be again if I could escape this awful island."

In the days to follow, Mario made a documentary of the abysmal life of the islanders. They refused to be interviewed and Mario found it difficult to film their daily activities because they didn't have any. Mostly they sat and scratched insect bites and wallowed in the shallows and cursed each other in the languages of their origin. Wally made a survey of *Leonardo's Dream*. It had held together rather well in its mad dolphin-powered dash over the waves, but the notion of re-launching her through the towering surf seemed impossible. Penelope spent much of the time tending to Montclair's grooming. She bathed him in the clear water of the lagoon, removing years of accumulated filth. It took many sessions, because prolonged scrubbing reddened his skin, especially his privates that, even toughened by life in the raw, were still quite sensitive. The most difficult task was grooming his matted thatch of auburn hair and his beard, which was encrusted with years of fish oil and scales, and the yellow yolk of Blue Footed Booby eggs. With a sharp chip of obsidian, she cut his hair and beard to a manageable length and then began the odious task of untangling what remained. They obviously had no comb since everything had been burned, years before, with the ship, so she used her fingers. She worked slowly and gently and, Wally thought, with a certain sense of dedication and proprietorship, as if the humanizing of her charge was the most important thing on earth. Little by little, Montclair began to resemble, though still naked, the handsome and committed diplomat he had once been.

Occasionally, others of the ignoble clan, in passing by, would spit in their direction. It became more and more apparent that they found the reclamation of their former mate disturbing and an intrusion on their abhorrent society. Soon they were observed carrying sticks and hitting them upon outcroppings of rock, as if practicing for more serious violence. Where once the islanders had lived silent, individual lives, they now seemed to gather in groups and were seen in long, often violent discussion. Then one morning, Wally woke to find the prophet was missing.

Penelope was distraught. "Where could he have gone?"

"I believe he's been kidnapped," Montclair exclaimed. "I think they see him as one of their own."

Later in the day, the islanders approached the cave, displaying the prophet like a trophy. They had stripped away what was left of his rotted Mariachi uniform, so he was wearing the accepted island attire, which was naked as a baby jaybird, and he was easily as scrawny and pitiful. Penelope checked to see if he was wearing any Veraugee penile adornment; he was not. The villagers paraded the awful old man before them, waving their sticks and hurling feces.

That night a huge, pale moon rose from the sea, tipping the tops of the waves with tracings of silver. Soon the stars came out, one by one by one million, so bright that some could even be seen riding the edge of the moon. Wally and the others crouched in Montclair's cave, seeking a solution to their twin problems: rescuing the prophet and escaping from the island.

"Penelope," Montclair asked, as they dined on seaweed and raw clams, "do I understand that you can speak with dolphins?"

"I can."

"Have you spoken with any other animals?"

"Well, burros, jackrabbits. Why?"

"When I heard you had the gift of communicating with dolphins it gave me an idea. Have you talked with birds?"

"Often. Ravens, doves and falcons, and once with an eagle."

"Where is this leading, Montclair?" Wally asked.

"There are some great birds that nest on a cliff high above the sea. I believe these birds are the Quetzal that was so important to the spiritual life of the Mayans."

"I thought the Quetzal was a myth," Wally said.

"There are a few Lesser Quetzals still in the forests of the Maya. But these are Greater Quetzals, considered to be a myth or extinct. But there may be some here."

Montclair pointed to one of the murals on the cave wall. It depicted a woman being attended in her bath by giant, extravagantly colored birds.

"Are these the birds you mean? The ones in the painting?"

"Yes. Obviously, these birds were close to the people who lived here, long ago. Not just mythological creatures, but real companions. There must have been communication between the people and the birds."

"But not between these islanders and the birds?" Mario asked, taking a wide-angle shot of the woman and birds depicted by the pool.

Wally noticed that one of the women in the pool looked very much like Penelope.

"As you can see," Montclair continued, "the people who lived here before were beautiful. The current occupants of the island are horrible and nasty, so the birds remain in the heights, avoiding the disgusting islanders. My idea is that Penelope would remind these few remaining Greater Quetzals of the people they once loved and she could convince them to help us. They must detest the sloth and nasty manners and disreputable appearance of the islanders—the disreputable appearance that, thanks to Penelope, I no longer possess." He turned to Penelope. "What do you think?"

"But the people in the paintings must have lived here thousands of years ago. The birds in the painting would no longer be alive."

"But I believe these are their descendants. I believe the memory of their human companions might have been passed down through the generations. I believe that, somehow, the memory might be buried in their genes." Montclair turned to Penelope. "Will you try to talk with the Quetzals?"

"Of course I will," she replied, eyes sparkling, obviously excited about the idea.

"You have a lively imagination, Montclair," Wally said, a bit lightheaded from struggling to believe they were going to depend on a mythical bird to save them.

"Yes. Imagination. It is one of those possessions I have refused to discard."

"Have you ever seen one of these birds?" Mario asked.

"Not really. They are very reclusive. Sometimes, in the full of the moon, I have seen the shadows of their wings—huge wings—and the sound those wings make in the night, as they power back into the peaks, is like the beat of drums. But you can see from the paintings that they were here. I believe a few remain."

The climb up to the home of the Quetzals was difficult. The rocks were very hard and the climbers, especially Penelope, were very soft. It was fortunate they had brought their Mariachi boots ashore or it might have been impossible to climb the sharp rocks. As they reached the summit, Wally looked back at the blue-black Pacific and the reef and the pounding surf and the small beach where they had come ashore. Below, on the white sand lay *Leonardo's Dream*, a dozen or more portraits of the brave matador El Cordobes looking up from the bullfight posters toward the moon.

Wally was looking out to sea when a shadow swept between the island and the moon, a great wing spiraling through the night. Then came other swift shadows, powerful wings drumming on the air, then gliding to a landing a few feet from where they stood. There were five of the great birds silhouetted against the night sky. The birds and the humans stood facing each other, each astonished at the encounter, as if wondering what would happen next. There was a sense of nobility about the Quetzals. They reminded Wally of pictures he had seen of Mayan warriors, fierce and proud. Even in the light of the stars he could tell that their feathers were riotously vivid, reds and blues, greens and yellows, much like the colors in Mexican paintings. They stood tall as a man, ominous, yet somehow comforting; wary, yet curious. For a long time, the birds merely stood, watching, perhaps feeling for some fragment of memory. Then they formed a kind of huddle, their heads close, making a bass harmonic sound deep in their throats, as if they had swallowed bassoons. Wally and the others simply stood mesmerized as the Quetzals conferred.

Penelope took a step forward. One of the birds moved toward her warily. The moonlight glinted off its long, sharp, blood-red beak. Wally noticed that the bird's claws seemed sharp and wicked, but for all its fearsome appearance, Penelope did not seem afraid. She stood, proudly, majestic in the starlight, waiting for the Quetzal. As the bird drew nearer to Penelope, Wally noticed it had retracted its claws and he could now see that the bird's eyes were round like human eyes, brown and soft, and they were filled with something like love at the sight of Penelope, the woman painted at her bath on the wall of the cave. The bird reached out a wing and touched her face, her hair, her breasts, her hands. Wally was certain he saw tears in the Quetzal's eyes. Penelope stepped into the folds of the great bird's wings and they stood together, swaying slightly in the half-light, Penelope singing some old song from the arroyos, the birds answering with their deep basso orchestra of bassoons.

They spent the night with the Quetzals. Except for the one that had embraced Penelope, they seemed quite shy, but not so shy that they did not examine their naked guests with the tips of their wing feathers, a touch that Wally found extremely ticklish. It was all he could do to withhold laughter, which would have been an awful thing to have happen in this historic interspecies moment. Their nest was covered with soft layers of feathers molted in previous seasons. Penelope and the leader of the Quetzals, who they named Manuel Benitez, after the brave matador Manuel Benitez El Cordobes, sat together on the feathered nest, conferring, it seemed, in some language not of earth or heaven. Just before midnight, the birds seemed to grow drowsy. Unable to keep their eyes open, one by one, even Manuel Benitez fell asleep, not standing up like some birds do, but lying down like men, their wings as comforters.

Penelope lay down with her human companions. She exuded happiness and wonder. In whispers, she told them about her conversation with Manuel Benitez. He had told her that they were the last of the Greater Quetzals. Once they had numbered in the thousands, living like demigods in the forests surrounding Tikal, Uxmal, Palenque and the other great Mayan cities. But there came a time when they became more revered for their feathers than for their spiritual significance. They were hunted down to make the extravagant feathered robes of the Mayan kings and warriors. Because of their brilliant coloring, there was no way to hide from the hunters. And although they were physically powerful and looked fierce, fighting was not in their nature. So, within a generation or two, they were nearly wiped out.

Manuel Benitez and a few others fled north, reaching Baja California. But they were pursued again for their feathers. There was no peace. And so they fled west, out to sea, blindly, not knowing where they were going or if they were flying to their deaths. But they found this place, and it became the home of the last few of what had once been thousands. The island was inhabited then, by the people depicted on the wall. And the people grew to love the Quetzals, not for their feathers but for their generous hearts. And the Quetzals grew to love the people.

"How did the people get here?"

"According to Manuel Benitez, they were shipwrecked, seeking their ancestral home in the Southern Oceans."

"What happened to them?"

"Manuel Benitez said that there came a time when the people longed to continue their voyage. After two generations, they rebuilt their ship and set out again for their ancestral home. They begged the Quetzals to go with them, but the Quetzals reluctantly refused. They preferred the safety of the island to a journey across the wide and dangerous seas. After emotional goodbyes, the people departed and the Quetzals were left alone. Generations went by. Young Quetzals were hatched, but year after year, their numbers diminished until only these five remained. I don't mean to make this about me, but they see me as the return of something they almost lost. Over the generations, they almost lost the memory of the beautiful people they had loved and the woman in the bath. All that had assumed the quality of myth. But then I showed up and suddenly the myth was real again; what they had wanted to believe all these generations had come true."

"What about saving the prophet?"

"It will be difficult for them. After all, the prophet is exactly like the islanders they detest. They are afraid, since all the islanders look alike, they won't be able to know which of the disgusting humans he is. But we decided that I would go with them when they fly down to rescue our old friend."

"How?"

"I'll fly down on Manuel's back, holding my arms around his neck. He said I'd be light as a feather. Two Quetzals will fly down. After I identify the prophet, the other one will grab him, and we'll all meet back at *Leonardo's Dream.*"

"What then?"

"Manuel Benitez said they will dream up a plan for us to escape."

"Won't the islanders interfere?"

"Apparently, they are terrified of the Quetzals. Manuel Benitez doesn't think they'll be too much of a problem." Penelope stretched and yawned and then kissed Wally's lips and said, "It's been a very emotional day, Wally. Do you mind if I sleep with Manuel Benitez?"

Wally's first thought was of Leda and the Swan. Shocked at the thought, he looked into her eyes. "You wouldn't..."

"Of course not, Wally! What do you think I am?"

In the morning, the Quetzals were the first to rise. They stood silhouetted against a pearl grey sky, their wings outstretched to a length of what Wally supposed must be at least thirty feet, tip to tip, their feathers ruffling in the morning sea breeze. They seemed in either prayer or in serious discussion, making that deep harmonic rumbling that was apparently their signature call. Soon, Penelope came out of the cave, wiping sleep from her eyes and bright feathers from her coal black pubic hair.

Mario came out with his camera to document the first flight of a woman on a bird. One of the Greater Quetzals made a preparatory flight, perhaps so Mario could know how to position his camera. The Quetzal moved to the edge of the cliff, spread its mighty wings and stepped off into thousands of feet of nothing but air. Wally's heart hurt when he thought of Penelope making that dreadful plunge.

"Manuel Benitez asks that you help me get on his back." As Wally should have expected, she showed absolutely no hesitation nor fear. Wally and Montclair lifted Penelope onto the bird's back. She shifted around for a comfortable position, her legs tucked up beneath her, like a jockey, arms around the bird's neck, her hands full of feathers. "I told him I didn't want to pull out his feathers. But he said the red ones on his chest were very secure." Mario made a note of this bit of Quetzal biology, probably never before disclosed in the literature.

Wally stepped to the edge of the cliff and looked down. "Manuel Benitez says you might not want to watch," Penelope said. "With the extra weight, we might have to free fall for a while before we gain enough speed for his wings to catch the wind."

Then, too soon, they were gone, plummeting like a stone into the abyss, wings furled at the great bird's side, Penelope's hair a dark flame against Manuel's bright feathers, Mario catching it all with his camera. Just when Wally thought he would die with horror and grief, the wings unfurled and the Greater Quetzal took flight and soared among the peaks. The second Quetzal leaped off the cliff and joined them in the wind. The two birds circled the cliff twice then were soon out of sight.

Montclair, Wally and Mario began the long climb back down toward the beach. Wally wondered if he shouldn't have been the one to fly the Quetzal. But he knew he was too heavy. And he was also mortal and he supposed, by now, that Penelope was not. He thought of the times he had exposed her to danger and he felt even worse about what new dangers she might be facing. As they reached the lower peaks they began to see the detestable islanders creeping out of their caves, waving their sticks and the hoe they had stolen from the prophet.

They walked faster, then broke into a run, their Mariachi boots clattering on the stone trail as Montclair's former companions gave chase. Ahead was *Leonardo's Dream*, rising and falling in the light ripples of the lagoon. They were outpacing the islanders, who huffed and puffed, apparently out of shape from their slothful inactivity. They reached the former helicopter, leaped aboard and Wally pushed it a few feet out into the lagoon. The angry islanders stopped at the water's edge, shouting abuse and making obscene gestures.

"They hate water," Montclair said. "But I've never seen them so worked up."

The naked islanders appeared unable to contain their rage. The women tore their hair and a few fights broke out among the men. It seemed only a matter of time before the mob would descend upon them. Wally was afraid he was going to have to fight, something he had never liked doing, especially without any clothes on. He had never understood how the ancient Greeks, armed with swords and axes, would go to war naked. Just the thought of that cold steel slicing into his warm body made him gasp. But the islanders were only armed with sticks and loathing, lesser weapons against his naked flesh. Then Wally remembered the box containing Billy Bucket's seemingly endless store of Moonwart concoctions. Billy had prepared packets, each containing a particular strength, calculated to produce a particular olfactory effect, ranging from simple pleasure to sexual stimulation, to unconsciousness, to packets containing a mixture producing potentially lethal explosions, like that planned for the ill-fated detonation of the Reventador volcano. Not wanting to kill the islanders or provide them simple pleasure, he selected packets of powder designed to stimulate sexual desire. Making sure the wind was blowing on shore, he opened the packet and released the Moonwart derivative into the air. What happened then, though grotesque in the extreme, was a highly successful defensive maneuver. The islanders lost all interest in attacking, and having abandoned sex for so long, they fell upon each other. The beach became alive with horrible clusters of filthy, copulating couples. Mario was so disgusted he turned off his camera and closed his eyes.

It was then that the five Quetzals rounded a distant outcropping of rock, glided gracefully down to circle *Leonardo's Dream*. Penelope waved and smiled and Wally felt relief, as love fill every molecule of his body. One of the Quetzals hovered a few feet off the deck and dropped the prophet from his talons. He fell like a sack of rutabagas at Wally's feet. Penelope slipped down off Manuel Benitez, rubbed his scarlet beak, kissed his eyes, then threw herself into Wally's arms, kissing him with a passion he had not felt from her since Mario filmed them pretending to make love.

"It was wonderful, Wally. Thank you for bringing me here." And then she kissed him again and said: "I love you for everything. Without you I would have never ridden a dolphin or flown with the Greater Quetzals. Without you I'd be back in the arroyos, healing *los camposinos*."

"It looks like some of the islanders have become sated," Montclair said. "If we have a plan, maybe now is the time to execute that plan."

Penelope stepped into the water and whistled. Almost immediately the surface of the lagoon was broken by the dorsal fins and bottle noses of dolphins. Penelope swam to them and hugged them and they answered her whistles with more whistles and clicks. After she had welcomed her friends the dolphins, she climbed back aboard. Wally looked out at the towering surf breaking across the reef.

"Riding the surf *in* is one thing," he said. "Riding it out again, against the flow, is another."

"Manuel Benitez has an idea. Greater Quetzals and dolphins have always been allies. He believes with the Quetzals and the dolphins working together, his idea might work. It's just a chance, but a better chance than facing the awful rage of the islanders. I have mentioned it to the dolphins and they agree to do their part." Penelope instructed Wally and the others to select the strongest of the traces made from their Mariachi uniforms and weave and knot them together into five ropes, one for each of the Greater Quetzals. The great birds were perched on various parts of the former helicopter, making occasional threatening gestures at the islanders with their wings. Montclair, Wally and Mario attached the lines to the strongest parts of the former helicopter. Penelope handed the other ends of the lines to the Quetzals, the last being Manuel Benitez. Then she walked into his enfolding wings, disappearing in his embrace.

For a long moment, they stood motionless, saying their good-byes, Wally supposed.

Then she stepped away, tears flowing down her face, bright feathers on her lips and in her hair. She moved to Wally, leaned against him, sighed, touched his face, then whistled a strange command. The dolphins surged beneath *Leonardo's Dream*, as before, lifting the craft almost clear of the water. Another wordless command and the Quetzals began to pull on their traces, their powerful wings pounding the air, and they rushed closer and closer to the surf that towered like a moving mountain above them.

"Hold on!" Montclair shouted, and they did, making sure the prophet was securely tied in place. Then they were into the belly of the surf.

For a moment, Wally thought they had been driven to the bottom of the lagoon and that all was lost. The world was drowning in a rushing caldron of water. But rather than being driven down, he felt they were rising. He opened his eyes, looked up and saw they were being guided at a diagonal to the line of the surf, riding within the curl, pulled forward by the Quetzals, upward by the dolphins. The sound was horrendous: the thunder of the breakers, the creaks and groans of the helicopter's sinews struggling to hold together, the whistles and clicks of the dolphins, the deep rumbling voices of the Quetzals, the pounding and slaps of their huge wings on air and water, to say nothing of the hellish howling of the prophet. He and Penelope were holding onto each other as if their lives depended on it, and they did.

Then, in one last great surge of power, the dolphins and Greater Quetzals lifted the belabored craft to a point where it seemed that a mighty sea would break over them, but instead, it rose almost gingerly to the crest and then slipped over and down into a rolling, but benign, sea. Exhausted, the Quetzals alighted on the craft, spread their great wings to dry them in the sun. For a long while, they all sat quietly, enjoying the comparative silence beyond the breakers. Penelope moved to each of the Quetzals and placed her cheek against their scarlet beaks and they touched her, almost reverently, Wally thought, with the tips of their wings. She went to Manuel Benitez last, but they did not embrace as before. Wally assumed they had already said to each other all that their hearts held.

"They are not good at saying goodbye, especially to humans," Penelope said. "But they wish us well on our journey and in our lives."

"What will happen to them?" Mario asked, drying his camera lens.

"They will go back to their peak," Penelope said. "And we will become a memory. But we will be a beautiful one. Then, in time, we will become a myth."

Then, with a powerful performance of their bassoon concerto, the last Greater Quetzals rose into the air and their wings became a shadow between the sea and the sun.

CHAPTER 7
THE *SPRUCE GOOSE*

Wally wondered if they hadn't leaped from the frying pan into the frying pan. Here they were again, drifting in the middle of the Pacific Ocean, right where they had been a few days before. They had managed to create an area of shade from one of the former flying machine's wings, but it was still terribly hot. There was not a whisper of wind; the sky was cloudless and the sea seemed oily and sluggish, the color of slate. 'Perhaps this is the doldrums,' he thought, 'or one of those dead zones that environmentalists warn are becoming more extensive in the world's oceans.' He glanced over at Penelope. Her naked body had become even more golden; she glowed as if from some inner light, and yet, as much as he enjoyed the view, he longed for the day they could find some clothes to wear. In his full-body exposure to the sun and the elements, his flesh had assumed the tone and texture of a tangerine.

He watched her for a while and then called her name. She turned her head and smiled. "Are the dolphins still with us?" he asked.

"Yes. They said they were sorry but wouldn't be able to pull us to land. The distance is too great and they have babies to make here in their home waters. But they will stay with us to keep sharks away until we are rescued." Then, after a pause, she said, "Come swim with me, Wally." She took his hand and they plunged into the sea. A few dolphins came to greet them and circled and played. Wally marveled how difficult it was to tell the difference between the touch of Penelope's body and the bodies of the dolphins. Maybe they shared more than language; certainly they shared grace, as they pirouetted and leaped and came slip-sliding against him. He listened to the clicks and whistles but could find in them no meaning, merely mysterious and compelling music, and even when he concentrated and focused, wishing the sounds would form words in his mind, the words would not come. What capacity of spirit must Penelope have, to know the language of the creatures God made on that morning and evening of the fifth day of Creation! And he wondered why God didn't create man and woman first, then the beasts of the field and the birds of the air last. Could it be that He intended the birds and beasts of the field to be the principle life forms of earth, and man and woman were merely secondary creations?

Wally swam until he was tired and then returned to the deck and the shade of the awning. Soon Penelope climbed aboard, her wet perfection gleaming in the sunlight. She flopped down next to him and smiled, and he was astounded again that such a splendid creature had managed to find something within him to love. In the late afternoon, it rained and they managed to fill their sombreros to the brim.

That night they were awakened by a slight change in the motion of the sea, a lifting and falling, and there came a small chill wind and a new subtle, whispering sound along the surface of the sea. The first thing Wally saw when he looked up was an absence of stars, and to the southwest there loomed a huge, roiling bank of cloud, a black wall, pierced by blooms of light. Now the others were awake.

"What is it?" Penelope asked.

"I don't know," Wally said. "But it's really very big."

"I believe we're in for a rough night," Montclair observed.

"It's suddenly so cold," Penelope said, hugging her arms around her chest, shivering in the rising wind.

Wally held her close to share his warmth. From the prophet came a low growl. Soon jagged spears of lightning carved golden wounds across the sky, followed by violent slaps of thunder. The dark wall of cloud moved closer until they were consumed in its heavy gloom. More lightning punctured the darkness—incisions of fire in the night—some sweeping horizontally, other bolts stabbing straight down into the sea. Now came the rain, cold and fierce, whipped by the wind, so much rain and spray in the air that it was hard to breathe. The air became sea; the sea became air. The pitiful, vulnerable little crew of the former helicopter huddled low and held to each other and to anything on their craft that seemed the least bit able to withstand the onslaught.

Enormous seas swept over them, the thunder became a continuous rolling rumble and the night became day as Thor cast down his bolts of fire. Wally listened to the voice of the storm.

He thought of the sound as a great chorus, an anthem sung by a Russian choir, a blending of deep male voices. Then the sound would become an orchestra of oboes, or the howling of a pack of wolves, or the scream of Banshees, or the lament of drowned sailors. Whatever the source of this voice, it was obvious that it was very much alive, a being with some important truth to tell, if he could only understand the language.

The night seemed endless, a violent offensive against spirit and flesh. It swept away all thought, all memory, all past, all future. There was only this terrible, elastic *now*, the violence and the cold, and the desperate struggle to cling to their craft and to their lives. Even fear had fled in the face of the storm. Then, somewhere in the night came the awesome realization that they were more powerful than the storm. These five, fragile, naked creatures would survive all that the gods of the storm could hurl their way.

Dawn brought a pale sky streaked with dark, windblown streamers of cloud. Large swells generated by the storm were rolling in, not steep and breaking as before, but smooth and lazy. The sea was the color of liquid steel, awash with foam, and the wind still whipped wisps of spray like smoke, and it seemed as if the sea was afire, smoldering beneath the surface. Occasionally flying fish scudded by, but otherwise, they seemed alone on the vast wilderness of the Pacific. In every direction, the sea was empty and colorless as a blind man's eye.

Penelope was sandwiched between Montclair and Wally, trembling violently, her eyes bright with wonder. "It was terrible, Wally, but beautiful. Thank you for giving me the storm." The survivors, all except the prophet, who had rolled up into a knot of sinew and bone and seemed impervious to the cold, took turns roughly massaging each other, seeking to restore circulation, and to snatch warmth from each other's bodies. To prove they were alive, they sang every song they knew, as loud as they could, until dolphins surfaced to see what the racket was.

Soon, with the appearance of the morning sun through the haze, the air grew warmer and they no longer shivered as violently as before. They lay together in each other's arms, listening to the beating of their hearts, holding each other, touching each other, marveling at the warmth of their flesh, rejoicing in the sweet, warm thrill of being alive. Wally felt a deep love for these companions who had experienced so much together. 'How close we are,' he thought, 'in body and spirit, made new by the storm, washed clean.'

"It was wonderful," Penelope breathed, "But please, Wally, don't give me any more storms. Think flowers. I've seen a storm now, but I still haven't seen a rose."

As he felt the first warm touch of the sun, Wally thought about the life and the voice of the storm. He decided that, if he were to believe there was a God, he would worship the Storm. Here is an unknowable, yet infinite power beyond the control of man or beast. It creates itself from nothing, grows terrible and beautiful and majestic, fills the world with its omnipresence, then slips away to nothing again. 'If I were to pray,' he thought, 'now I would pray to the Storm.'

Later in the morning, as they were soaking up the blessed rays of the sun, they heard a familiar sound in the distance, the unmistakable whump and chatter of a helicopter. Then, out of the sun it came, flying low. It began to circle, its rotors lifting coils of spray from the sea. It was Penelope who first recognized the emblem painted on the chopper's side: a naked woman riding a lightning bolt—the cartooned signature of Swamp Sweeney's Road.

"It's Major Tom!" she cried, jumping to her feet and waving frantically.

The helicopter hovered for several minutes and then a rope with a loop on the end descended. Tied to the rope was a pouch, and within the pouch was a note. It contained a simple stick figure drawing of a person with the loop of a rope under its arms being lifted into the helicopter. On the drawing was a message. "What are you doing out here and where are your clothes?" It was signed, *Major Tom.*

The prophet was the first lifted aboard, then Penelope, then Montclair, and then Mario, who carried aloft his case of the exposed film he had shot since Crystal City. Wally was the last to leave their beloved *Leonardo's Dream.* He had observed the others kicking their feet wildly as they were pulled into the unstable air beneath the helicopter. Even Penelope, who usually was the essence of grace in motion, seemed awkward. Wally decided that, since being dangled naked at the end of a rope was undignified in the extreme, he would at least keep his legs together and point his toes, as the best divers do.

After they hugged and shook hands all around, Major Tom introduced them to his copilot, an old comrade from his test pilot days. The man's name was Adam Thunder. 'Now, there is a real man's name,' Walter Woodrow Pillow thought to himself, as he shook the man's offered hand. Adam Thunder seemed perplexed and embarrassed by the entire scene, especially when the naked prophet, the naked former diplomat, and then the naked Angel of the Arroyos offered themselves for hugs.

"See what you can find them to wear," Major Tom said to Adam Thunder. As the co-pilot scavenged some towels to drape around the passengers, Wally recounted their adventures since they had last seen Major Tom. At first he doubted that Major Tom would believe the crazy things that had happened to them, but then he remembered, the former astronaut had had the unbelievable experience of falling out of a Mercury space capsule over New Jersey, and had also been a part of what unfolded on Swamp Sweeney's Road. Both those experiences had strained credibility, far more than anything that happened to them in Mazatlan or on the Greater Quetzals' island.

Then Major Tom filled them in on what he had been doing since he had seen them last. "I flew up to Baja California and landed for fuel at this little airport at a town on the coast. It's an eco-tourism center. People from all over the world come there to watch the grey whales. I got a job whale spotting from the air, searching for the greatest concentrations of whales and then reporting the locations to boat captains below. That's how I spotted you guys. I couldn't believe my eyes. It's not often you find a bunch of naked people floating on an ancient flying machine in the middle of the ocean, especially people you know."

"I thought you were going to get a job with Howard Hughes." Mario said.

"I wasn't able to contact him. No one knows precisely where he is. So, I've come up with a better idea. I'm going to do something I've wanted to do for twenty years. I'm going to fly the *Spruce Goose* again."

"Wow!" Wally said. "Will Hughes give you permission?"

"Not likely. I guess you could say I'm going to borrow his flying boat like I borrowed Swamp Sweeney's helicopter. But I'll tell you all about it when we land."

The airport was merely a hard-packed dirt strip on the coast. The town itself retained the primitive simplicity of a fishing village, its seawall lined with boats that would depart each morning, in search of sea cucumbers, the town's primary export. Major Tom said that the Chinese, who eat them as aphrodisiacs, covet the sea cucumbers and pay top dollar for the slimy little grubs, which is why so many of the village fishermen had fancy new trucks. He said the town itself was shared by the fishermen, their families and a growing population of new age spiritualists, crystal healers, moon meditators, yogi practitioners, hippie smokers and dopers, Indian saddhus and various other pilgrims on their journey through the Age of Aquarius. Then, with the coming of eco-tourism, wealthy pseudo-adventurers, scuba enthusiasts and environmentalists joined the crazy social patchwork. So, when Wally and his half-naked friends departed the helicopter and walked through town to its only hotel, they hardly attracted notice.

Major Tom secured adjoining rooms for the company and sent Adam Thunder out into the town to secure suitable attire for his guests. Soon he returned with Bermuda shorts for all, and T-shirts that said: "HUG A WHALE." Penelope looked beguiling in her HUG A WHALE T-shirt, an extra-large that fell to mid-thigh. Wally noticed that Montclair was quite handsome in his HUG A WHALE shirt, thanks to the constant grooming and civilizing attentions of Penelope.

Once they were settled, they met in the bar to get reacquainted and drink tequila shots. It had been many days since they had eaten anything besides raw fish, so Major Tom ordered them food, heaping bowls of *ceviche*. 'A cruel irony,' Wally thought.

"So, what's this story about flying the *Spruce Goose*?" Wally asked. And this is the story the one-armed former astronaut told:

"You knew I was on that first flight with Howard, flying as co-pilot. For one reason or another, Howard never flew the plane again—never allowed it to be flown. He was too busy with his many businesses, making movies or making love to Hollywood movie stars. Yet the plane was always maintained, ready to fly. But Howard was also getting more and more peculiar. I suppose, in those days, Cary Grant and I were Howard's best, maybe his only, friends.

"You mean *the* Cary Grant, the movie star?" Montclair asked.

"The very one. For some reason, he and Hughes were very close." Major Tom told them that Hughes was a recluse and had begun wearing disguises when he went out in public. But he could be charming, and with all that money and power, he was pursued by the most beautiful women Hollywood had to offer. "It was my job to fly Howard and his women-du-jour to New York or Las Vegas or Lake Tahoe or Miami. Often, Cary Grant would come along. Howard would be with Rita Hayworth or Olivia de Havilland, and I would be with Olivia's sister, Joan Fontaine. Jane Russell often came along. He had discovered her and made her the star of his movie *The Outlaw* in 1943. But for all the years he tried—forgive me, Penelope—he was never able to get in her pants. It was one of the few defeats of his lifetime. Cary, at the time, was living with actor Randolph Scott in a Malibu beach house. He didn't join in with the women. I think, maybe, he liked watching the erotic escapades of his good friend."

"But you were his good friend, too."

"I was a good pilot. Howard respected that. I was loyal, even when it seemed he was being assailed from all sides, and I believe I was a good wingman. Maybe more important, I was discreet. He knew I could keep his secrets."

"Until now," Mario observed.

Major Tom paused, looked down at his hands, as if wondering if Mario's subtle rebuke was justified. "Things changed. Howard became more bizarre. It became evident the *Spruce Goose* would never fly again. Then came rumors that the great old flying boat would be dismantled. I just couldn't let that happen. And then, there is the matter of Howard and the circus animals."

"Circus animals?"

"Howard always loved the circus. He would often dress up in a disguise and would have me fly him and his current movie star companion to the great circuses of the world. We went to Paris, Berlin, Bombay and wherever the most famous circuses were performing. At one point, before I became an astronaut, he told me his greatest ambition was to create his own circus. Sworn to secrecy, he had me fly him to foreign locations to collect exotic animals: tigers, bears, monkeys even a baby elephant."

"This is *the* Howard Hughes?" Montclair asked, obviously not quite able to keep up with the lunacy. "The famous aviator, movie producer and billionaire?"

"Wally, your friend seems of a skeptical frame of mind."

"He's new. He's only known us for a few days. Actually, he's only been civilized for a week. Before that, you wouldn't believe how skeptical he was."

"Where did he keep these circus animals?" Penelope wanted to know.

"You won't believe this," Major Tom said.

"I'll give it an honest effort," Montclair said.

"Well, he had this huge, barn-like empty space."

"Not the *Spruce Goose*?"

"You guessed it. He selected a few of his most loyal associates to secretly create a place aboard the *Spruce Goose* for the care and feeding of his circus animals. He even had a ring installed to train them."

"And they're still there?"

"In the flesh. And on occasion, Hughes sneaks aboard and works with the animals."

"To what end?" Wally asked.

"No one knows. He's completely crazy. He probably doesn't even know himself. But the point is, when his many enemies discover that his flying boat is filled with circus animals, his secret won't be secret for long and he will finally be sent to a lunatic asylum. And the *Spruce Goose*, the world's largest and most amazing airplane, will be dismantled and sold as scrap."

"So, you have a plan?" Wally asked, hard-pressed to believe Major Tom's revelation. It was much harder to believe that Howard Hughes was an apprentice circus animal trainer than the fact that Major Tom was the astronaut in David Bowie's song.

"Well, actually, I could use your help. Of course Adam Thunder will be co-pilot. But it takes a big crew to fly a plane that big. It takes someone to monitor the electrical systems, the hydraulic systems, the fuel systems, communications."

"But we don't know how to do that stuff," Wally said.

"I can teach you."

"But what about the circus animals?" Penelope asked.

"We take them along." Major Tom said this as if it was the most natural thing in the world.

"But where would we fly to?" Mario asked.

"I calculate, we have enough fuel to reach China."

"Why China, for heaven's sake?"

"Because you guys are fugitives, at the top of the Free World's most wanted list. And when I steal Howard's flying boat, a major symbol of American exceptionalism, I'll be right behind you on that list. The entire Free World will be our enemy. So let's make friends with the enemy of our enemy, the Unfree World. And that would be Red China."

"As a former United States ambassador," Montclair offered, "I can see that making friends with the enemy of our enemy makes perfect sense. The art of diplomacy is one of elegant deception, convincing people that truth is a lie and a lie is the gospel truth. It is the art of getting what you want without pissing anyone off too badly. And as for American exceptionalism, that implies there are international rules of behavior that everyone must obey but America. For instance, it is illegal to overthrow a foreign government, except when we do it. That's American exceptionalism."

Penelope was impressed with the man she had civilized, and she looked at him with admiring eyes. "We could use diplomacy, or maybe we could win their trust by offering them free admission to the circus."

"Excellent idea," Major Tom agreed. "They love circuses in China. Howard has stowed everything we'd need for a circus. Besides the animals, there's gear for aerialist acts and all the musical instruments for a circus band. He even has a cannon to shoot a man out of."

Wally poured another round of tequila all around. He looked into Penelope's eyes to gauge her reaction to all this nonsense. Her face reflected a joyous acceptance of Major Tom's absurd plan. She turned to the former astronaut and asked, "Baby elephant? We'd have a baby elephant?"

"Yes, and its mother, along with lions and tigers and all the other animals. Also, two white horses."

"Oh, Wally," she said, caressing him with her blue eyes. "I've never seen an elephant."

It occurred to Wally that Penelope had not seen very much of the world before their adventure Not a rose, not a mountain, not the sea, not an elephant. She had experienced nothing beyond the desert arroyos and the Rio Grande. Yet, she seemed to inhabit worlds of the spirit denied to mere mortals. She was a serial stranger-fucker but was also a complete innocent.

"What a hell of a documentary!" Mario exclaimed. "Major Tom and his Flying Circus! Penelope can be the beautiful aerialist. I love it. In addition to his diplomatic chores, Montclair can be the barker. The prophet can headline our freak show." He went on to say that he would have to buy a new camera and the other equipment lost in the storm. "I also need to get all the footage I've shot processed."

"What better place than Hollywood?" Major Tom said. "Just down the road from Long Beach, where Hughes keeps the flying boat."

"But who will be the lion tamer?" Penelope asked.

"I'd like to give it a try," Adam Thunder said. "I've risked my life in every kind of experimental aircraft in America. How hard could it be to step into a cage with a lion?"

"Don't forget, we're still fugitives. We'll need disguises," Wally said, dumbfounded, yet thrilled, that his statement seemed to lend credence to their nutty venture, as well as his tacit approval. They discussed going as a rock band, but realized they had not fared so well as musicians in Mazatlan. Then they discussed the possibilities of going as anti-war protesters or a squad of marines returning from a tour in Vietnam, but decided in either case they would be vilified and perhaps assaulted. Finally, they decided, since Major Tom and Cary Grant were old chums, they would go to Hollywood as board members of a Cary Grant fan club.

The flight to Southern California was uneventful. Flying in a helicopter registered in the name of Swamp Sweeney offered them protection from American authorities, because Swamp Sweeney's Road was considered a highly patriotic experiment in capitalism and nation building. They were met at the LA airport by none other than Cary Grant, and they all piled into his chauffeur-driven Mercedes. All the way to the Beverly Hills Hotel, Grant and Major Tom traded stories about their adventures. Since the days of flying with Howard Hughes. Mario recounted another aviation story: Penelope's status as the first woman to fly solo on a Greater Quetzal. Montclair offered further observations on the art of diplomacy, including the necessity of knowing something of the truth, in order to lie convincingly.

They made quite a stir, making their way up the red carpet to the lobby of the hotel in their HUG A WHALE T-shirts, in sharp contrast to the elegantly attired Grant. Cary had reserved a bridal suite for Wally and Penelope, assuming they were a couple because they were nearly always holding hands and because of the lingering, soulful looks that passed between them. The suite was magnificent—all white and gold—and the bed was the size of a small aircraft carrier. For a long while, Penelope stood in the middle of the room, her eyes lingering on an opulence she had never known existed.

"Oh, Wally, it's beautiful." She moved to the bathroom with its huge clamshell bathtub and gold fittings. She stood in front of the mirror for a long time, looking at her reflection, pensively, shyly, as if she were seeing the person there for the first time. Wally wondered if it was possible she had never seen a mirror, certainly not a full-length mirror, and her only bathing might have been in the Rio Grande or a sponge bath from a bucket pulled from her mother's, Little Dove's, well. Finally, she turned and said, "Am I beautiful, Wally?"

"You are perfect. The very essence of beauty."

"I hope so. I want to be beautiful for you." She stepped into his arms, kissed him, then turned, skipped toward the bed, and took a flying leap over the footboard and onto its pillowed surface. She bounced for a while on her knees, higher and higher, as on a trampoline, then flopped again on her back, her arms and legs spread-eagled, as if to measure the size of the bed. "Is this where we will sleep?"

Wally said it was, his heart fluttering. He thought for a moment about Jasmine, the human factors engineer, and how she would have loved to make love in this magnificent bed instead of the cockpit of the *F-111* supersonic fighter-bomber.

"Come lie down by me," Penelope said, stretching out her arms toward him. He moved to the bed, took her hands and then lay by her side. She nestled against him. Then something amazing happened. So exhausted were they from their recent travails, and so soft was the huge bed, and so comfortable were they with each other, that without another word or thought, they both fell sound asleep in each other's arms.

Cary Grant had invited them all to dinner in the hotel's elegant restaurant. To replace their HUG A WHALE T-shirts, several boxes from Hollywood's top fashion boutiques were delivered to the room by Grant's style consultant, who had selected a Pierre Cardin suit for Wally and a lovely Mary Quant sheath dress for Penelope. She also provided them with documents proving they were certified board members of Cary Grant's fan club, including rubber Cary Grant face-masks. She made much of Penelope's natural beauty, comparing her to the young Italian movie actresses that were invading the Hollywood scene. The consultant said she would return later, after they had bathed, to help them dress and properly accessorize.

"Accessorize?" Penelope asked. "Do you know what that means?"

"I think it means shoes and hats and things, maybe jewelry."

"I have never worn shoes," Penelope said, looking down at her feet. "I wore those Mariachi boots that time, but that's all."

"I think the consultant was hinting we should take a bath before we dress," Wally said. He had been a little offended, but it was true; they had spent the last week or so on the run and they probably reeked of seaweed and raw fish. But then, as he watched Penelope slip out of her HUG A WHALE t-shirt, he was certain it would be impossible for this splendid creature to reek. Still, he said, "You can take your bath first."

"Don't be silly, Wally. We have been naked together for days and days and nights and nights, there's no reason we can't bathe together."

And so it happened that they filled the huge clamshell tub with hot water from the gold faucet and one bottle of fragrant oils after another and bottles of liquids that made towering columns of bubbles until they were almost invisible to each other. As she scrubbed beneath the surface she sang Mexican folksongs in her rich contralto and scooted back and forth on the slippery porcelain, her butt making musical squeaks in time, if not tune, with her singing. Only occasionally could he see her smiling blue eyes through the mounds of suds. This was the child that he loved in the woman with the old soul. After a while, she scooted behind him and scrubbed his back, where he couldn't reach. Then she lay against him; they added more hot water from the gold faucet, and they let the fear and frigid cold from the storm fade away into the universe.

Finally, as the water began to cool, she said, "This is not me, Wally. I love this for the moment: the luxury, the beautiful dress, the hot water. But I am the woman you met beneath the Lone Star Beer sign in a Crystal City, Texas bar, the daughter of the *curadero*, the girl who heals men's souls and doesn't wear shoes so she can feel Mother Earth beneath her feet." She turned toward him, "Do you know what I'm saying?"

"I don't know."

"This beautiful honeymoon suite, all white and gold. Wally, you know I love you, but you must also know I can never be your bride."

Wally remained silent.

"I'm not even sure we can ever really make love. Don't you think it's strange that we haven't? How we can be so in love and never make love? I know you feel the ghosts of all those other men. And you don't want to be just another lost soul in the arroyos."

Wally said nothing.

"How sad it is to be in love and not make love. But what we share is far greater than anything in the arroyos or among the fishermen. It is a love without boundaries. It fills me with joy and with pride."

"Why me?" Wally asked.

"Because Little Dove said you were the one."

"Not one of the many?"

"Wally, do you have to have all of me? I could change... if you wanted me to; maybe I could be your bride." For a long while, she lay against him in the great porcelain clamshell, rubbing fragrant oils into his shoulders.

"I don't want you to be anyone other than who you are," Wally said, feeling a tracery of tears that had begun to ease from the corners of his eyes. "I wouldn't want the risk of your changing. I don't want to risk what we have, although I'm not at all sure what that is."

Penelope reached over and brushed away his tears. "We will find a way, Wally. We'll find a way because we are magic."

"You got soap suds in my eyes." He laughed, embarrassed at his tears. "You just don't want to be Mrs. Walter Woodrow Pillow. Can't say I blame you, a sissy name like that."

She scooted around to kiss the suds from his eyes, her butt making an unlovely squeal. "Try it, Wally. Let's hear your bottom sing." And so he did, and she did, both sliding the length of the tub, both butts singing a duet, a powerful anthem to creative skills unrealized, the water splashing out over the rim of the tub, both laughing until they sank beneath the water.

After drinks at Bar 1912, they joined Cary Grant and Major Tom for dinner at the hotel's Cabana Café. The restaurant was filled with celebrities and movie stars. Yet Penelope in her bright red, clinging, sheath dress was the most striking woman among all the striking women in the elegant café. She had refused to wear the low pumps the fashion adviser had selected for her and, instead, was barefoot. She was the only woman in the room who wore no makeup or jewelry, and her long, black-blue hair was gathered in a single unfashionable braid. Not long after they were seated, a number of other diners approached their table to chat with Cary Grant and seek introductions to the beautiful, barefoot stranger with the electric blue eyes who was eating her poached salmon and truffles with her fingers. Peter O'Toole, after being introduced to Penelope, seemed incapable of speech. Stanley Kubrick pressed his card into her hand and whispered something in her ear. Clint Eastwood took her hand and seemed unable to give it back.

"Who were those people, Wally?" she asked, licking the cream sauce from her fingers.

"Movie stars, the most famous men in Hollywood. One was a famous movie producer. What did he whisper in your ear?"

"I don't know. It didn't make any sense. Something about a screen test or something."

After dinner, Cary Grant invited them to his suite for a strategy session. Major Tom took charge of the meeting. "Cary has checked to make sure Howard is in Las Vegas. He appears to be settled in with a new starlet, but you never know what he may do or where he may go. So I believe we have to move fast." He told them that the plane was in its hangar on Long Beach Harbor, the largest wooden building in the world, and arrangements had been made to lead them through security at five in the morning. They were to show up, wearing their new Cary Grant fan club T-shirts and rubber Cary Grant face masks.

"What about the guards?" Wally asked.

"There are only a few. And they are so disgusted with Howard's behavior they have decided to look the other way. And they are tired of cleaning the cages of the circus animals, especially the elephants. It's also quite possible that Penelope will be a distraction. She was certainly a distraction in the restaurant."

"I could let the guards have a little feel," Penelope said. "That's often disarming."

Wally rolled his eyes.

Mario asked if the plane could carry all that weight, what amounted to a whole circus, plus two elephants.

"The *Spruce Goose*, with its eight 3000-horsepower Pratt and Whitney engines, was designed to carry General Sherman tanks and artillery pieces and a battalion of marines. So, no problem with weight."

"But suppose we do manage to take off, won't we be seen?"

"People won't believe their eyes. They are conditioned to believe that Howard won't take the plane up again. And who would have the gall to steal a flying boat, anyway."

"What about radar?"

"Remember, the *Spruce Goose* is made entirely of wood. It will have a very low radar profile. Once we get in the air, we'll be home free."

"I just can't imagine we could get away with it," Wally said. "Stealing a little plane would be one thing, but stealing the biggest airplane in the world is something else."

"What about that silly man who is chasing us?" Penelope asked. "The Lynx? Do you think he knows we're here? He always seems to show up, wherever we are."

"We just have to keep our eyes open. If he and his henchmen are here, they'll probably also be in disguise."

Because they would meet again so early in the morning, Major Tom called the strategy meeting to a close. When Wally and Penelope opened the door to their suite, they were confronted with what appeared to be a florist shop, a number of beautiful bouquets, artfully arranged, and all with notes addressed to Penelope. There were a dozen red roses from Peter O'Toole, a dozen white roses from Clint Eastwood, mixed red and white roses from Stanley Kubrick.

"What are these wonderful flowers, Wally?

"Love, they are roses. At last you've seen a rose."

"Oh, Wally, they are so lovely, just how I dreamed they would be. Thank you, Wally, for giving me a rose."

"Not me. Thank Peter O'Toole and Clint Eastwood and Stanley Kubrick—and whoever gave you these beautiful yellow roses.

Penelope opened the envelope, removed the card and read the note. "Oh, Wally, this is not good." She passed the note to Wally. It was signed THE LYNX.

They needn't have been worried about being recognized on the way to Long Beach. The streets were relatively empty and there were few people abroad so early. They did get a start when they reached the harbor area and they ran across the most frightening group of men Wally had ever seen. Beneath the light of the full moon they were monstrous: one a terrible little hunchback, another had long fangs and hair all over his face, another seemed to have been created of mismatched body parts. Then Wally noticed the sign they were carrying. It said: THE BELA LUGOSI FAN CLUB." The leader of the group, wearing a Count Dracula costume, approached them. "Do not be afraid, my little one," he said to Penelope who was cringing behind Cary Grant, who seemed to have no fear of Frankenstein, the Wolf Man, Igor, The Mummy or the other awful members of the Bela Lugosi Fan Club. "My name is Bela Lugosi," he continued in a thick Hungarian accent. Just then, the terrible prophet leaped in front of the fan club members, growling and swinging his hoe in a threatening manner, and all the monsters, except the leader, screamed in terror and ran away. "I will see you again, my lovely, and I will drink your blood," Bela Lugosi said, and then turned and followed the other fan club members into the shadows.

"What was that?" Penelope asked when she had recovered her composure.

"An actor playing Bela Lugosi."

"Who is Bela Lugosi?"

"An actor who played Count Dracula."

"This is all very confusing," Penelope said, crouching down by the prophet to thank him for coming to her rescue, even though the monsters were apparently not real. "Who is Count Dracula?"

Wally explained that he was a vampire who lived long ago in Europe, a fictional character based on a man who really lived. He slept in a coffin and only came out in the full of the moon to drink the blood of beautiful women. Hollywood has made many horror movies about his terrible deeds.

"He said he wanted to drink my blood, Wally. That's not very friendly."

"Well, that's what he did. And all those other members of his fan club were also featured in horror movies. One became part wolf when the moon was full. One was called Frankenstein, made from dead people. They were all very popular."

"Why would they make movies about such horrible things?"

"People love to be frightened, I guess."

"Do you?"

"No."

"Me neither. Why would anyone want to drink my blood?"

"He was in love with these beautiful women. I guess it was some strange expression of his love. Their blood became part of him, the ultimate intimacy."

"Would you want to drink my blood?"

Wally looked down at her lovely blue eyes peering at him from within her Cary Grant mask and he felt a momentary tug of guilt when he had to think about it before he said no.

They were not challenged when they approached the huge hangar. There was only one guard at the door and when Penelope offered him a little feel, he lay down his automatic rifle and was no longer a threat. But when they entered the huge hangar, even Wally, who knew every detail of the construction of the *Spruce Goose*, was nearly overcome by its massive scale. It towered above them, like a huge, winged whale, but much larger—larger than any flying thing had a right to be.

Right away, from within the fuselage, they could hear the growling of the big cats and the trumpeting of the elephants. But when they entered the plane through a hatch in the nose, they were met with a scene even Hollywood, with all its special effects, couldn't have created. The lions and tigers had escaped their cages. In order not to be eaten alive, the guards, who were entrusted with the care of the animals, had found the only possible place where they could escape the rampaging beasts. They had locked themselves in the cages from which the beasts had escaped. Adam Thunder and the prophet found the whips and chairs Howard Hughes had brought aboard, and they valiantly protected Major Tom, Montclair, Cary Grant, Wally and Penelope from the big cats' claws and terrible teeth. Wally was amazed at how quickly Adam Thunder and the prophet mastered the art of lion taming.

Then the mother elephant thundered into the huge cargo area, its mighty trumpet echoing in the great hollow chamber, a sound that would have felled the walls of Jericho. Penelope moved to the elephant and they had a brief conversation and then, with her trunk, the elephant lifted Penelope onto her back. Two white horses galloped onto the scene. Penelope grasped one of the horse's mane and swung down onto its back, an unexpected move, graceful as a ballerina. Then the elephant and the horses approached the biggest of the tigers and Penelope reached down and patted its great shaggy head. Soon all the great cats were lying down, looking up at Penelope with loving kitten expressions.

"What just happened?" Cary Grant asked.

"She can talk with animals," Wally said. "I don't know how, but she does. She says she can talk with any animal that has a beating heart."

Assured by Penelope that it was safe to do so, Major Tom released the imprisoned guards who, after expressing heartfelt gratitude, recovered their machine guns and headed for the door.

It was then that the Bela Lugosi Fan Club rushed through the door. "I'VE GOT YOU NOW, WALTER WOODROW PILLOW," The Lynx shouted, stripping off his Bela Lugosi mask. Penelope gestured to the big cats and the elephant and, still mounted on one of the white horses, led the charge on the terrified fake monsters, finally instructing the big cats to round up the fan club members, including the man called The Lynx, and force them into the cages where the guards had so recently been hiding.

The Lynx was apoplectic. He could only fume and swear at the other members of the Bela Lugosi Fan Club. Meanwhile, the members of the Cary Grant Fan Club, including the real Cary Grant, celebrated the moment, and each other, and prepared for the greatest airplane heist in history.

"But this can't be happening," Mario said. He had filmed the strange events of the last hour with his new camera and was now loading another magazine. "It's unreal. It's absurd."

From some distant classroom, Wally remembered what the philosopher Albert Camus once said. What he said was something like, "When seeking the meaning of life, it is necessary to embrace the absurd."

CHAPTER 8
MAJOR TOM'S FLYING CIRCUS

Once The Lynx and his CIA colleagues had been securely caged, Wally had a chance to reflect on the majesty of Howard Hughes's most noble accomplishment. The *Spruce Goose* was a miracle of design and craftsmanship. Built entirely of wood, the joinery work was perfection. Wally was overly familiar with the steel and aluminum components of modern jet aircraft, but here was an aircraft built with all the care and precision of a fine violin or a classic yacht. It reminded him of the sailing craft of the 1930s he had seen featured in *Wooden Boat Magazine*, and in a sense, as a flying boat, it was a first cousin to a topsail schooner. Its laminated frames and beams and longitudinal members brought back memories of his youth, working with balsa and tissue paper and airplane glue to create models of the great airplanes of aviation history. How strange and wonderful that Howard Hughes had the genius and imagination to go back to a time-honored material for the *Spruce Goose*, which actually was not spruce but laminated birch, but that didn't rhyme.

Still marveling that such a gigantic airplane could be made from trees, he climbed the spiral stairway to the flight deck. Once again, he was nearly overcome with the scale of the space and the complexity of the gauges and switches and controls and the impossibility that two pilots, with only three arms between them, an Italian movie director, a prophet, a former diplomat, an angel, Cary Grant and he, himself, would be able to get this beautiful monster off the ground, or in this case, off the water. It seemed even less likely even than *Leonardo's Dream* rising off Ice Box Hill in Mazatlan. When Wally joined the others, Major Tom gave them a briefing.

"First," he said, "We don't have time for any pre-flight checks, primarily because we don't have a normal crew to monitor the instruments. I'll be in the left-hand pilot seat, Adam Thunder on the right. Wally, you will be flight engineer, Cary will be radio operator, Penelope will be electrical and hydraulic engineer and Montclair will keep a lookout for the Long Beach Police and the Coast Guard and anybody else who might try to stop us. Mario will document the entire thing on film."

Wally recalled that there were thirty-two miles of electrical cables and more than five hundred gauges and switches controlling and monitoring the engines, the electronics and the hydraulic systems, and he wondered if even the magical daughter of the magical Little Dove Segura was up to the task. But she seemed eager as she climbed into her station. Several other vacant stations were now occupied by circus animals that Penelope had invited onto the flight deck, to share the excitement of the takeoff.

"Now!" Major Tom called. "Is everyone ready?"

"Of course not!'" Wally said, with some force. "I don't mean to whine, but we don't know what to do. And we're still in the hangar. And we've got circus animals where engineers and aviators and technicians should be."

"One thing I learned from Howard Hughes is that you can do anything you set your mind to. So I suggest you all set your mind to doing this."

"But the hangar!" Cary Grant called. "We're in a hangar."

"Not to worry. Mario mixed up a little Moonwort explosive from Billy Bucket's endless supply. It's a variation of what he would have used to blow up the Reventador Volcano. In exactly three minutes, it will blow away the hangar door."

Major Tom started up all eight engines, two at a time, listening to the sound and watching his gauges until all 200-plus Pratt & Whitney cylinders were running smoothly. He called out to Penelope, "Can you give me fifteen-degree flaps, my dear?"

"*Si, puedo*," she answered, in her excitement reverting to her native tongue. Wally winced as she began flipping switches in what he thought was a terribly indiscriminate manner, but soon he could hear the whine of the hydraulics as the flaps were extended. And then Major Tom called out, "Thank you. We have fifteen-degree flaps."

"*De nada*," Penelope called.

It was then the great door to the hangar was blasted away, and Major Tom pushed all eight throttles forward. The mighty engines roared with the power of their 24,000 horses, the flying boat lumbered down the ramp and they were afloat, clear of the hangar and the dock. Soon they were pounding through the chop of the Long Beach Channel as Major Tom gradually increased the speed to forty miles per hour. Then, when he reached the Long Beach end of the channel, he turned and headed for the open sea. He gave it more throttle and the Goose's speed inched up to fifty, then sixty miles per hour. The noise of the engines and of the great plane pounding through the waves was deafening. Major Tom gave it full throttle and suddenly the pounding ceased. It grew almost silent as the flying boat reached a speed of about ninety miles per hour and lifted up onto the step, barely skipping along the tops of the waves. Wally knew that if he lived to be one hundred, he would never forget the heart-pounding thrill of this moment as the *Spruce Goose* lifted from the channel and soared out over the open sea.

Terrified by the noise and the sensation of flight, many of the circus animals found refuge on the flight deck, particularly the great cats, who were able to manipulate the spiral stairway. Her eyes blue as gas flames, Penelope moved among them, offering comfort, calming their fears. Later, they would find that one of the zebras had apparently died of fright, but now everyone was in a congratulatory mood, hugging one another, all except Major Tom, who took their triumph in stride and remained at the controls, as if this second flight of the *Spruce Goose* was the most ordinary thing in the world.

When they reached cruising altitude, Major Tom turned the controls over to co-pilot Adam Thunder and he turned and addressed the crew. "Before we get too far from land, we have to jettison our prisoners."

"You mean throw them into the sea?" Penelope asked, obviously opposed to the idea.

"Not exactly." He reached into a locker and removed five parachutes. "It's a bit of a risk, because these are the only chutes we have, but I don't see any choice." They returned to the great cargo hold where The Lynx and his agents were cowering in their cages. One-by-one they were removed from the cage and instructed to put on a parachute. Then one-by-one they were asked to step out of a hatch into the void, which they each did gladly, preferring a leap into space to the teeth and claws of the big cats. The Lynx was last to go, shouting curses at Wally until he was lost from sight.

Once rid of their prisoners, they made a survey of what Howard Hughes had stowed aboard. Here, indeed, was everything one might need to establish a circus, including such thoughtful side show items as a cotton candy machine, a merry-go-round, even a cannon, meant to shoot a daring circus performer high into the air and into a net. Also stowed aboard was a large colorful canvas tent and plenty of poles and rope to raise it. Penelope was singing a Latin lullaby to the baby elephant when Cary Grant called them back to the flight deck.

"We've got trouble," he said. "I've been monitoring the radio and it's all about us. The Air Force is scrambling its jets with orders to force us to return." Almost before they could assimilate this bad news, more bad news arrived in the form of an Air Force *F111* supersonic fighter-bomber.

"Crap!" Wally said. "It's the twelfth *F111*."

"I thought you destroyed them all."

"All but one. That one," Wally said, as the *F111* made a threatening pass and then swerved away into a climbing turn. Its wings, Wally noticed, were sliding back into the aft position. It reminded him of how a police dog's ears go back before it bites the mailman. Then the *F111* spiraled back, extended its wings to the forward position, and assumed a flight path quite near and parallel to The *Goose*.

"He says we should turn back immediately," Cary Grant said. "If we don't, he will shoot us down."

"He wouldn't, would he?" Penelope asked. "He wouldn't shoot down an unarmed plane, would he?"

"They must be pretty pissed at Wally for what he did to their Air Force," Mario said, "so they just might." Then, after watching the jet and listening to Cary Grant passing on the threats of the pilot, Mario said he had an idea. "Maybe we aren't so unarmed after all."

He led them back down below and dragged out the cannon and its sign that said: "See the Death-defying Human Cannon Ball fired into the air!"

"You mean to shoot down a supersonic fighter-bomber with that thing?" Wally asked. "Who would we shoot out of it? I doubt you'll get many volunteers."

Then Mario revealed the rest of his plan. "We don't load the cannon with a man. We don't even load it with the prophet. We load it with a zebra."

Mario handed his camera to Wally and asked that he document what was to happen next. They had lain the literally scared-to-death zebra aside, to await a proper burial at sea, but plans do sometimes change. Now, placing a quantity of Billy Bucket's supply of Moonwort explosive in the breach of the cannon, they gently loaded the zebra into the cannon's barrel. They opened a hatch and there was the supersonic fighter-bomber, flying side by side with them, so close they could see the eyes of the pilots. Without further ado, Mario aimed the cannon and fired the zebra. What happened then was a wonder to behold. The zebra flew through the air, directly into the jet's air intake to be ingested into the engine. It was only moments before the 12th *F111* fell out of the air, and the cockpit-jettison system Wally had invented blasted the entire cockpit from the aircraft. Its parachute bloomed open and the two pilots drifted safely into the Pacific.

"Good shot, Mario!" Penelope shouted, hugging him close. Then she turned to Wally. "And you saved their lives." She hugged him, as well. "By my count, that's twenty-four pilots whose lives you've saved."

After a brief moment of silence in honor of the departed zebra, they flew on toward China.

The next two days were filled with preparations for the circus they would establish when they reached China. When Major Tom wasn't at the controls, he was below in the lion-tamer's ring practicing with whip and chair. Penelope worked with the horses and the elephants. Wally tried to make sense of all the aerialist gear, finally improvising a high wire, with a net below, reaching the length of the cargo bay. He also rigged a high trapeze and found that he could perform tricks with Penelope without fear of falling. He imagined he was Burt Lancaster, the catcher in the movie *Trapeze*, or Tony Curtis, the flyer, and that Penelope wasn't Gina Lollobrigida, but the far more beguiling Penelope Segura. Adam Thunder revealed that when he first started flying in the barnstorming era, he and his sister had entertained at air shows by climbing out on the wing of their ancient biplane, where they would walk on their hands. He looked out at the immense wings of the *Spruce Goose* and realized what a singular thrill it would be to wing-walk on the world's largest wing, and before long he had convinced Major Tom to reduce speed. He climbed out onto the wings and walked from wingtip to wingtip, a distance longer than a football field, certainly a wing-walking achievement worthy of the Guinness Book of Records, especially for walking the distance on one's hands.

Occasionally, a flight of jets would come into view, but they kept their distance, perhaps fearing the strange lethal weapon that had downed the last *F111* fighter-bomber. At one point, Cary Grant heard reports on the radio that a team of CIA agents had been rescued from the sea, off the coast of Southern California. He heard no radio conversation regarding the crash of the twelfth *F111*. Strict radio silence was being maintained, certainly to prevent the embarrassing word spreading that the supersonic jet had been downed by a zebra.

Wally could feel China long before its coastline came into view, something enormous and alive and formidable and ancient and very, very human. He imagined he could hear the deep, imperative beating of 700 million hearts, an actual sound, like an orchestra of muted drums that seemed to come from both the distant horizon and from within. Penelope was standing by his side, watching where a bank of clouds to the west proved the existence of a great land mass.

"Is it China?" Penelope asked.

"Yes. China," Wally breathed aloud. The very thought filled him with a high-hearted excitement, his mind dancing with images of dragons, plum boughs, warlords, peaceful philosophers and incredible depths of wisdom, time, and mystery.

Major Tom throttled down, and the *Spruce Goose* descended, settling slowly along the coast, over what appeared to be a river delta with myriad silver tributaries winding through hundreds of small, green islands. The eternal mists, so often depicted in Chinese paintings, hung low above the hills and seemed to hide the islands away from heaven's eyes.

Major Tom eased the *Spruce Goose* down through the mists, slowly skimming over the larger tributaries and along the green slopes, searching for some clue to where they were. "I believe it is Guangdong Province," he said, checking his Rand McNally World Almanac. "If so, Hong Kong would be to the south. And we are well into Red Chinese air space."

Mario seemed uneasy. "You know what they'll do if they catch us."

"Remember," Wally said. "We're famous Communist spies, destroyers of American air power, assassins of Popeye, symbol of the enslavement of the working man. They will probably welcome us as heroes of the Revolution."

They followed a course to the northeast, above the islands, seeking a stretch of water wide and long enough that they might land on it. It was growing dark when they made their final approach and then, far ahead, they saw a glimmering of what appeared to be a thousand floating stars, a celestial city rising from the depths of the sea. "What could it be?" Penelope asked.

"No idea," Major Tom said. "But whatever it is, we're committed. We have to land.

So smooth was the landing that it failed to wake the tigers, sleeping like house cats at Penelope's feet. The great flying boat slipped through the sea as if sledding on ice. Soon, Major Tom cut the engines and they were consumed by a monumental silence. Then, out of the strange constellation of faint flickering lights on the horizon, sailed a classic Chinese junk, a vessel little changed since the Song Dynasty, a thousand years ago. High at the bow and stern, it was graceful as a new moon, its tanbark triangular sails leaning against the wind. As it approached, the sails were furled, one by one, until the ancient craft was within hailing distance.

"Who do you think they are?" Penelope asked. "They look like pirates." The men aboard the junk were barefoot. They wore simple but threadbare cotton tunics and trousers; some wore headbands, others conical hats. Most wore their hair long, often plaited into long braids. Although they appeared to be unarmed, there was, about them, an aura of menace. Soon, one of the pirates called out in Chinese. Not surprisingly, since he had once been a diplomat on a mission to China, Montclair answered in the same language.

"He welcomes us and asks us to come aboard," Montclair reported. "He says we have nothing to fear. He says they are the enemy of the Communists and friends of America."

Deciding to leave Adam Thunder, Major Tom and the prophet to stand watch on The *Goose*, Wally, Penelope, and Montrose climbed out on the wing and then down to the deck of the junk. The crew of the junk was about as hard and rough as any group of men Wally had ever seen. Yet, when Penelope stepped aboard, they seemed to be merely boys again, entranced by her beauty and perhaps intimidated by the ceremonial Oddfellows sword at her side. Their captain was tall and thin with broad shoulders and a flat, hollow chest. He had the hands of a pianist, and there was a sense of intelligence and sensitivity about him. He had a long, white Fu Manchu mustache and beard, and kind eyes. His movements were fluid and sure, as if he was a man in perfect control of a vast inventory of physical, mental, and spiritual powers. He greeted them cordially, offered them rice wine, and, with Montclair interpreting, said his name was Charley Oh. He informed them that they were approaching one of coastal China's many typhoon shelters.

He explained that the shelters were originally created for the obvious reason: a place where fishermen and other mariners could ride out the terrible storms that struck the coast regularly. However, with Chairman Mao's rise to power, the shelters had become havens for refugees fleeing the excesses of Mao's Red Guards, an army of teenage madmen determined to stamp out anything classical in Chinese society. Millions were being persecuted, publicly humiliated, and having their property seized. Many were being tortured and imprisoned without cause.

"The Red Guards are destroying our temples, our religion, our customs, anything that does not pay homage to Mao Zedong's cultural revolution. These days, the typhoon shelter is occupied by people fleeing persecution, an altogether different kind of storm.   Like most of the boat people, I, too, am a refugee," he told Montclair. "I was a poet. But the Communists don't like poetry, especially classical poetry. So, they put me in prison and tortured me until I promised not to write any more poems. Of course, I promised. Of course, I lied."

"Promises and lies," Montclair interjected. "Ever the fine art of diplomacy."

As they drew closer to the typhoon shelter, Wally could make out the shapes of boats, maybe thousands of vessels, all rafted together between the mainland and the lee of one of the larger islands. Wally had never seen so many boats at one time: wonderful old Chinese junks, sampans of every size and description, small rusting coastal freighters. All were rafted together to form a floating village. The night was dark, moonless, and an offshore wind had raised gentle swells, causing the flotilla to rise and fall as if the harbor were a living, breathing organism. Fish oil lanterns and cook fires on the sampans and junks winked like fireflies. The motion of the boats set up a muted racket of hawsers and halyards and the sound of teak hulls straining and moaning. As they moved closer still, they could see families gathered on deck—the women tending clay cook stoves, men smoking, children watching the newcomers, fascinated, wondering who these strange visitors from another world might be.

When they were within a hundred yards or so of the typhoon shelter, the crew lowered all sail and cast out an anchor. Charley Oh said they would proceed in the small sampan they had been towing. The junk was too large to navigate the intricate avenues that meandered through the world of the boat people.

The typhoon shelter was a vast cove in which a million tiny ghost boats drifted, their magic lanterns winking like Disney wands upon the black water. A curtain of peace settled like a wandering prayer. The poet stood at the stern, stirring the sea with a single oar that creaked and sang in its rope harness. From every direction came the answering call of the oars pulled by other timeless mariners. Alien conversations hung close to the water and other boats, teak hulls polished by generations of voyages, slipped silently by, seemingly on their way nowhere.

They passed the hulks of great junks, no longer fit for sea but still the homes of masters too old for voyages and too sad to do anything but die with their ships. One of the many sampans glided by, wiggled close, and a handsome old man held his lantern high to show them the San Miguel beer and tiny bottles of White Horse scotch he had to sell. Wally bought a quart of warm beer, and they shared it in the dark. They passed a row of sampans set somewhat apart. On the bow of each little boat, a young girl sat, sometimes sewing, sometimes merely looking out to sea. Diaphanous curtains formed a little cabin where cushions lined the floor, and lanterns cast soft half-light. A few of the sampans rocked gently, oddly, and even though the curtains were closed, Wally could see the silhouettes of the lovers within. "Oh, Wally," Penelope whispered, "this is the most magical place I have ever been. To make love out here among these people must be very close to God." She slipped his hand up her thigh beneath the folds of her Mary Quant dress, and Wally wanted nothing more than to sail with Penelope forever, out to sea in a curtained sampan.

But soon, as they moved deeper into the world of the boat people, Wally and Penelope began to see beneath the magical surface to the harsh reality of the typhoon shelter. Here were thousands of human beings, packed together in appalling conditions. Charley Oh revealed that many of the boat people lived all their lives on their boats in the shelter, had never touched shore, and that poverty, starvation, poor hygiene and improper disposal of waste has created high levels of disease. But the refugees were trapped here, between the sea and the Red Guards.

"Can't they just sail away in their little boats?" Penelope asked.

Charley Oh said that many did try to leave. "Some even try to swim to freedom with bottles tied under their arms to keep them afloat. But if they are caught by Red Chinese patrol boats, they are never seen again; either imprisoned or simply drowned. If they do make it to British Hong Kong, the British merely turn them over to the Communists, because they are already overflowing with refugees. And so, they too are imprisoned or killed."

Wally could tell that Penelope was overcome by an emotion that could only prove that angels, like devils, could rise to anger. Her knuckles were white where she gripped the hilt of her Oddfellow's sword.

"This is wrong!" she said, a blue fire sparking in her eyes. "Why don't you do something?"

"We do what we can," Charley Oh said, meeting her angry eyes with the kindness within his own. "We take as many as we can through the New Territories to Kowloon and Hong Kong to freedom. But for each refugee we save, ten more flow into the typhoon shelter, driven south by the Red Guards. The boats only become more crowded. Disease spreads and more children die."

"Are there doctors?" Penelope asked.

"There are a few unlicensed doctors," Montclair translated. "They call them *Wenmi Po*. They cure with herbs and animal parts and a manipulation of the body's energy flow. But sickness is rampant and there is now only one *Wenmi Po*. The children still die."

Wally looked out at the lovely lanterns dancing on the sampans and he wondered how a place could contain, all at once, such beauty and such misery, such peace and such violence to the human spirit. Once again, he reflected that things often are the opposite of what they seem. He glanced at Penelope and realized it was even true of angels. There was nothing angelic about the fire and fury in her eyes as she stood and demanded that Charley Oh take her to see the *Wenmi Po*. "Tell him I am the daughter of Little Dove Segura, a famous *curandera,* and I have experience with herbs and traditional healing."

When Montclair had passed on the message, Charley Oh bowed low, and he rowed them into the labyrinth of vessels until they came to what the poet-captain said was the only medical facility serving the entire shelter. It was a large junk, its deck covered with dozens of patients, women in childbirth, children with respiratory problems, and men terribly emaciated from lack of food or debilitating disease. Charley Oh led Wally, Montclair and Penelope aboard and introduced them to the *Wenmi Po*, a wizened old man who moved among his patients as if they were all his beloved children. He was obviously exhausted, perhaps ill himself, and he appeared to be as dangerously diminished as most of the men, women and children in his care. When he learned that Penelope had knowledge of traditional healing, he bowed, placed his hands on her shoulders and looked deep into her eyes. She placed her hands over his and they stood like that for more than a minute. 'Looking past the eyes into the soul,' Wally thought, 'speaking to each other without words.' Then they embraced, the old man and the girl, and he took Penelope's hand and led her to a child, a boy about eight years old, who was obviously in great pain. His head was on his mother's lap, his eyes tight closed, his body doubled up like a steel trap, his fists clenched so tight his fingernails had cut into his palms. Penelope knelt at his side, touched the mother's hand, then lifted the boy from the woman's lap. She laid him down gently on the teak deck, and then she did something Wally would never have expected. First, she kissed each of his eyes and then she bent and kissed his lips. Their lips were barely touching, but they remained in contact as Penelope breathed in and out, the breasts above her good and generous heart expanding and contracting, perhaps to imbue his lungs with the ambrosian breath of angels. Then she took off his clothes and began to explore him with her fingertips, seeking, perhaps, blockages to the flow of his *ki*, his life's energy. After a few minutes, the enormous tension in the boy's body began to relax, the grimace on his face began to soften, and his fists began to open. Now he seemed merely a little boy, asleep. Penelope sang to him, some lost melody from the arroyos, kissed him once more on the lips and stood. The *Wenmi Po* bowed low to Penelope, his eyes filled with respect and thanksgiving. He then made available to her his ancient apothecary, a rosewood chest filled with the herbs and medicines of his profession. Wally would later learn that the chest contained herbs from the eastern slopes of sacred temple mounds and such other curatives as powdered seahorses, centipedes, Asiatic toad, various forms of fungi and animal parts. Penelope would augment the apothecary with small vials of medicinal Moonwort from Billy Bucket's supply.

The *Wenmi Po* pointed out a woman in the later stages of labor. Penelope started to follow the healer, then turned. "Wally, why don't you go on back. I want to stay here tonight. There's so much I can do."

Then Wally asked her about what he had been thinking as he had watched her heal the boy. "Is that what you did with the men in the arroyos? With the fishermen? Is that all you did to heal their souls?"

Penelope just smiled, said, "Maybe," and then turned to follow the *Wenmi Po* and tend to more of his patients.

The next morning, with the assistance of fishermen and pirates recruited by Charley Oh, they began to unload the cargo of the *Spruce Goose*. Howard Hughes had designed the flying boat so that the entire forward section of the fuselage could be opened. First came the animals: the elephants, the horses, the lions and tigers. Shepherded from the plane and up the beach by the whips and chairs and cajoling of Adam Thunder and Major Tom, they were led to the brow of a hill on the mainland, overlooking the typhoon shelter. As he watched the animals leave the plane and parade up the hill, Wally thought it looked like the story of Noah's Ark in reverse. Following the animals came the colorful canvas tent, which, according to circus tradition, was to be raised with the help of the elephants.

As Wally worked side by side with Charley Oh, he learned that the poet was leader of a growing number of dissidents pledged to resist the cruel deprivations of the Red Guard and the Cultural Revolution. He explained that a center of that resistance was in the typhoon shelter, but that it had spread to the mainland with acts of civil disobedience.

"Why haven't the Red Guards put down the resistance?" Wally asked.

Montclair interpreted. "First, they are afraid of the refugees in the typhoon shelter, especially the pirates. Second, they see no reason to attack. The people here are trapped. If they try to leave, they will be caught or killed. So they leave them alone."

Wally watched the Big Top rise, great expanses of red, green and blue canvas, wrestled atop its wood poles by the elephants and the strongest of the pirates. Surely, he thought, the circus tent could be seen for miles around. He asked Charley Oh why the Red Guards weren't attacking the circus. Charley Oh responded that fellow dissidents from the north had heard rumors that the Americans in the huge airplane were to be protected. Charley Oh said that there was more to the rumor, but he found it beyond belief and that he didn't want to spread false rumors.

When pressed, with some embarrassment, Charley Oh told what else he had heard. "They say you destroyed a large part of the American Air Force with some kind of explosive made from chocolate. Even now, in Beijing, Chairman Mao has ordered the erection of a giant replica of you, a fifty-foot-tall memorial carved from a single flawless block of chocolate. It resembles the picture of you on the American FBI's Most Wanted List. You are playing your guitar and looking out over the Forbidden City. Of course, I think this is absurd," he added.

Wally decided he liked the idea of being immortalized in chocolate. But the more he got to like the idea, the more anxious he became about such things as birds and rain. How frustrating it would be to be immortal like that for a day, or maybe a week, and then have rain wash the monument away or have a bird shit on your immortality. A thing like that, immortality, shouldn't be given lightly.

Charley Oh pulled Montclair aside, and they spoke together quietly. Charley Oh seemed embarrassed.

"There is more to the rumors from the north," Montclair said, "but our host is reluctant to spread the rumors. It is said Chairman Mao is in possession of Major Tom's arm. It was found in an elliptical orbit around the moon, during the first Chinese mission into space. It was brought back to Beijing and is now honorably displayed in the Chinese National Air and Space Museum." As Cary Grant hastened to tell Major Tom the good news, or perhaps the bad news, Montclair said he knew the rumor was true. "In my last diplomatic mission, before I rejected the world and everything in it, I was assigned to retrieve Major Tom's arm. Washington wanted the arm so that it could be hidden away and the public would never know that Major Tom existed. The Chinese wanted to keep the arm as a symbol of America's vulnerability and as proof of the superiority of the Chinese space program. Like Wally, they regard the Major as a hero of the revolution."

"So, what did you do?" Mario asked, ready to film the response in close-up.

"There are two kinds of diplomatic problems," Montclair said. "There are little ones and big ones. The little ones generally solve themselves. The big ones you can't do anything about anyway. So, the proper diplomatic posture is to resist the temptation to do anything at all. And that's what I did."

Later, Charley Oh took them to one of the last remaining temples in the province. It was a small shrine, its roof decorated with dragons, deities, and monsters. Inside were statues of gods and altars venerating ancestors, joss sticks and coils of incense as fragrant as any Billy Bucket had ever created. Entering the shrine, Wally felt the presence of gods as old as Earth.

"The religion here is far older than Buddha or Confucius or the Taoists," Charley Oh said. "Here, under the oppression of the communists, the people have reverted to the old gods. Animistic gods. Gods of nature, the wind, the sea, the earth, the harvest, the turning of the seasons.

"Do you believe in them?" Wally asked the poet.

"Yes," he said. "I believe in all gods. I just don't worship them. But they have inspired my poetry."

The old gods: the phrase itself seemed a part of the mystery and romance and tragedy of eternal China. Wally could see the lighted images of the gods, woodenly watching smoke curl upward from burning joss sticks. There was something vaguely humorous about the shrine—the colors too bright, the figures too theatrical—but then, he was sure the idea of Jesus rising up into the air surrounded by angels and the old, white-bearded father-God sitting on a cloud would surely evoke smiles from those who worship here. The Holy Ghost would probably lay them in the aisles. 'It all began with animism,' he thought. 'Maybe that's where it should have stopped. Simple, fundamental, utilitarian. But then we had to put faces on our gods, give them bodies, perfume them with incense.' Wally felt in his pocket for his mystic stone and warmed it reverently in his palm.

As they were leaving the temple, Charley Oh mentioned that he had managed to secure the release of a famous classical poet who had been imprisoned in Beijing for the content of his poems. "He had been a towering figure among Chinese intellectuals, known primarily for his uncanny gift of camouflaging the profound meaning of his poems and for his abhorrence of any lines that rhymed. For this reason, his code name is Ginzberg. When I knew him at the university, he was at the height of his powers. But I fear his years of torture at the hands of the communists might have dulled his sensitivities."

Then Wally learned that Ginzberg was now being held in a village on the Pearl River by the Opium People, a nefarious group of outlaws and drug dealers, and that Charley Oh and his pirates would attempt to rescue the poet the following night. He asked Wally to join them.

"Why me?"

"Anyone who can destroy twelve supersonic fighter-bombers and elude the CIA, the FBI and Interpol as long as you have, obviously has formidable skills."

Wally wondered if he had the stomach for such a mission. But as a writer of ballads, he had a great respect for poetry. Maybe the rescue of Ginzberg would move the world one step closer to justice and peace and civility. Penelope said that, in any case, it would make good material for a ballad. But she refused to let him go on a potentially dangerous mission without her. "I don't want to hurt your feelings, Wally, but I don't think you could have survived the last few weeks without me. I'm the one who seems to get us out of trouble and you're the one that seems to get us into it."

Wally's feelings were hurt, but he felt better when Penelope kissed him so passionately and for such a long duration that the zipper of his Pierre Cardin trousers got so hot that he suffered second-degree burns. Penelope was crestfallen when she saw his injury and made amends by massaging him with healing herbs from the Wenmi Po's ancient apothecary.

They set out toward the lair of the Opium People just after sunset. Charley Oh led the way, followed by six of his toughest pirates, then by Wally, who had brought his guitar, in case he was inspired to create song fragments along the way, and then by Penelope, bearing her unsheathed Oddfellows sword, as rear guard. It was a grueling passage through rough terrain. Beneath a pale moon, the countryside seemed as if no one had ever passed this way before. But Wally knew, could actually feel the weight of human presence in the darkness, generations of ghost pilgrims accompanying them through the night.

Even from a distance, there was something foreboding about the lair of the Opium People. It appeared to be an ancient palace fallen into terrible disrepair. Mostly rubble, it rose at the edge of the river, where the hulks of ancient river freighters rusted at tortured wooden docks. There was a nauseating, sweet stench clinging to the air, and it grew stronger as they came closer. A great rat lumbered down a mooring line and disappeared into a terrible clutter of garbage and broken things vomited by the river. There was no reception, no sign of life.

"It's as though everybody is dead," Penelope whispered as they moved through the darkness into the foul and broken palace. Then, the deep shadows began to move and shapes eased loose from the black mouths of doorways and over the walls of rubble and up from the depths of the earth itself. They came like the ghosts of drowned men, the spectral crew of some pirate ship lost at sea in a storm. They moved closer, and now Wally could see their awful faces; the gaunt Oriental faces with patches of wild, sparse hair; haunted negro masks with deep, hooded eyes; faces with jungle beards nearly hiding wan memories of Anglo-Saxon features; Arab faces scorched and drained of any expression save reflected torment. With sightless eyes, they came, as if from hell.

Then, from the bowels of the palace came a voice. "Who has come to the palace of Pappy Poppy?" The voice was gentle and melodious, and it echoed through the ruined rooms like the ringing of deep bells. "Who seeks an hour or more of Paradise?" The advancing specters hesitated and held their ground, swaying against the voice. "Who will dream the great dream? Who will breathe the gentle, everlasting pause?"

"It is Charley Oh. We have come for Ginzberg."

"Come, my children, and I will give you dreams enough to fill your souls."

They passed into echoing chambers where the light from fish oil lamps fell on the wretched faces of the Opium People. As he passed by these ruins that were once men and women, Wally felt more pity than fear. It was that fear-shame-pity one might feel when walking through an insane asylum, the special pain born of being in the midst of immense human suffering, the fear felt when a man with no legs wheels by on his tiny scooter and pauses to look up into your eyes, the fear that sweeps the heart at the sound of a leper's bell.

Then they were in a kind of amphitheater where an incredibly old man sat in the lotus position upon a pile of decaying mattresses. He was small, very frail, and the ruins of his clothing suggested the uniform of one of the world's navies. He had a thin, white beard and a pale, unlined, sensitive face. It was obvious he was blind, for his wide, white eyes fluttered from side to side like an insect, feeling.

"We have come for Ginzberg," Charley Oh repeated, "not for pipe dreams." He turned away from Pappy Poppy, who seemed to have fallen asleep, and walked back to where the others were watching.

"Who is he?" Wally asked.

"He was a powerful man," Charley Oh said.

"Doesn't he know what's going on here?" Wally asked. "I mean all these dreadful people and the ruins and everything. You don't need eyes to tell what a hellhole this is."

"I suppose he doesn't want to know. It was quite a place— this palace was. He built an empire here on the river, unlike anything on earth."

"How?"

"Opium. Opium for the pipes of fifteen million Chinese passed through here. People from all over the world came here to dream the Great Dream. Pappy Poppy held court over revelries unrivaled anywhere in history."

"What happened?"

Charley Oh said that when Pappy was a young man, the opium market was wide open. In a single year, he imported thirteen million pounds into China. He believed he was performing a great service for the Chinese who used it. He conducted his business in an atmosphere of evangelistic fervor. He was a spellbinding character. He entertained lavishly. Then, shortly after the turn of the century, the Empress Dowager cut down on the opium traffic. It was the beginning of the end. The communists took power, and there was no more room in China for the Great Dream.

"Come," Charley Oh said. "We must find Ginzberg." He led them through a shadowed hall.. On each side of the hallway, darkened doorways suggested rooms beyond. In some of the rooms, Wally could see the shapes of the Opium People. They lay here and there like heaps of old rags and bits of bone and flesh, and around them rose the tragic aroma Wally had first noticed on the dock. A few smoked pipes of opium, their faces in awful rapture. Others rolled in the rubble, their sensuous dreams cloaked in nausea and fever, groans and yawning, and slow, spastic movements of their limbs. And then he saw what had once been a woman. She was on her hands and knees and she was forcing a crumbling chestnut of opium up her rectum.

Wally turned his face away. He felt sick and was consumed by a numbing wrath. He was angry at Pappy Poppy, the human race and himself for being a part of it. 'What has become of mankind?' he wondered. 'What has become of that transcendent creature born of love and blessed with the capacity to smile and to whistle and to write a sonnet?'

Then Wally heard himself say: "I'm not going to leave them this way."

"What?" Penelope asked, incredulously.

"I'm going to stay here with the Opium People." It seemed suddenly quite clear. "This is what I am meant to do. No moral hang-ups here. No ambivalence or shuffling of convictions. Everything pure and simple. Just as you civilized Montclair, I'll immerse myself in an effort to make the Opium People human again."

"What would you do?"

"Maybe I'd clean up the place, plant parks and gardens. Maybe teach them to play the guitar."

"You only know minor chords, Wally."

"I'd organize folk dancing, arts and crafts, classes in personal hygiene and creative withdrawal from their addiction. Maybe they could develop some useful industry; perhaps weaving."

Wally was horrified that he had begun to cry. Penelope pulled him into her arms. "My poor, poor crazy man," she said, kissing away his tears and then holding him tight against her good and generous heart.

Charley Oh had been listening quietly. "This isn't what you are looking for, Wally. This place is too far gone. There's nothing left. The people have been on opium so long their souls are gone. Their bodies and their minds are destroyed. They have been neglected too long."

"How can you be sure?" Wally asked.

"Indeed!" said a man, whom Charley Oh introduced as the illustrious classical poet with the code name Ginzberg. The poet was an elderly gentleman with an explosion of wild white hair. He seemed pleasant, yet forceful, and had the voice of a young boy. They shook hands all around and he hugged Penelope, and then Ginzberg began to tell them that he agreed with Wally about the resurrection of the Opium People. He had a plan.

"I'm not going to tell you about the plan in rhyme," he said. "People always seem disappointed when they realize I'm not speaking in rhyme. But actually, I hate rhyme. I would rather have a boil than a rhyme. Now you take the classic line about Jack Spratt. Mr. Pillow, recite the line for us, please."

Wally did. "Jack Spratt could eat no fat."

"Now," Ginzberg said, "see how the poet was restricted by the need to rhyme something with Spratt? The whole meaning, and flow and tone of this classic work were dictated by a need to find a rhyme for Spratt. Now, suppose the poet would not have been restricted by the necessity of finding a rhyme for Spratt. Consider the following line." The old poet paused again and drew himself up on the tips of his toes and said, "Jack Spratt could eat no shit! Now, consider the creative possibilities here. A revolutionary anthem! Jack Spratt just couldn't take any more shit off the goddamned fools who ran his government and his life."

Ginzberg then said he would demonstrate his plan to resurrect the Opium People. He led them into what must have been the palace ballroom, where Pappy Poppy was now passing out pipes of opium, moving slowly with the aid of a cane. The poet moved to the old addict's side, whispered a few intense phrases in his ear, then turned to his awful audience and rang a small bell to capture their attention.

"Ladies and gentlemen," he said to the creatures. "How pleasant it is to be in your company. I trust you and your families have passed a rewarding day." He paused then, and smiled, as if to give his audience a moment to reflect upon a day well lived. "In my long life, I have discovered that poetry is essential to human dignity. Therefore, with Pappy Poppy's permission, I would like to introduce the miracle of poetry to your lives." Then Ginzberg began to pass small pieces of paper and pencils to the crowd. "From this day forward," he continued, "we will all write a poem a day. It will affect your lives in marvelous ways. Of course, if you don't write a poem a day you will be shot. It's only fair."

It seemed incredible to Wally, but the room was soon filled with the scratching of pencils on paper. 'Could it be possible,' he thought, 'that these tormented beings could actually create poetry?' In spite of doubt, he felt a growing excitement. He found Penelope's hand was squeezing his, as if she, too, was aware that something good was about to happen. Soon the scraps of paper had been collected, placed in a box, and brought before the classical poet. In deference to Pappy Poppy's magnif-icent voice, Ginzberg asked him to read the first poem. And this is what he read"

> There is nothing I feel
> More frightening than remembering
> Things once told
> Like a wheel
> Feeling round
> Remembers it rolled.
> I remember.
> I feel.
> I remember.

There was a stillness delicate as crystal. Wally was touched beyond measure and he looked out at the ghastly hoard and wondered in which ruin could such tender melancholy lay hid-den. He felt tears pooling again in the corners of his eyes.

Suddenly Ginzberg's boy-voice called, angry and high, into the stillness. "I want the damn fool son-of-a-bitch who wrote this trash to get his or her ass up here where I am!" Ginzberg was furious and was leaping about in a snit. Wally was horrified at the old poet's behavior, following, as it did, such a profoundly beautiful moment.

Then, from the crowd emerged a small, frail figure, ragged and old as a root. So light and insubstantial he seemed, that Wally imagined he weighed nothing at all. The figure stood still and shallow as a shadow before the Classical Chinese poet.

"Do you realize what you've done, you ass?" Ginzberg screamed.

"I wrote a poem," the shadow said.

"But it rhymed, stupid! The goddamned thing rhymed," he screamed again and then he whipped a revolver from his shirt and shot the shadow, dead in the head. The shadow didn't bleed at all.

The sound of the gunshot echoed around the ruined ballroom like claps of thunder, like old boards slapped together, over and over. Then a new sound came from high above, as ancient timbers, weakened by the vibration of the gunshot, began to creak and scream and snap, and plaster and tile began to rain down on the gathered Opium People. Then the first of the great chandeliers broke loose, fell, and Ginzberg and Pappy Poppy were crushed beneath shards of broken crystal. Charley Oh's pirates grabbed their captain, Penelope and Wally, and they half carried them and half dragged them from the palace. Wally looked back once and knew that the Opium People would never dream again.

The would-be rescuers moved away from the river and back down the rugged hills in shocked silence. Wally was inconsolable, but Penelope tried with kisses and soft words to comfort him, and she sang to him the lost songs of the arroyos in her soothing contralto. "It was my fault," Wally said, when he could finally speak again. "It was my idea about making their life better. I wanted to save them and I ended up killing them. Just like I killed Gaspar, like I kill everything I touch."

"It was my fault," Charley Oh said. "I should have known Ginzberg was insane."

"How could you have known?" Wally asked.

"Because I'm a poet. I knew him long ago in the University. I should have known he was mad then. But I was awed by his reputation. And I shouldn't have embroiled you and Penelope in this terrible travesty."

Suddenly something occurred to Wally. "How is it I can understand Chinese?"

"How can it be I understand English?" Charley Oh responded.

Then they both looked at Penelope, who was walking between them and holding both of their hands.

When they returned to the typhoon shelter, Penelope spent most of her time working with the *Wenmi Po*. Her stylish Mary Quant dress had by now fallen mostly apart and the women of the typhoon shelter had made her a knee-length tunic and a pair of free-flowing trousers, which did nothing to diminish her radiant and sensuous beauty. She still found time from her healing to work with the horses and the elephants and to perform on the high wire and trapeze with Wally, who was beginning to recover from his terrible depression following the death of the Opium People. He had always suspected Penelope could fly, was not restricted by the force of gravity, and now, as she soared through the air from one trapeze to another, performing the elusive quadruple somersault that had been so difficult for Tony Curtis to master, he was certain. But each time she leaped from her trapeze, his heart stopped until he felt the twin slaps of her hands in his own and knew she was safely in his grasp.

As the days went by, more and more people from the typhoon shelter and the surrounding countryside came up the hill to the circus. They were especially attracted to Adam Thunder's death-defying lion-taming act, little knowing that Penelope had babied the beasts to the point that they were as lethal as kittens.

Perhaps the crowd's favorite was when they fired the prophet from the cannon that had downed the twelfth *F111*, and he landed in a grotesque heap in the safety net. Several times, he missed the net altogether, landing on the sawdust floor with no ill effects. Ultimately, they dispensed with the net altogether, saving the trouble of aiming.

Like children all over the world, the Chinese children were drawn to the outlandish magic and reality of the Big Top. They came in droves, thrilling to the animal acts, eating whorls of cotton candy from the machine Howard Hughes had so thoughtfully provided, laughing at the clowns recruited from among the pirates and the more fun-loving refugees.

Whenever possible, Penelope and Wally stood unseen, to watch the joy on the faces of the children. "You know, Wally," she said, "there is a kind of healing going on up here. It is a miracle. You gave me a mountain, the sea, a rose, and now you have given me a purpose."

"Healing has always been your purpose, ever since Little Dove taught you how."

"But never like this, Wally. The boat peoples' need is so great. And to help them, to ease their pain, to make them whole, gives me a feeling that I'm a part of Creation. It is a good thing that we are doing, my love, you up here with the circus, me down below with the refugees."

There were times when Penelope would gaze out at the ancient terraced rice fields where ragged and gaunt men worked to coax a crop. Her eyes would grow misty, and then she would be gone for hours at a time, and an unbearable sorrow would force Wally almost to his knees. She would return, radiantly alive, her trouser cuffs soiled, her spirit soaring, and she would gather Wally in her arms, kiss him passionately, and tell him she loved him more with each passing day.

One day, Charley Oh and a delegation of pirates asked Wally and the others for a conference. Major Tom was there in his Bermuda shorts and flip-flops, still a bit testy about the theft of his arm and its use as communist propaganda. Adam Thunder was in jodhpurs, styled after those of his hero Clyde Beatty, and Mario was covering the conference with his new Aeroflex movie camera. Montclair served as translator. "We were wondering," Charley Oh began, "What are your plans for the big airplane?"

The question seemed to come out of the blue. Wally realized they had never discussed what would happen next. He was uncertain how to reply.

Charley Oh continued, "The circus is established and is changing lives day by day. We can't imagine you would take it away. And since that big airplane has no cargo, we were wondering if you might fly refugees to freedom. Perhaps to Taiwan, beyond the reach of Chairman Mao and the Red Guards."

Wally looked at the others, and they looked at him. The question had come as such a surprise that they could find no words to answer. After an uncomfortable silence, Montclair and Charley Oh spoke briefly, then Montclair said, "He respectfully asks that we consider the possibility." Then, the captain-poet and the pirates bowed low and turned back toward the typhoon shelter.

They met on the flight deck of The *Spruce Goose*. It was obvioius that flying refugees to freedom would be a good and generous thing, but the risks would be great. Did they have enough fuel? After checking his Rand McNally World Almanac for the location of Taiwan, Major Tom said it wasn't that far and they could probably make it, and they could probably refuel in Taiwan for the flight back. Although Chairman Mao had ordered his Russian MIG fighters not to fire on the flying boat, they still worried about being attacked by the Taiwanese air force. Major Tom reminded them that the Taiwanese were allies of the Americans, who had given them their old *F-86 Saberjets*. Those were shopworn, but with their machine guns and rockets, they would be more than a match for a twenty-year old flying boat fresh out of zebras. They estimated the *Spruce Goose* could carry as many as 300 refugees, and it was a sobering thought that they might be carrying this human cargo into danger or possibly to their deaths. Then they considered the fact that they would be abandoning the circus and Penelope would be abandoning her patients. They discussed the pros and cons until sunset without reaching a firm decision.

As they left the plane, they thrilled to the lines of refugee families moving up the hill, to where the evening performances would soon begin. It appeared to be the largest attendance so far, and the crowd's excitement was palatable, a joyous gathering anticipating the danger, surprise and delight of the hours to come. The circus band had already begun to play. Unable to master such western band instruments as trumpet, trombone and clarinet, a volunteer band of refugees utilized such classical Chinese instruments as the four-stringed lute, the seven-stringed zither, the Cantonese two-stringed fiddle, the Chinese zither, bamboo flutes and various wooden clappers, stone chimes and metal gongs. Wally had taught them the rhythm to "When Johnny Comes Marching Home Again," and had given each of them license to play any melody that came to mind. As Wally stepped under the tent flap, he was met with an orchestration of unparalleled originality, which climaxed with the resounding HOORAH, HOORAH that always followed the song's verses.

Cary Grant had proved to be an excellent barker. Handsome and charismatic, he announced each act with the clipped precision for which he was known. First came the grand parade, led by the mother elephant and her baby, then came Penelope riding the two white horses, executing daring flying leaps from the back of one to the back of the other. In her performances, she always wore the conservative peasant tunic and trousers that the women of the typhoon shelter had made for her, but what Wally saw was a beautiful exotic in a brief, form-fitting, sequined costume, and he was fairly certain that's how every other male beneath the Big Top saw her. Next came the big cats. Although they were perfectly harmless, they were rolled out in cages to preserve the illusion that they were man-eaters. The illusion was further perpetuated by the fact that one of the lion-tamers only had one arm. Penelope had taught the tigers to roar and growl and snap at Major Tom's empty sleeve.

It was a triumphant night. The aerial act and high-wire acts kept the audience on the edge of their seats. The elephants performed flawlessly. Once Penelope had performed her signature quadruple somersault on the high trapeze, Cary Grant, accompanied by a crescendo of lutes and flutes and clappers and gongs, announced that she would attempt the impossible. Penelope Segura would attempt a quintuple somersault, five complete revolutions in the air.

Wally was horrified. "I won't have it!" he shouted at her.

"I can do this, Wally," she pleaded. "You know I can fly. I don't really even need the trapeze."

"I won't catch you!" he said.

"Yes, you will," she said, and she grasped the trapeze and swung away from the high platform. As she swung like a pendulum, higher and higher above the crowd, Wally looked down at the circus rings so far below. He remembered the fear he felt watching Penelope rocket down the side of the cliff on the back of the Greater Quetzal. He was somewhat comforted by the thought that this might not be near as dangerous as free-falling off a mountain on the back of an extinct bird. Besides, this time he was not simply standing by helplessly. He had a role to play. He watched her gathering momentum, her loose tunic and trousers whipping in the wind, her blue eyes smiling and absolutely unafraid. The circus band's gongs and clappers and chimes simulated a drum roll. The voice of the crowd rose in waves as the trapeze swung higher and higher. And then there came absolute silence. Penelope released her grip on the trapeze and flew even higher, tucked and then began to spin in somersaults of dizzying velocity. As she spun, Cary Grant counted the revolutions in English; the crowd counted in Cantonese. One. Two. Three. Four. Five. Six. Seven. Eight. Then she opened from her tuck, her arms wide, and Wally could have sworn she was gliding as gracefully as a falcon through the high, upper reaches of the Big Top. Then he felt the glorious slap of her hands on his, her body against his and her lips at his ear, and she whispered, "Told you so."

Only two things marred the success of the evening. The first was a misadventure with the cannon, which shot the prophet, not only high above the circus floor but blasted him through the tent itself and out into the night. It took several hours before they found him in a rice paddy.

The second unpleasant thing began when Wally noticed there were several clowns he had not seen before. Actually, since the clowns were all volunteers, there were probably many he wouldn't recognize. But these had black, highly shined shoes. One of the clowns moved to Wally's side and said, "I've got you now, Walter Woodrow Pillow! You won't get away from me this time." And before Wally could react, he pulled out handcuffs and handcuffed himself to Wally and swallowed the key.

Wally's first thought was, who has got whom? And he would have said so out loud, but he wasn't sure of the grammar. None of the circus performers had witnessed this strange apprehension except Penelope, who was so high from her performance that she only said, "Oh, Wally, it's the silly man. The Weasel."

"Lynx!" The Lynx corrected, offended at the slight. "You will not think me silly for long." He grabbed her arm with his free hand.

The Lynx took them to a gunboat hidden behind one of the islands. Wally recognized it as a Swift Boat used by the Marines in Vietnam. The other FBI agents had gone to the typhoon shelter to have carnal knowledge of the prostitutes in the sampans. The Lynx had let his men go because there was no way Wally could escape him now. He was also pleased to have some time with the beautiful Penelope, whom he hadn't seen since he had threatened to drink her blood in Long Beach. He had never been able to get her out of his mind and was even now mesmerized by a pulse in her throat.

The Lynx gestured to a bottle of vodka by the gunboat's helm. "Since we are such old friends," he said, "we might as well share a little elixir of the potato. Then we'll talk about what will happen next. I assure you, it won't be pleasant." Instead of bringing the bottle, Penelope poured three glasses and handed two of them to Wally and The Lynx.

"Here's to the good old U.S. of A!" he toasted. "And to lovely barefoot senoritas who traipse around with terrorist traitors." He took a large swallow, then almost immediately turned to hardwood, stiff as the pine boards in Jose's Buenaventura's *carpenteria.*

"What did you put in his drink?"

"A bit of newt urine. It's a trick I used when I was doing tricks on the border. He will be out for a while."

"How will we get the key?"

"I will heal his soul," she said, and she began to remove the man's clown suit. It was difficult because of the handcuffs, but she managed, until he was naked except for one arm. She lifted his head into her lap. "You may not want to watch this, Wally." Then she kissed the comatose counterspy's eyes, and when she lowered her lips to his mouth, Wally turned away. The time went by slowly and Wally imagined she was using the same healing technique she had used on the boy. But he wasn't sure. He didn't like the idea of her touching the man's naked body with her fingertips. Perhaps an hour went by and then he heard a metallic clink that sounded very much like something small and metal hitting a steel bulkhead. He turned. Penelope was smiling. She was holding a key. She unlocked the handcuffs, climbed into Wally's lap and kissed him long and hard.

"How did you get the key?" he asked, not sure he wanted to know.

"It is a magical thing *curanderos* have done since time began. Little Dove taught me when I was young. It's a way to reach within the body to remove tumors and such. Or keys."

"Is there blood, a scar?"

"Not if done right."

When The Lynx showed signs of awakening, they dressed him back in his clown suit and poured another drink, sans the newt urine.

The change in The Lynx was immediate and profound. At first he seemed confused, especially when he noticed the handcuffs had been removed. Then he seemed resigned, even relieved, as if a great weight had been lifted from his soul, as, indeed, it had. He looked at Wally as one might look at an old friend who had returned after a long absence. He looked at Penelope with what could only be love. Then he looked down at his wrist where the handcuff had been. "I know now, Walter Pillow, that you were never who I thought you were. But I had lived a life so filled with deceit that I couldn't imagine anyone else living without it. I am sorry for all the trouble I have caused."

Wally couldn't immediately accept The Lynx's apology. He was still a little angry with the man, and after all, he hadn't had the advantage of having his soul healed, as the counterspy just had. His soul still contained a truckload of negative thoughts and garbage and feelings of rage and guilt and confusion. And, besides, he really didn't like the silly shit.

The Lynx confided that he was going to retire and buy a kumquat orchard, live in the lap of nature, and perhaps write sonnets. When he asked Wally and Penelope about their plans, they looked at each other and shrugged. They simply didn't know and hadn't thought beyond the moment. They told him about Penelope's work with the refugees and Wally's management of the circus.

"Noble work," The counterspy said. "It would be a life worth living."

Not sure how far he could trust the former lying, deceitful counterspy, Wally was reluctant to tell him about the possible plans to smuggle refugees out of Red China. "Do you still have contacts in Taiwan?"

"Of course, they are America's close allies."

"What would they do if the *Spruce Goose*, loaded with refugees, flew into their air space?"

"Ah, I see, another noble endeavor. I could put in a good word with Chiang Kai-Chek or perhaps more importantly with Madame Chiang Kai-Chek, my good friend Soong May-ling, with whom I spent many enjoyable evenings playing Mah Jongg and listening to Elvis Presley records. Elvis was the avenue to Soong May-ling's heart, and I went there often."

For another hour, the former enemies chatted and sipped vodka. The Lynx's soul had been so completely healed that he didn't even suspect Penelope might give him another Mickey Finn.

Eventually, The Lynx said they should part. His men would be returning.

"What will they say when they see we have escaped?" Wally asked.

"They won't be surprised. After all, you always have."

As Charley Oh selected the refugee families who would make the flight to Taiwan, Wally, Penelope, and the other fugitives gathered to consider their future. Major Tom said that once his mission with the refugees was complete, he wanted to return the *Spruce Goose* to California, back to its creator, Howard Hughes. Cary Grant said he wanted to go with him. He missed Randolph Scott and the glamour and excitement of Hollywood. Mario also wanted to go to Hollywood to process his footage and edit his documentary. Montclair said he planned to go to Washington to re-open diplomatic negotiations for the return of Major Tom's arm. They all begged Wally and Penelope to come along, but they tearfully declined. They would stay in China, continue with the circus and the healing, and watch over their awful old friend, the prophet.

And so, one spring evening, they watched the mighty *Spruce Goose* rise from the sea and wing its way east toward freedom. They continued to watch as the flying boat grew smaller and smaller, until it was only a memory. Then Penelope took Wally's hand and led him up the hill toward the ancient Chinese temple. There they found the awful old prophet, leaning against a brightly colored dragon and gazing toward the far mountains to the west. On the end of his hoe was tied a cloth bag, much like the bindles in which hoboes carried their belongings. The old man stood, walked forward, and showed them what the bindle contained. There was rice, bok choy, and cotton candy, and it was all wrapped in the ancient parchment on which Leonardo da Vinci had drawn his flying machine. Wally had forgotten all about the drawing because it always made him feel bad about the death of Gaspar Lopez. If there was a reason why the prophet had kept the drawing, Wally didn't want to know it, or even think about it. 'Just let it be,' he thought. The prophet retied his bindle, pointed to his chest and then to the distant mountains.

"What's over that way?" Penelope asked Wally.

"India, the Ganges," he answered. "It would appear the prophet is going home. Maybe to find his lost prophecy along that sacred river." Wally remembered how the people in Gaspar's village had said the old man had the look of one who must travel.

Penelope reached for the old man, but the prophet turned away, apparently, like the Greater Quetzals, he abhorred good-byes. Then the prophet took the first steps on his long way home.

When the prophet had gone, Penelope and Wally entered the temple. It was dark inside, and they shared the task of lighting the incense, the joss sticks and candles. The little shrine soon glowed with a mysterious, ethereal light, blooming through clouds of fragrance. Then Penelope took off her tunic and her trousers, undressed Wally, and they lay down together on the earthen floor. "And so we are alone," she said. "It feels strange, but good."

"What fine companions we have all been; what adventures we have shared! I already miss them all."

"What will happen now, Wally?

"What would you like to happen?"

"I would like to stay here with you, performing in the circus and working with the refugees. Maybe we could build a small house overlooking the South China Sea. I think I remember how the man who makes good bricks and sweats made those lovely adobe bungalows. And maybe we could have a child, a little girl."

"And you could teach her how to heal souls."

"And under your guidance, the circus will become famous throughout the Orient."

"And one day, when we are old and it is time, I will build us a little airplane entirely of bamboo and we will fly together to the ends of the skies."

Then Penelope rose and knelt between his legs. He reached for her breasts, and she kissed his eyes; then her lips lingered on his and he felt her spirit flowing into his consciousness. As her fingertips explored his body, he felt all the darkness and clamor of his inner life seeping away like a forgotten dream, only to be replaced by starlight and silence. Then he found himself slipping into a warm, moist sanctuary fashioned of silk and rose petals. As they moved together, the passion between them grew like a storm, all thunder and sunlight, fire and rain, an infinite power, beyond the control of man or beast, that creates itself from nothing, grows terrible and majestic, fills the world with its omnipresence, then slips away to silence again. And so the cycle of storms raged and subsided, raged and subsided, again and again, through the night, as they made love on the earthen floor under the watchful and envious eyes of the old gods.

The End

Marshall Riggan

Over the past four decades, Marshall Riggan has written more than 200 scripts for film and television. Twice films he wrote were selected for the PBS Eudora Welty Americana Award as the Best Short American Film of the Year. Two years running, his films were selected by the Outdoor Writers Association as the best nature films of the year. His assignments have taken him to the far reaches of the globe, including projects in China, India, Vietnam, Thailand, Africa, Indonesia, the Arctic, the Caribbean and many countries in Central and South America. Along the way he has written many short stories and ghost written three novels, one of which was made into a successful tv mini-series starring Angelina Jolie. Under his own name, he has published several novels, including *Sulu Sea, The Lost Caravan,* and the children's adventure novel *The Last Traveler.*

For nine years, Marshall and his wife Betty wrote, lived and cruised aboard their 32-foot sailboat in tropical waters. They now live in Dallas near their children and grandchildren.

SULU SEA

BY

MARSHALL RIGGAN

One night, off the coast of Nicaragua, the luxury liner *Sulu Sea* runs aground on a reef and sinks with great loss of life. Her captain, Joaquin O'Hara, is blamed for the disaster. His reputation ruined, he goes into decline, drinking to excess. Eventually he is reduced to being skipper of a little tramp steamer carrying cargo between the islands and ports of the Caribbean.

While delivering a consignment to a dealer in Cartagena, he is approached by a beautiful woman who offers him $30,000 to take her and several crates of her personal belongings from Cartagena to Miami. Once at sea, O'Hara discovers that the woman, Gabriella Torres, is the runaway wife of one of Colombia's most powerful drug lords, and one of the crates she brought aboard contain millions of dollars she has stolen from her husband and the cartel.

The chase is on. Juan Torres wants his wife back, but he wants his money more. O'Hara initially eludes pursuit by sailing directly into the path of a hurricane, but then he decides that if they are to survive, they must become the hunter, not the hunted. When they reach Cuba, using some of Gabriella's stolen money, they purchase powerful weapons intended to defend their little ship against their enemies.

PENMORE PRESS
www.penmorepress.com

A Falcon Flies

by

James Boschert

The fifth book of Talon

Talon returns to Acre, the Crusader port, a rich man after more than a year in Byzantium. But riches bring enemies, and Talon's past is about to catch up with him: accusations of witchcraft have followed him from Languedoc. Everything is changed, however, when Talon travels to a small fort with Sir Guy de Veres, his Templar mentor, and learns stunning news about Rav'an.

Before he can act, the kingdom of Baldwin IV is threatened by none other than the Sultan of Egypt, Salah Ed Din, who is bringing a vast army through Sinai to retake Jerusalem from the Christians. Talon must take part in the ferocious battle at Montgisard before he can set out to rejoin Rav'an and honor his promise made six years ago.

The 'Assassins of Rashid Ed Din, the Old Man of the Mountain, have targeted Talon for death for obstructing their plans once too often. To avoid them, Talon must take a circuitous route through the loneliest reaches of the southern deserts on his way to Persia, but even so he risks betrayal, imprisonment, and execution.

His sole objective is to find Rav'an, but she is not where he had expected her to be.

PENMORE PRESS
www.penmorepress.com

Local Resistance

by

J. G. Harlond

WWII in England, Cornwall smugglers, Intelligence agents, detective story, locals and war in the UK, German navy operations on the coast of the UK. Murder thriller. Espionage.

On a stormy night in March 1941, Maisie Rose Hawkins leaves her drunk husband, Stan, out in the rain—and he disappears. Detective Sergeant Bob Robbins and young PC Laurie Oliver are called out to investigate and discover that Stan's small fishing boat is gone, the rope sawn through. As Bob searches for answers, it becomes apparent that in this small Cornish village where everyone knows everything about everybody, nobody quite knows the truth.

Beneath the surface of village life, a fierce battle is being waged against wartime deprivations. Shopkeepers quietly evade rationing restrictions. Food inspector Archibald Bantry, charged with enforcing those restrictions, dies in a suspicious car crash. Various leads connect a sea cave full of smuggled black-market goods to the missing Stan Hawkins. And what seems like the work of local malcontents becomes more complex and dangerous when Bob stumbles on the truth in a disused copper mine, where a much deadlier affair is underway.

"Uncanny happenings and warm characterization. . . . The realities of wartime life in this novel combine with a lovely sense of place to create a distinctly Cornish mixture of secluded charm and the unsettlingly mysterious." —Robert Wilton, prize-winning author of the Comptrollerate-General historical thrillers.

PENMORE PRESS
www.penmorepress.com

Historical fiction and nonfiction
Paperback available for order on line
and as Ebook with all major distributers

9 781957 851549